Praise
Savanna

"*The Vampire's Betrayal* is by turns romantic, tragic, horrific, fantastic and fun—a huge range for just one book! Jam-packed with vampires, werewolves, voodoo, demons, zombies and faeries there is plenty here to entertain fantasy and vampire fans alike."
—LoveVampires

"Raven Hart's *The Vampire's Seduction* and its sequel, *The Vampire's Secret,* held me captive from the very first page! I love the world she's created and the incredible characters who live there. I can't wait for the next installment!"
—ALEXIS MORGAN, author of the Paladins of Darkness series

"An excellent treat . . . An excellent read!"
—Fresh Fiction

"An exotic, exciting thriller."
—Futures MYSTERY Anthology Magazine

"One can almost feel the heat rising from the pages . . . A stimulating read."
—Curled Up with a Good Book

"Dark, seductive, disturbingly erotic, Raven Hart drives a stake in this masterful tale."
—L. A. BANKS, author of the Vampire Huntress Legend series

Also by Raven Hart

THE VAMPIRE'S SEDUCTION
THE VAMPIRE'S SECRET
THE VAMPIRE'S KISS
THE VAMPIRE'S BETRAYAL

The Vampire's Revenge

RAVEN HART

BALLANTINE BOOKS • NEW YORK

The Vampire's Revenge is a work of fiction. Names, characters, places, and incidents are the products of the author's imagination or are used fictitiously. Any resemblance to actual events, locales, or persons, living or dead, is entirely coincidental.

A Ballantine Books Mass Market Original

Copyright © 2009 by Raven Hart

Published in the United States by Ballantine Books, an imprint of The Random House Publishing Group, a division of Random House, Inc., New York.

BALLANTINE and colophon are registered trademarks of Random House, Inc.

ISBN 978-0-345-49858-8

Cover illustration by Kathleen Lynch, based on photographs © Digital Vision (woman), RWP/Almay (Spanish moss), and Wesley Hitt/Almay (gate)

Printed in the United States of America

www.ballantinebooks.com

OPM   9 8 7 6 5 4 3 2 1

This book is dedicated to that *old* gang of mine, the McEachern class of nineteen—well, never mind. Ken(ny), Dobbo, Warren, Judy, Frieda, Cindy, Vicki (aka Lizzy Myrtle), Lynn, Bev, and especially Sandra and Jeannine, the inspiration for Doc Barton. All for one and one for all.

ACKNOWLEDGMENTS

Thanks to Jennifer Labrecque, Rita Herron, and Stephanie Bond for their guidance and encouragement. You're the best!

The Vampire's Revenge

Letter from Jack, a Vampire

My so-called life has become a nightmare. Each time I climb into my coffin at sunrise and the deep death-sleep claims me, I think I'll wake up and things will be normal again. As normal as a vampire's existence can be, anyway.

In my dreams I'm back in my old, ordinary life. My maker and mentor, William Thorne, is whole and with me again. Connie Jones, the woman I love, is just a regular human being coping with nothing more complicated than being a cop and the girlfriend of a vampire—as if that wasn't tough enough. Melaphia and Renee, my human family, are untroubled by their own nightmares and secure and happy, as a young mother and daughter have every right to be.

But when the moon rises and the shadows lengthen to hide the monsters that exist on the fringe of human consciousness, my sweet dreams of normality implode under the weight of the here and now. When I wake, the real nightmare begins.

William, my sire and the friend who had my back for more than a hundred years, is dead, slain by Connie, the woman I love most in this world. That leaves me alone to protect Melaphia and Renee. Already tortured and traumatized by the most evil of my kind, the crowning blow of William's death was nearly too much for them to take. As the most powerful *mambo*s in this hemisphere, the daughters of my heart might not be as vulnerable as ordinary humans, but because they bear the priceless voodoo blood that can give vampires otherworldly powers, they are now hunted for their life force by the most evil and determined of fiends.

If that weren't enough trouble, there's a whole menagerie of monsters out to challenge me for the role of chief enforcer that I inherited from William. Now I have to ride herd on all things nonhuman around here. Without me to watch over the local monsters, they would be free to threaten the mortal population of Savannah, which is one of the most haunted places in the world. And for the first time I have to do it without William and his formidable power at my side.

Oh, and let's not forget the worst enemy of all. I have been left to contend with a council of the most evil vampires in history. They are trying to harness the elemental powers of the universe to enslave peace-loving bloodsuckers like me and turn us into killing machines. Their most recent show of force briefly opened a portal to the underworld, through which dozens of reanimated vampires clawed their way top-side in every demonic form imaginable. The only way I was able to convince Connie to let me live was to promise to help her track down and destroy these double-dead demons before they can wreak enough havoc to send the human world into a full-scale panic.

Yeah, Connie wanted me dead. You see, the moment Connie murdered William, she turned into a creature that I barely recognized—part demon, part avenging angel. As the vampire Slayer sworn to kill me and my kind wherever she finds us, Connie is the new favorite target for every evil blood drinker on the planet. So I have to try to protect her from them while I protect myself from her and hope to God it'll be a while before she figures out that she doesn't really need my help. She's lethal enough all on her own.

Oh, and incidentally, Connie's pregnant with my child but doesn't know it yet. A child that is an abomination of nature and has no right to exist, but whom I already love with a ferocity that frightens me. I would do anything to ensure the survival of Connie and our baby, even if it means giving them over to the care of another kind of monster altogether. Probably just as well that she hates me now, don't you think? At least that's what my rational brain tells my shattered heart.

So as you can see, reality bites. Even worse than I do.

Welcome to the new normal. Welcome to my nightmare.

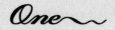

One

"Hey! Watch where you're swinging that ax!" I yelled as the blade whistled through the air, grazing my cheek. "I'm helping you bring that demon down, you know. The least you could do is try not to lop off my head."

The demon, a nasty little number, was covered with slimy brown scales. It ducked, but not before Connie's ax connected with its shoulder. The demon howled in pain and outrage and backed further into the corner of the alley where we had trapped it.

"Is head-lopping one of the ways you can kill a vampire?" Connie asked. She never took her gaze off the demon, but her eyes lit up with a deadly fervor that made me cringe. I knew her question was a reference to me.

"Well, yes," I admitted. "One of the few." The demon made a break for it, but I caught him in the jaw with my fist—if that lump below its mouth *was* a jaw—and spun him back into the corner.

Connie sighed. "I have so much to learn. So many vampires; so little time."

Our friend Werm, who'd acted as bait to lure the creature into the side street where Connie and I were hiding, danced back and forth. I knew he was looking for an opening so he could use the ninja throwing stars he'd ordered from a martial arts catalog. He'd gotten each of them specially engraved with an ankh, which is the ancient Egyptian symbol for eternal life. The ankh is also a good-luck charm for vampires—or so he told me. Werm can be ridiculous at times. Even though his greatest weapon is his ability to make himself invisible, he'd still rather play with kung fu toys.

"And as for you," I warned, pointing at him, "if I wind up with one of those chunks of steel sticking out of my forehead, I'm going to make you rue the day you begged to be made into a vampire."

"What makes you think I don't rue it already?" Werm asked, holstering his ninja stars with a pout. The little goth had thought being a vamp would be all fun and games and give him a chance to scare the shit out of guys who used to kick sand in his face. He didn't figure close-quarters demon fighting would be part of the deal.

The demon charged me and I kicked it in the side, slamming it back into the wall. Connie raised her ax again and swung with almost as much speed and strength as I myself could have mustered. The demon's head left its shoulders with a spray of blood. As its body fell forward onto the pavement, it instantaneously turned into a pile of dirt. The smell mixed with the sickening-sweet stench of the nearby Dumpster and made my nose twitch with disgust.

"Another one bites the dust, uh, huh," Connie sang with a little victory dance. I watched in awe as she shimmied her shapely booty. I wasn't quite sure whether I should be grossed out by her bloodlust or turned on by it, but I seemed to be a little of both. Maybe I'd inherited William's infamous death wish along with all his responsibilities.

"I'm going back to the club," Werm said. "Call me when you need me."

As I waved him off, Connie turned her attention to me, noticing the trickle of blood running down my cheek. Her eyes dilated, the pupils turning into slits. Her irises were bloodred. She grabbed me by the neck and pulled my face next to hers so quickly it startled me. I searched her eyes for a sign of my old Connie, and didn't see it. Would she ever be back? Or was she lost and gone forever, lost in the shell of this vicious, half-human killer standing in front of me now?

When she pressed her lips to my cheek, I felt myself go weak in the knees. She hadn't shown me any affection since. . . well, since the night I tried to kill her. Of course that had been for her own good.

I quickly realized it wasn't her lust for me that had caused her to move her lovely lips along my skin, though it had sent a shiver down my spine and a throb of desire running everywhere else. As a *dhampir,* she was part vampire, part human, part goddess. She was savoring my blood for its flavor and its power. She was a predator now, and I was her prey of choice. She flicked out her tongue and lapped away the dribble of my blood.

"Mmm. Good to the last drop," she murmured in a throaty whisper.

Even as I glanced down to see her pull back her lips and reveal her small fangs, I felt more yearning than terror. She was driven to kill me, after all, and I swear if it weren't for Mel and Renee, I would have let her. I was tempted to just tell her to get it over with, as long as she made love to me one last time.

I closed my eyes, relishing the serrated rasp of those fangs across my skin, and nearly swooned. I know, I know. Kick-ass vampires with superpowers like me don't swoon. But you don't know Connie. Her hot breath burned from my cheek to my neck.

"Please," I heard myself beg.

"Please what?" Her tongue probed the hollow of my throat, searing my cold, dead flesh.

I bit my tongue to keep myself from murmuring, *Kill me.* It was tempting, but too many innocent people depended on me for their safety. I couldn't take the easy way out. As much as I might want to die in Connie's arms, perish at the point of her fangs and be done with it, I couldn't.

I took hold of her shoulders and gently pushed her away from me, breaking the suction lock she had on my neck. "Remember our agreement," I muttered. "I help you with the demon killing, and you don't eat me."

"You're going to get a nice bloodred hickey," she teased, ignoring me.

I rubbed at the spot on my neck. It was difficult getting used to the new Connie. Before, she had been a no-nonsense woman. Oh, she had a great sense of humor and could be as playful and fun-loving as anyone, but when it came to matters of life and death—which it came to often because she's a cop—she was as serious as a heart attack and always in control. But the way she went about catching demons as a slayer was altogether different from the way she went about catching regular bad guys as a detective.

When she was activated as the Slayer, she'd turned wild, unpredictable, and vicious. Travis Rubio, who was her father and one of the only vampires who had faced down slayers and lived to tell the tale, said she would achieve more self-control as she matured. But for now, to her way of thinking, the only good vampire was a dead vampire. I hoped that as time went on, she would develop some discrimination. I longed to be able to reason with her, to convince her to fight at our side against the evil ones. I only hoped I could keep her from killing me before we reached an agreement.

And I also hoped to keep my beloved Melaphia, the voodoo queen, from killing Connie to avenge William's death. What was done was done. He was the first vampire whom Connie had slain, and nothing could bring him back now.

The whole situation really was a nightmare, but William would have been the first to approve of my strategy of convincing Connie to come over to our side. And he would have been the first to forgive her, too. An evil vampire named Damien, with the help of two other vampires, Eleanor and Reedrek, had manipulated the time and place of Connie's official switchover into slayer mode, and William had been in that wrong place at the wrong time.

As I studied the predatory gleam in Connie's eye and the way she licked the last drop of my blood from her ruby lips, I figured my efforts to keep her from killing me had at best a fifty-fifty chance. She made a little feint toward my neck and I dodged away.

"You're no fun," she said, thrusting out her bottom lip in the pretty pout that still drove me to distraction. "And you and Werm are not much help, either. The only demons we've killed are the ones I could have identified myself because they have scales and stuff. I thought you were going to help me sniff out the ones who aren't so obvious, the ones who chose to take over human bodies."

"Oh, yeah, that," I began as if I'd forgotten our deal. "I'll be doing plenty of that. But we have to get rid of the obvious ones first so the humans won't panic." I pointed to the pile of dirt that used to be a monster. "I mean, if this guy had decided to wander into Clary's, sit down at the lunch counter, and order up a plate of humans on the half shell, it would have made the national news, and we can't have that, can we?"

"No, I guess not," Connie agreed reasonably. I wondered if her fellow cops had noticed the recent change in her. Maybe she went back to acting normal when she wasn't in the presence of vampires.

"And don't forget that Saint Patrick's Day is in a few days. Tourists are already flocking in here from all over the country. Humans drunk on green beer and staggering around unfamiliar streets in the dark are going to be easy pickings for the demons. On the other hand, maybe you and the other cops can write off any demon sightings as the ravings of knee-walking-drunk tourists. Either way, we've got to work fast."

"Is this fast enough for you?" In a move too quick for me to see, she grabbed the collar of my denim shirt and brought my face close to hers again. "Just make sure you're ready to step up when the time is right. And be fast yourself or I'll send you back to the underworld so quick your head will spin faster than that monster's did, *lover boy*."

I winced at her sarcastic tone. Technically, my heart stopped beating the night William made me a vampire on a Civil War battlefield, but it truly died the night Connie stopped loving me.

The police radio on her hip squawked and distracted her enough for me to slip out of her grasp. I don't do cop-speak but the code the dispatcher announced made Connie frown. "I'm on duty, so I've got to take that call," she said. "We'll pick this up later. Keep your cell phone turned on or I'll have to come looking for you."

"Yes, ma'am." This whole situation might have been a lot easier to deal with if I wasn't so damned turned on by authoritative women. The closer Connie came to killing me, the hotter I was for her. As she turned to walk away, the sight of her handcuffs jingling against her hips gave me a thrill all the way down to my toes. Man, oh man.

It was harder to stick with *the plan* every day that

passed, and a major part of it was to keep my hands—not to mention the rest of me—off Connie Jones. Because the plan was the only thing that might save her, the good vamps, my human family, and my unborn child. It was a good plan; unfortunately, it depended on elements that I couldn't control as closely as I needed to.

That thought reminded me that I needed to check on the status of Seth Walker, because even though I was the man *with* the plan, Seth was the key to its success.

Seth was the werewolf I hoped would take Connie and my baby away to safety—and as far from me as he could get them. Every time I thought about that my chest felt like someone was twisting a stake in it. I guess you could say Seth Walker was both my best friend and my worst enemy.

From his usual place behind the bar, Werm mixed me a Bloody Mary without the celery but with real blood—my favorite kind. I saluted him with the glass. "Here's blood in your eye," I muttered.

As usual, my diminutive vampire pal was festooned with silver-colored piercings. His ears bristled with hoops. Bars with balls on the ends garlanded his lips and eyebrows. He'd had to give up the actual silver in favor of surgical steel because the sterling had started giving him hives. Silver's not much better for vampires than it is for werewolves.

On top of that his hair was dyed goth black and spiked with enough gel to stop up the Savannah waterworks. He wore silver-studded black leather from head to toe.

"So, what are you hearing about the demon situation now that we offed that latest slimeball?" I asked. I'd agreed to invest in Werm's bar, the Portal, in exchange for the information he could wheedle out of people from behind the bar. And I use the word *people* loosely.

The Portal attracted a diverse clientele composed of everyone from young art students from SCAD to tragically hip professionals to adventurous yuppies to the downright dangerous denizens of the dark like us. That is, folks who hid in plain sight by masquerading as human. Werm kept his ear to the ground, plying the shadow dwellers with the poisons of their choice to get them to cough up information that might prove useful.

Werm lowered his voice to a pitch only another vampire could hear. "I think you and Connie and I have destroyed almost all of the double-dead vampires who were careless enough to come up from the underworld in the forms that Satan cursed them with," he said. "The ones who are left are the ones who had enough brains to take over human bodies."

I drained the blood cocktail. "That's good blood," I said. "Bovine?"

"Equine," Werm corrected. "You don't seem surprised by my news."

"Connie says the reports of obvious monsters have dwindled down to a trickle, thank the gods. She grabbed all those calls as they came in from dispatch, but they were getting really hard to explain away.

That guy we just took care of not far from the historic district might have been the last of the easy pickings. At least that's the way I've got it figured."

"The historic district is too close to the tourists for comfort," Werm said, wincing at the memory. "Especially with Saint Patrick's Day only a few nights away."

Saint Patrick's Day in Savannah is quite a citywide party. We have a large community of Irish immigrants who have put on a legendary annual celebration for almost two hundred years. There is a real Mardi Gras atmosphere, complete with a parade, and pubs dye the beer green and make sure a good time is had by all. If you don't have a good time, chances are you'd be too drunk to remember it.

"We've been really lucky that the existence of the demon world—us included—didn't explode onto the front pages and lead stories of every news outlet in the country," Werm said.

"Tell me about it." The police department wrote off the public's initial reports of monsters stalking the city as mass psychosis following the earthquake that had rocked Savannah less than a week ago. Unbeknownst to the humans, the trembler was the old lords' attempt to open the gates of hell, freeing twice-killed vampires to rise again and wreak havoc on humanity. Mel had gotten the voodoo gods to close the portal but not before a couple dozen double-deads were freed and William was trapped in the underworld with no way to get back to us.

"So now the real work begins," Werm speculated,

pulling on a longneck beer. "The balance of the demons will have to be sniffed out one by one."

I heard the slight break in Werm's voice as he described the situation, and I tried hard not to grin. He was my second now, and although he wasn't much of a fighter, he was learning and getting tougher by the day. Even more important, he was willing to do whatever I asked. "Things are going to be dicey all right," I said. "As long as it takes, you, me, and Connie will work our way through the rest of them. Hopefully, though, Seth will take Connie away soon. Be prepared for you and me to soldier on by ourselves."

"You've got so much on your shoulders, Jack. I want to be able to help more." Werm slid a catalog onto the bar in front of me. "I'm going to order a pair of these sai. Aren't they great?"

I looked at the picture of the sharp objects. They looked like rotisserie forks. "Son, how many times do I have to tell you? A vampire's already got his weapons." Glancing over my shoulder to make sure no humans were near, I unsheathed my fangs.

"But yours are so much bigger than mine," Werm complained, fingering his own fangs.

"They'll grow in. Meanwhile, you do what you can." Werm had never been vampire material, but he'd realized that much too late. He'd been a wannabe, begging me to turn him, shadowing my every move until he'd come to the attention of William's evil sire, Reedrek. Dear old Granddad Reedrek forced William to turn Werm and the rest is history. But the lad wasn't entirely useless. What he lacked in muscle he often made up for in smarts. If I had to be honest, he'd saved my bacon a time or two.

Werm continued to look uneasy. "What is it?" I said, motioning him to hand me a longneck.

"Are you sure this plan of yours is going to work? I mean, what if Connie figures out she's pregnant before Seth gets a chance to seduce her? Then she'll know the baby isn't his. And what even makes you think he can talk her into moving away with him when Connie knows she's needed here in Savannah to fight the double-dead demons? She's a really dedicated cop, ya know."

"It's gonna work," I growled, "because it has to. Have you heard from Seth?"

Werm inclined his head toward the door. "Speak of the werewolf."

Before I had a chance to turn around, the scent of shape shifter wafted to my sensitive nose. I glanced behind me to see a tall, broad-shouldered man wading through the crowd. When he saw me he scowled. I could hear the rumble in his throat from my bar stool.

Seth was the police chief of a small town in north Georgia. He had been on sabbatical in Savannah to straighten out a drug-dealing werewolf pack, but wound up becoming their new alpha after he'd had to dispatch their old leader to that big kennel in the sky. He volunteered to help the Savannah PD in the aftermath of the earthquake, then had briefly disappeared to take care of business back home. He and Connie had a history: he'd fallen in love with her when he was her firearms instructor at the police academy. I suspected she'd loved him back in those days.

When they met again here in Savannah, Connie and I were already involved; Seth, my best friend, had the decency to keep his distance. But it was a new ball game now, and Seth was more than willing to pick up where he left off.

"Hey, Seth, welcome back," Werm said, handing the werewolf a cold longneck.

"Thanks," he muttered, seating himself on the bar stool next to mine.

"Did you get things ready for you and Connie to move north?" I asked him as casually as I could.

"She didn't tell you?" Seth asked.

"What?"

"Before I left she told me she wouldn't move. I tried to reason with her. I told her that if she came with me to north Georgia I could protect her from those European vampires who are gunning for her now. But she says she has to track down all those vampires that came up from hell."

"I can do that without her," I said, trying to keep the desperation out of my voice. True, it would be easier with her help, but I could do the job myself one bloodsucker at a time. Especially if Werm pitched in now and then.

"She says she's the Slayer and it's her responsibility." Seth held up his hand when I started to sputter out all the reasons he had to get Connie away *now.* "I know. I know. I tried. Remember we're dealing with a force of nature here. Even more now than she was before."

I ran my hand through my hair in frustration. This just wouldn't do. William had been smuggling peace-loving European vampires into Savannah for the last couple of hundred years. They would come into port and be assigned a coven somewhere else on the Continent, but eventually the Council got wind of his activities. The old lords, a.k.a. the Council, targeted William as a warning to others not to try to escape their influence. Savannah became a hotbed of evil vampire attacks.

The Slayer had succeeded where the old lords failed, and her coming-out party would be old news to the Council by this time. Reedrek—through his contacts on the Continent—would have already warned them of the Slayer. They would come for her any day. Seth was the only person she trusted completely, and with good reason. He had to get her away.

The only way I could see this working was if Seth got her to sleep with him and later appealed to her to leave town to protect what they both thought was his baby. She might not go for herself, but maybe she'd do it for the sake of her child. I had to count on that. Even though Connie was part monster now, I had to believe that her maternal instinct was still alive. She had lost one child. I just knew she'd do anything she could to prevent losing another.

"So, what are you going to do?" Werm asked Seth with a sidelong glance at me.

"I resigned from the force," Seth said glumly. "My old deputy is the new chief and is going to hire someone to help him. I told him I'd be here in Savannah indefinitely."

"Listen," I said to Seth, trying to stay calm. "Since you've been out of town for a couple of days, why don't you go see Connie tonight? See how she's doing, you know? She should be off duty by now."

"You don't know how she's doing? You've been demon killing with her the last few days." Seth looked at me with suspicion in his yellow-green wolf eyes.

"It's hard for me to judge. It's all I can do to keep her from killing me. She's not . . . herself."

Seth nodded solemnly. I had warned him about the change in her. Fortunately for him, her urge to kill didn't extend to shape shifters. Some monsters had all the luck.

"Okay," Seth said, tossing back the last of his drink. "I'll go see how she is." He bumped my shoulder hard when he stood up and turned to go—just another he-man way to say *go to hell*. He was still pissed about the whole thing. Mostly about how I'd tried to kill the woman we both loved. Connie had told him so.

I tried to tamp down the pain I felt just thinking about Connie sleeping with somebody else—not to mention my best friend. I was trying to rub the ache out of my temples when the scent of vampire hit me in the nose like a backhanded slap. "What the hell?" I asked Werm.

In unison, we turned our heads to stare as a short vampire, clad in a khaki trench coat, matching fedora, and sunglasses glided through the door and perched himself on the bar stool one spot over from where I sat. He laid a small notebook and pen on the bar and looked toward Werm expectantly.

"What's your pleasure?" Werm asked.

The vampire's nose twitched and he pointed to my empty cocktail glass. He could smell the blood residue. "One of those, if you please," he said in a British accent. He had sharp, angular features and buck teeth. With the glasses, hat, and pointy nose, he looked like he just hopped out of one of those spy versus spy cartoons in *MAD* magazine. I know that dates me, but what the hell. I'm almost a hundred and fifty years old.

Werm raised one eyebrow slightly and set about to mix the creature a drink. The little blood drinker eyed me pleasantly. I looked around at the crowd of clubgoers. If anyone had even noticed the newcomer, nobody showed it, which was miraculous because the guy looked like he might have been the love child of Nosferatu and Pee-wee Herman. His getup could have caused a stir even if his pallor and hard, shiny skin didn't put you in mind of the kind of marble used for tombstones.

He followed my glance toward the crowd. Lowering his voice to a whisper only other vampires could hear, he said, "What a delightful establishment. Do you southern vampires often rub elbows with unsuspecting humans?"

"Yes, but no tapping into the vein," Werm said. "House rules."

"That goes for all of Savannah," I added.

"Oh, of course. I, like you gentlemen, am a civilized man." He extended a slender hand to me and said, "My name is Velki."

Reluctantly I shook his hand. If his skin looked like marble, it felt more like leather. "I'm Jack McShane," I answered. I thought I saw a little spark of recognition, but it was gone in a flash. Probably my imagination. I had a lot to be paranoid about just lately.

He touched the brim of his hat. "I am pleased to meet you." He said it in an oddly formal way, like someone in a period movie.

"What's with the shades?" I asked.

"My eyes are a little . . . sensitive. You see, I've recently taken a rather long rejuvenating sleep underground."

"I thought only vampires in Anne Rice novels did that," Werm observed.

"Anne who?" Velki asked.

"Never mind," I said.

Werm set Velki's drink in front of him. He took the celery stick from the glass and sniffed it experimentally as if he didn't know what it was.

I tapped my forehead to signal Werm to open his mind and thoughts to me. Since we were the vampire equivalent of brothers, Werm and I could communicate psychically if we tried really hard. A sire and offspring could do it easily, but Werm and I had to practice. We'd gotten good enough to speak through our minds from a distance of a mile or more. For privacy's sake we kept our minds closed most of the time. I didn't want Werm to know my every thought and action, and I damn sure didn't even want to *think* about his if I didn't have to.

What is he, Jack? I mean, I know he's a vampire but what the hell?

Double-damned if I know. Besides Reedrek, he's the only vampire I've ever seen who actually looks like a vampire. He must have been underground a helluva long time.

Werm shuddered. *I hope the humans don't notice him. Halloween was over a long time ago and some of them aren't drunk enough not to go running out of here screaming if they get a good look. Do you think he's using glamour on them?*

No. I can't feel any glamour from him. I think they just haven't noticed him yet.

Maybe he's one of the double-deads.

I was thinking the same thing. Either that or he's heard that there's a slayer in town and he's come to check it out. I'll see if I can get any information out of him.

How are you going to do that?

Ask him.

Oh. Uh, if you have to rough him up, would you mind taking it outside?

You're no fun. I wondered if Werm was ever going to vamp up.

"So, you're new in town," I stated. "We don't get many of . . . our kind here in Savannah. Where did you come from?"

The newcomer finally decided the celery stick was unfit for vampire consumption, turned up his strange nose at it, and laid it aside. "Oh, here and there," he said vaguely.

I lowered my face near his and felt my nose twitch

at his odd sulfury smell. Glancing around to make sure no humans were in earshot, I whispered, "That answer won't cut it with me, Scooter. Now, tell me where you came from before I send you directly to hell without you passing Go and collecting two hundred dollars."

The little blood drinker gulped some of his cocktail and pink droplets of sweat popped out on his bumpy forehead. "I—I'm from the Midwest," he stammered. "I don't belong to any coven. I just keep to myself and keep moving. I thought it was time to wander back east, see what William is up to."

The mention of William's name still pained me and I winced. "You were a friend of William's? Are you one of his European imports?"

"Yes," he squeaked.

"How long ago?"

"I was one of the first. That was before the formal clans were established. So I just went off on my own."

Werm looked at me. *What do you think? Is he telling the truth?*

Could be. If he was one of the first to come over by boat, that would be before my time. And I don't think we can expect your garden-variety double-dead to know about the smuggling operation. It was always a pretty well-kept secret.

Didn't William have records?

I never thought about it before. I'll ask Deylaud. He'd know.

Records like that would come in handy in case any of the other double-deads have a similar cover story.

Good point.

I turned back to Velki when he tapped me on the arm. "You said *'were'* a friend of William's," he pointed out.

It took me a second to catch his meaning. "William's dead," I said.

Velki's face fell. "Oh, no. When? How?"

"A few days ago," I said. "*How* is classified."

"I am so sorry," he said. "You were a friend of his also?"

"He was my sire."

"And mine," Werm muttered.

"What an incalculable loss. You both have my most profound sympathies." Velki raised his glass. "To William."

Werm looked at me. *He seems sincere.*

Yeah. But if I decide to let him live and he starts hanging out here as a regular, you keep your eye on him.

Will do.

"Thanks," I said to the little blood drinker and clinked my bottle against his glass. "So, are you just passing through or are you planning to stay awhile?"

"I'm planning to stay for a bit," he said between sips of his cocktail. "I'm working on a book about killers."

"Killers? What kind of killers?" I asked.

"Human ones, of course." He set down his drink, took up his pen, and opened the first page of his notebook. "What famous serial killers were from Savannah?"

"I can't think of any," I said. Werm shrugged and shook his head.

"Mass murderers?" Velki asked.

"None that I know of."

"Terrorists?"

"Not as such, no."

The little man looked flustered. "But I was told Savannah had a most violent past," he insisted.

"It does," Werm put in. "There were all kinds of battles from the Revolution onward."

"Savannah was home to pirates, brigands, and cutthroats of all kinds," I added. "People got robbed, murdered, shanghaied, and dragged off by privateers, you name it."

"Names! I need names!"

Werm and I exchanged a look. "Not that many individuals stand out in terms of body count," Werm said. "Sorry we can't help you. Why don't you try the historical society?"

Velki pulled himself together and closed his book. "Very well. I shall enquire elsewhere. Thank you so much for your hospitality." He laid a bill on the bar and stood up.

"You keep in touch, you hear? Werm and I like to keep track of the other vamps passing through town."

"Naturally you are protective of your territory. I applaud your vigilance. Shall I drop into this club from time to time while I'm here?"

"You shall," I said pleasantly.

The little creature nodded and left, not drawing any notice from the humans on the dance floor. Of course, Werm's patrons were a motley crew in their own right, so I guess one weirdo more or less didn't seem strange to them.

"Man, he was creepy," Werm observed.

When a metal-studded, spiky-haired vampire wearing black leather from head to toe calls you creepy, you know you're pretty much in a class by yourself.

As for me, after spending the last few days staking scaly, slimy demons, my creepy quotient had maxed out. I had a sudden urge to go after the new vampire and kill him just on general principles. What can I say? I'm a bite-first-and-ask-questions-later kind of vampire. I had Connie to protect and some evil fiends to ferret out, and for all I knew this Velki character might be one of my new enemies. My life would be a lot simpler if I just offed him.

I'd taken a step toward the door when Werm appeared in front of me, blocking my way.

"What?" I demanded.

Werm swallowed hard. As close as we'd become, he'd never lost his fear of me. That was a good thing for him.

"Jack, please don't get mad at me for saying this, but before you go after that guy, I think you should ask yourself something."

"Oh, yeah? This better be good, little man. What should I ask myself?"

He shifted his weight nervously from foot to foot as if he had to be ready to run. "You should ask yourself—what would William do?"

He couldn't have rocked me any harder if he'd punched me in the gut. Actually, Werm couldn't have rocked me at all if he'd punched me in the gut, but the point is—he was right. My role had always been to be the enforcer—the brawn to William's brain. Now I had to be the brain *and* the brawn. I had to learn to think before I acted.

Werm looked up at me expectantly. "Was it good?"

"Huh?"

"You said if I stopped you it had better be good."

I squeezed his shoulder gently. I would have ruffled his hair like a little brother if I could have, but there was too much gel in it.

"Yeah," I said. "It was good."

Two

I stood in the shadows outside Connie's town house feeling as dead inside as the vampire I was. A cool breeze whispered through the dry leaves and swayed the Spanish moss in the oak branches overhead. The chill stoked the mist that rose from the earth, swirling around the benches and street lamps and into the dark street corners.

I had to cloak my presence using glamour. Connie was getting as good at smelling out vampires as I was. It was just another skill that would help her kill me when my time came.

Seth's truck was parked by the streetlight, which meant he was still there with her. I wished someone would kill me now as I saw the light behind the bedroom curtains go out. I waited for ten of the longest minutes of my life, but he didn't come out. Trying not to think about what was going on beyond that curtain, I bit my tongue until the blood ran.

How had I gotten myself in this mess? Hadn't bitter experience taught me that long-term relationships with human women always led to heartache? The fact that the woman I finally tried to keep for my own turned out to be a vampire slayer was just a big old cosmic joke on yours truly.

With a final glance at the window, I slid back behind the wheel of my convertible and roared away. A few minutes later I was at my garage on Victory Drive.

The bays were full so I parked out back where I found my detail man and resident zombie Huey digging an ever-deepening hole in the ground. He'd been digging the hole for weeks, and he'd almost reached his goal when the earthquake had caused it to collapse, ruining all his work. He'd started over again and was going at it harder than ever. His pet crow, Ginger, was supervising this process. At the moment she was hopping along the ground complaining bitterly about mites.

"Dammit!" she squawked. "Can't somebody around here get me a flea collar or something?"

"I can get you some Sevin dust," Huey offered.

"I don't want to be poisoned, hamburger-for-brains! I just want to get rid of these cooties."

I winced. Ginger had been in a foul—if you'll pardon the expression—mood since her former boss, Eleanor, had tricked her out of her human body. Ginger's soul had taken up residence in the nearest living thing. Which, unfortunately, was a female crow, one evidently lousy with biting insects.

When Ginger fixed her beady little bird eyes on me, she said, "Speaking of bloodsuckers—what have you done for me lately, fang boy? Have you found my bitch of a boss yet?"

I sighed. Eleanor used to run a fancy brothel and Ginger was one of her girls. But William had made Eleanor a vampire and, when she'd betrayed him, cast her into the underworld. Eleanor had returned, though, and now Ginger was flapping around as a crow.

"Believe me," I told Ginger. "I want to find her as bad as you do. If it wasn't for her, William would still be undead and I wouldn't be up to my ass in devils." What I didn't tell her was that I wasn't all that sure I knew how to get her body back from Eleanor. One problem at a time, I figured.

Ginger lifted one wing and probed for a mite with her beak. "Seriously, Jack, I'm going out of my mind already. How do you propose to find her?"

That was a good question. Until Eleanor decided to show herself again, there wasn't much I could do. Unless she made a mistake, like feeding on the wrong human or killing one, I might just have to wait it out. That was not the answer Ginger wanted to hear.

"I'm hunting the double-deads as fast as I can, Gin. I give you my word I'll get her sooner or later."

"Make it sooner, or I'm going to go all Alfred Hitchcock on your sorry, bloodsucking hide. I guess I'm just going to have to look for her myself." With that, she flew off into the night.

"She sure is sore," Huey said. He was so deep into the hole he was digging that his voice sounded far away. I peered over the rim to discover that he had finally freed up the Chevy Corsica we buried him in back before he'd returned as a zombie. All that was left was for Rennie to haul it out for him with the wrecker hoist.

"Don't worry about it, Huey. Now that you've reached the Chevy, you can find another hobby." I find that having a pet zombie is kind of like having a pet border collie. You have to have work for them to do or they're just not happy. Feeding them red meat helps, too.

"I think I'll just keep on digging. I think something else is down here."

"Whatever, dude."

I still felt bad about bringing Huey back. He was having a grand old time in his own personal version of heaven before I accidentally raised him from the dead after a drunken rant. I have certain powers when it comes to fellow dead people, and to tell you the truth, sometimes I don't know my own strength. A few ill-chosen words in a prayer to a voodoo god and old Huey was clawing his way up out of the ground and making himself right at home again. Melaphia's anti-rotting spell kept his flesh more or less intact—enough so that the customers couldn't quite put their finger on just what was different about him. If they knew he was a zombie they'd all run screaming into the marsh, but the policy around the garage had always been don't ask, don't tell, no matter what manner of creature you were.

Speaking of creatures, Rennie and the irregulars were at their usual places at the poker table when I walked inside. Despite the way it sounds, "Rennie and the irregulars" are not a garage band. They're a motley group of hangers-on and hangers-out made up of one human, one werewolf, one other shape shifter of indeterminate species, and one faerie.

The faerie, Otis, and the mystery shifter, Rufus, were best friends. At least they had been until Otis had revealed himself to be a faerie. Not the homosexual kind—the leprechaun kind. Or something close to that, anyway. Otis was a fey creature in the Irish tradition. He could lay on the glamour even better than me. Good enough to masquerade as a coverall-wearing, grease-under-the-fingernails, good-old-boy blue-collar redneck. In reality—if you could call it that—his hair was blue and as shiny as Christmas tree lights and his skin glowed with perpetual youth and otherworldly beauty.

And that wasn't the half of it.

He'd been sent to watch us vampires for a group of high-falutin' Sidhe royalty who were afraid our activities had some connection to an end-time scenario.

I had enough on my plate without worrying about the end of the whole freakin' world, so I told Otis to do what he had to. Hell, he or his supervisors might prove useful one of these days. All he'd ever been good for so far was playing cards and drinking my coffee.

"Evening, boys," I greeted them on the way to the open coffee area.

They grunted their hellos. "Say, Rennie, can I talk to you a minute?" I asked.

My business partner sauntered over and looked at me from behind his thick glasses. He was walking a little stifflike and rubbing his abdomen.

"You okay?" I asked.

"Ulcers," he said. "I'm taking medicine. It'll be okay. What can I do for you, hoss?"

"Sorry you're sick, man," I said, patting him on the shoulder. I reckon being partners with an evil creature of the night would be a mite stressful on a regular guy. It made me feel a little guilty. "Uh, the last time I went by the hospital I noticed that the city work crews had finished repairing the street and were working on putting the foundation of the hospital to rights."

"Yeah, I noticed that, too," Rennie said.

"Do you feel up to doing a little job for me?" I asked. Rennie nodded. "Okay. Here's what I want you to do . . ." I gave him explicit instructions for a project I hoped would help me get Reedrek back under control. Now that William was gone, I was going to have to start thinking ahead, anticipating all kinds of situations, and figuring out solutions to problems that might or might not happen. The way William used to.

When I was finished giving him directions, Rennie nodded. "No problem," he said. "Consider it done."

"Thanks, man. I knew I could count on you." I clapped him on the back and waved my coffee cup in the direction of the card table. "I notice Rufus still isn't making eye contact with Otis." In fact, he was holding his cards in front of his face like a geisha holding up her fan, giving him a coquettish look that was a mite incongruous on a redneck.

"Yeah. His nose is still out of joint because he had to hear about Otis's other persona secondhand. He's mightily pissed." Rennie rejoined the card game as Jerry was dealing and I walked over to the others.

"Hey, Jerry, Seth's back in town," I said, taking a sip of the stiff coffee.

"I'm glad to hear that," Jerry the werewolf said. "The pack's driving me crazy, whining about having to get real jobs and stay out of trouble."

Jerry was the beta, second in command of the local pack behind the alpha, Seth. Together they were trying to get the pack to give up drug dealing and bootlegging for more legal pursuits. It was an uphill battle.

"Hmmph," Rufus observed.

"What was that, Rufus?" Rennie asked. Although Rennie was the only human in the group, he wasn't afraid of any of us. He probably should have been, but he wasn't.

"Real jobs, he said. Not like *spyin'*, I guess."

Rennie winked at me from behind those glasses that made his eyes look perpetually bleary. "Here we go," he muttered.

Otis, his face indignant under the bill of his Caterpillar hat, threw his cards on the table. "Why don't you come on out and say what's on your mind, Rufus? I'm sick of you sitting there sniping at me night after night."

Rufus slapped his own cards down as well. "I just can't believe you've been hanging out here for years and spying on us the whole time."

"I thought I explained all that, you hardheaded coot. Even Jack isn't holding a grudge, so what's it to you?"

"It ain't that," Rufus said peevishly. "It's just—

well, dang it all, I thought we were friends. And you didn't even tell me who you really are."

I drew a chair up to the card table and straddled it. This was shaping up to be a good old-fashioned slap-down. Gods knew I could use some entertainment.

"Oh yeah?" Otis demanded. "And what about you? Everybody here knows you're some kind of shifter, but nobody knows what kind. We used to play all coy with one another—don't ask, don't tell, just like Jack always said. But now we've all had to come out for one reason or another—everybody but you. You're the only one left holding back and you got the nerve to complain about me keeping secrets? So I'm a freakin' faerie. Now it's your turn. Do it, if you're man enough! What are you?"

The silence was deafening. Rufus peered at us like a rat in a trap. Even Huey had appeared in the doorway and was waiting expectantly.

Finally Rufus squared his shoulders, thrust out his chin, and said, "I'm a werecat."

"I knew it was something like that," Jerry said smugly.

"Yeah, I figured that, too," I said.

"Cool," Huey added.

"What kind of werecat are you?" Otis asked, crossing his arms over his chest.

"What do you mean, What kind of werecat?" Rufus asked.

"I mean, are you a wereleopard?"

"No."

"A weretiger?" Jerry wanted to know.

"No."

"A werelion?" I asked, genuinely puzzled now. How many kinds of ferocious werefelines could there be?

"You are some kind of *big* cat, right?" Rennie asked.

Rufus turned beet red. "No! I'm just a were*cat*, all right? *Felis silvestris catus.*"

The rest of us froze in place for a second, trying to wrap our minds around it. I finally asked for clarification. "Dude. You're just a regular old cat?"

The five of us who were not part-time house cats exploded in laughter. "How in the hell did you wind up as a were*kitty*?" Jerry asked when he'd caught his breath. "That is just so wrong. Shape shifters are supposed to be dangerous, man! What happened?"

"I'm not a regular were," Rufus admitted glumly. "It's more like a curse. I have to spend nights as a human and days as a cat. Kind of like those two dogs of William's."

"Wait a minute!" Rennie wheezed, holding his side. "Don't tell me! You're the red tabby that hangs around here in the daytime, aren't you?"

When Rufus went all stone-faced and refused to answer, Rennie dissolved into hysteria. "Oh, my gawd! I've been feeding you Tender Vittles and table scraps for years and didn't even know it was you!"

Huey shook his head in wonderment. "I thought y'all knew. I've known that ever since I came back," he said and wandered out again.

I shook my head. "Zombies have a way with animals, I guess. So what was the curse all about?"

Rufus waved his hand. "Never you mind. Y'all

done made enough fun of me for one night without dredging up that ancient history."

I wondered how ancient that history was. You could never tell with curses and spells. Reyha and Deylaud—the "two dogs of William's," as Rufus had described them—were hundreds of years old, even though in their human forms they looked to be twenty-somethings. It was interesting that Rufus looked on his lot in life as a curse whereas the Rin Tin Twins considered theirs a gift.

Otis clearly did not agree that Rufus had been made enough fun of. He was still slapping his knees, laughing. "Here, pussy, pussy!"

Rufus dove across the table, scattering cards, chips, and coffee cups in his wake. He hit Otis in the chest, his momentum carrying both of them onto the concrete floor where they grappled, trying to get a clean punch off.

"Will the two of you look at each other?" I shouted. "You're acting like a couple of damn fools."

Jerry and I pulled them apart. "Otis, say you're sorry," I demanded, holding him by the scruff of the neck.

"Sorry." He smirked.

"Like you mean it," I said, shaking him like you would a stubborn child.

"Sorry," he repeated, looking at the floor.

"Now, Rufus, you say you're sorry for giving Otis the skunk eye lately," I said.

"Sorry," he muttered.

I released my hold on Otis, and Jerry let Rufus go.

"Y'all ought to be ashamed of yourselves," I scolded. "Acting out like a couple of kids while I'm out there fighting demons and trying to hold this city together. From now on you two are earning your keep."

"Huh? I work for the Sidhe," Otis said.

"Well, now you're working for me. And unless you want to be a blood donor, I would suggest you go out there tomorrow and use those faerie glamour skills to find Eleanor." Otis began to protest but shut up quick when I flashed fang.

"And as for you, hairball," I said, directing my attention to Rufus. "I would suggest that you use your talents to comb this city in your feline disguise and help Otis sniff out Eleanor's whereabouts."

I gathered them up into a man hug, one against each shoulder. "I can't believe I didn't think of this before," I said, squeezing them until they both gasped. "You guys are going to make a great team."

Rennie looked up at us, wiping away tears of laughter with his bandanna. "I just love it when a plan comes together for you pointy-toothed types. Especially when it doesn't involve me."

"How goes the demon hunting?" Melaphia asked, sipping a cup of coffee.

As usual, I'd made it back to the mansion just as the sun was coming over the horizon. Mel was convinced I was going to cut it too close one day and fry to a crisp. Maybe she was right.

"Not bad," I said. I didn't go into specifics. Any mention of Connie created a real tension convention between Mel and me, and I'd had a hard day's night.

"Tell me again why I can't kill that woman for murdering my father," Melaphia muttered into her cup. She had the aristocratic profile and beautiful golden brown skin tone of her foremothers, voodoo royalty all. She—and her ancestors before her—had in fact been William's adopted daughters, although they masqueraded as servants.

That deception had been necessary in the old days. Now it was just a convenient cover story for why Melaphia had remained in this home, working for William, when she could have done so many other things with her life. It was her home. Hers, and her daughter, Renee's. In the daytime I slept in the basement vault so I could protect them. Or at least try to. I hadn't been all that good at it lately.

I opened the fridge and took out a bottle of fresh blood. "You know why you can't kill Connie. If you do, you'll wreck some kind of ancient prophecy, and that'll put you on the shit list of the whole pantheon of voodoo gods and goddesses."

Melaphia was perfectly aware of all this. And I knew her well enough to know that she had gone over the situation from every angle. If she could have figured out a way to avenge William and not be relegated to the far corners of the underworld, she would have offed Connie already. She just needed more time to make her peace with the situation—and with the Slayer.

"She'll kill you, too, you know," she said solemnly, peering into her cup as if she could see the future there.

"Maybe she will. Maybe she won't. Time will tell."

"And who will protect us then?" She said this calmly, but I could feel the emotion coming off her in waves of raw pain and fear.

I groped for an answer, but none came. No good one anyway. "Mel, all I can tell you is that I'm going to do the best I can."

She worked her mouth but said nothing. Still the unspoken question hung in the air. *What if your best isn't good enough?*

"Dex came here today," Melaphia said, still not looking at me.

"What?" I nearly dropped my drink. Renee's father hadn't been around since she was an infant. "What did the sperm donor want?"

"Don't call him that," Mel said sharply. "He heard I'd had a nervous breakdown."

I didn't like the sound of that, or the implications. Melaphia had almost lost her mind when Renee was kidnapped awhile back. William had to go to England to rescue her, and Mel was nearly catatonic on and off while they were gone. "And?"

"And he wondered if he should try to get custody of Renee." Mel stifled a sob, and I sat down at the table beside her and took her hand.

"I'd like to see him try," I said fiercely. "William keeps the best lawyers in the south on retainer. There's no way in hell—"

"He says he can do it. He says he can take her from me legally."

"No, he can't. Not after we prove that he's been an absentee father who's never been much more than indifferent to Renee. Besides, surely he can see that you're better—I mean, that you're fine . . . now."

"He dredged up a lot of ancient history."

Dex hated the fact that Mel worked as a "domestic," as he called her. He thought having the mother of his child working as a housekeeper was bad for his academic career. He'd divorced Melaphia after Renee was born when she refused to leave William's household. But Melaphia had known she had a destiny to fulfill that Dex could not be a part of. He had no idea that Melaphia was the most powerful *mambo* in this hemisphere or that his child was fated to inherit the same ability. And, of course, he didn't know about the vampires she was living with.

"Let me deal with him," I said. "Tell him if he wants Renee back, he'll have to go through me." I cupped Mel's chin in my hand like I did when she was a little girl and kissed her on the forehead.

"Thank you, Uncle Jack," she said. Even though Mel and I looked about the same human age, I had helped William raise her from an infant after her beloved mother died. I felt, as William had, like she was my own daughter.

As I turned to go to the basement, Mel said, "Wait. There's one more thing I have to tell you."

I could tell by the tone of her voice that it was something bad. Was there any end to bad news around here? She handed me a newspaper clipping. It was Tilly Granger's obituary. "Oh, no," I heard myself whisper.

"She died right about the same time as William, poor old thing. We missed the wake because of everything that was going on. I called her staff and gave them our sympathies. I'm going to have a gourmet food basket sent over from Paula Deen's place."

If Diana, William's human wife, was the love of his life, Tilly was a close second. He'd offered her the gift of immortality when she was a blushing Savannah debutante in the roaring twenties, but she'd turned him down.

Tilly had aged like any other mortal while William remained perpetually young. After she rejected his proposal, he'd had to stay out of the country for a few years in order to fool Savannah society into thinking he was his own son. In fact, that was how Melaphia had decided we should handle William's death. We would simply tell people he was on an extended tour of Europe.

I didn't really see the point in not having William declared dead. If we did, Mel and Renee could legally inherit everything. But I think in her heart of hearts, Melaphia still harbored the hope that she could some-day figure out how to conjure William back to life. Gods knew she'd worked feats almost as miraculous in the past. Maman Lalee's word was law, though, and she had been crystal clear about the issue. William could never return from the underworld.

But like I was saying, Tilly had been one of the few constants in his life. It was somehow poetic that they had died at nearly the same time.

"I can't believe it," I said, staring at the paper. "I mean, I know she was nearly a hundred and all, but I just can't wrap my mind around the idea of her being gone."

"Sometimes I think you forget that not everyone's immortal like you."

I looked at her in amazement but said nothing. How wrong she was. I never forgot the fleeting nature of my human loves. I was as terrified at first to hold Mel as a newborn as I'd been with her mother before her. I would peek into her crib, marveling at the musical sound of her little cries, the tissuelike delicacy of her skin, the sweet freshness of her newly minted human scent. When I finally worked up the nerve to lift her up and hold her against me, she seemed so fragile, so helpless.

My succession of human daughters were like butterflies, all beauty and color, floating on summer air with delicate gossamer wings. And their lives seemed just as short. Summer turned into winter in the blink of an immortal eye and they were gone from me forever.

Human lives were brief enough without the *non*-human threats that Melaphia and Renee faced on a regular basis. I only hoped I could survive long enough to help them reach a ripe old age.

I couldn't bear the thought of seeing them fly away from me, but humans always did.

Three

I woke to someone banging on my coffin lid. I pushed the lid open and the sight that greeted me convinced me I was dreaming. It wasn't until Reyha started growling that I admitted I was awake. Reyha slept with me in her daytime dog form, guarding me as she had guarded William. I blinked a couple of times as I tried to understand what I was looking at.

Otis stood outside my coffin in his fey Stevie Sparkle persona, complete with his trademark spangly blue getup. Otis had hidden himself in plain sight in the seventies, showing his real nature as the front man in a glitter rock band. After that phase was over he had to go back to disguising his true form. Any human who saw him up close and personal would be totally freaked out by his otherworldly appearance. There was no way he could pass for human unless he cloaked himself in glamour.

He had a very nervous red tabby cat perched on his shoulder with its back arched and its tail puffed out.

I grabbed the coffin lid and tried to shut it again.

Otis-Stevie latched onto it and held it fast. Those faeries are strong shiny little sumbitches. I cursed him, his cat, and their interruption.

"What time is it?" I asked.

"It's still daylight," Stevie told me.

"Reyha, go upstairs," I ordered. She whined and jumped onto the floor. With one last snarl at Rufus the cat, she trotted upstairs.

"What are you two freaks doing in my boudoir this time of day, and why are you decked out in your faerie finery, Otis?"

Otis sniffed. "Sorry to interrupt your beauty sleep. You told us to find Eleanor, remember? And I do my best tracking when I'm in my true form. My human nose was all stuffed up because of the snuff."

"You're supposed to put it between your cheek and gums, not snort it, doofus," I told him incredulously.

"Not where I come from."

I wanted to argue some more, but there was no time to get bogged down in smokeless tobacco issues. I had to focus. "Did you find her?"

"Yeah. As a matter of fact, we did. Didn't we, Rufus?"

The cat issued a trill and kneaded Otis's shoulder.

"Ow," said the faerie. "You need a manicure."

"Not to mention a bath. The both of you smell like you've been rolling in a cat box."

"It's no wonder. We've been crawling through back alleys and lowlife dives all over this city trying to sniff her out," Otis said.

I got out of the coffin and went to pull on my boots. "I take it you found her in a place I can get to from the tunnels. I'm not that into sunbathing." Savannah had a system of tunnels that was left over from the time when the city's street level was raised as a defense against hurricanes. It was a right handy way for sun-sensitive creatures like me to get around in the daytime.

"Yeah. Believe it or not, she's holed up in that house that William was building for her, even though it's only half finished."

"Well, I'll be damned," I muttered as I buttoned my shirt and pulled on my jacket. "That was the last place I would have looked for her. It was too obvious."

"She knew that, so that's exactly where she went. If we hurry we can make it there by sundown so you can surprise her when she comes out in the night to feed."

"Sounds like a plan," I said. "Let's roll." Then I stopped short, thinking about what Otis had just said. *When she comes out to feed.* "Dammit," I spat. "I can't believe I didn't think—"

"What is it?"

"I have no idea if she's still a vampire."

"Huh?"

"Think about it. She's in Ginger's body now. Ginger wasn't a vampire."

Otis followed me out the door that led to the tunnels, and Rufus trotted along by his side. "But she *smells* like a vampire, Jack. That's how we found her."

I swore bitterly. Poor Ginger. I wouldn't wish the life of a blood drinker on anybody. Sure, I had chosen it, but I didn't know what I was getting myself into. All I knew was that I was dying, and a charismatic man in a Confederate captain's uniform had asked me if I wanted to live. I was, what—thirty years old? Of course I'd said yes. Would Ginger even want to go back into the body of a vampire?

As we made our way through the tunnels, I tried to remember what Eleanor had looked like when I last saw her, the night of William's death. William was bleeding from an injury he got in the earthquake and she said she smelled his blood. She'd been clearly terrified of the Slayer. Eleanor had fought William briefly before Connie killed him, but was it with vampire strength? He was gravely hurt but threw her off easily before she ran away into the night like a coward.

Was Eleanor holed up in her under-construction house because she couldn't go out into the sunlight or because of habit? As a madam, she had worked through the night and slept during the day anyway.

Whether Ginger's body was undead or alive, I was about to find out. We'd reached the heavy metal door that William had installed between the tunnels and the basement of Eleanor's house. "We've got to be quiet, you two," I said. "If Ginger's body is a vampire's, Eleanor will be able to hear the slightest noise."

On cue, Rufus the cat made a noise like he was about to cough up a hairball the size of a small sheep.

"What the hell's wrong with him?" I demanded.

"Damned if I know," Otis insisted. "Do I look like a cat herder?"

Rufus hissed and began to stretch, but not in the slow, languorous way that a cat usually stretched. It was in the horrifying way a wereanimal began to shift. I winced when I heard long bones reforming and ligaments popping. Living with Reyha and Deylaud, I'd recognize those noises anywhere. The brutal sounds of shape shifting signaled the beginnings of Rufus's daily metamorphosis.

"The sun is out," I said. "He's about to turn."

Otis looked toward the floor in disgusted fascination. "Whoa! That's really ugly."

"Ain't it?" I averted my eyes.

"You should watch this."

"I've seen enough weres shift to last me a lifetime. Listen, you stay here and watch over him until he rears up on his hind legs. He'll be defenseless midshift. I'm going to go and try to get the drop on Eleanor before she leaves the house."

"Okay," Otis agreed, still mesmerized by the sight of Rufus's turning. "Wow, this would make some crazy reality show."

I looked at the faerie and the mancat. "You remind me of Beauty and the Beast," I said.

I opened the metal door as quietly as I could. Good thing it was new so the hinges didn't squeak. The basement had been finished in the last couple of days, so no light from the rising sun shown in. I saw a form covered in cloth near the far wall and could sense that it was Eleanor. As I crept closer I saw that the cloth was the silk shawl William had given her to use in her voodoo rituals.

I slipped up on her silently and grabbed her from

behind, catching her around the shoulders and pinning her to my chest. Instantly awake, she flailed against me with all her strength. Her heels struck my kneecaps and her head banged against my collarbone, but I held her fast.

"Tell me why I shouldn't kill you for what you did to William," I hissed into her ear.

"William deserved everything he got for sending me to the tortures of hell."

"You need a new song. I've heard that one too many times. Try again."

She struggled in vain to free her arms but only managed to claw at my thighs with her long nails. "Okay, how about this one? You and I both know you can't kill me because I'm the only one who can get your little birdbrain friend back into a human body. Your voodoo witch could study all the old spells she can find and she won't be able to help."

"So we're at a Mexican standoff. If you have any ideas, I'm listening."

"I'll let Ginger have her body back if you protect me from the Slayer."

Eleanor's proposal surprised me. It seemed too easy. What made her think I could protect her? She probably figured that since I had managed to keep Connie from killing *me* I had some influence over her. I wasn't about to set Eleanor straight on that point. And what made her think I wouldn't double-cross her? There was something missing here and I couldn't decide what it was.

"Okay," I said. "Agreed. There's just one thing,

though. If Ginger wasn't a vampire and you're in her body, why are *you* still a vampire?"

"Because the body takes its cues from the spirit," she said.

"You mean that when Ginger gets her body back she won't be a vampire?"

"Yeah."

"What will happen to your spirit?"

"I'll take the body of the nearest living thing," she said.

Still too easy. She was being much too agreeable. "I'm going to be right there when you make the switch and I'm going to make sure you go into the body that Ginger's in right now."

"Whose body is that?"

"More like 'what.' A crow's."

"A crow's? Well, hell, I always wanted to fly."

It hit me then what I was missing. No wonder Eleanor was so sanguine. "Wait a minute. What's to stop you from taking over some other poor unsuspecting human's body? And don't even think about lying to me."

Eleanor sighed and stopped struggling, hanging limply in my grasp. "Because every time I switch bodies, my vampire spirit gets a little weaker."

"How do you know all this?"

"Remember when the Council made that deal with the Devil in order to get him to open the underworld?"

"Yeah?"

"Part of the deal was that us demons who were released from the underworld could choose to take over the body of a human, but every time we switched, we would lose power."

"Is that why some of the vamps decided to come back in full-tilt demon form, scales and all?"

"Bingo. Those are the ones who decided to put all their eggs in one infernal basket."

"Which was still a bad bet."

"Thanks to you and the Slayer."

"So you're not as strong a vampire as you used to be?"

"No. I realized I was weak when I tried to use glamour on Deylaud that night at the bar and it didn't work. Then I tried to draw strength from William when I was still pretending to be Ginger. Tried to trick him into another blood exchange in the back room of the Portal, but he saw through me."

"Good for him." Eleanor was still being too reasonable and forthcoming. Something about it bothered me, but Ginger was desperate to get her own body back, so I decided to roll the dice and take her up on her offer. "Let's go, then. You've got some body swapping to do."

"Wait, Jackie. I want one more thing before I do this." Eleanor squirmed against me, grinding her bottom into my crotch and massaging my thigh with her hand. "I want you to give me strength. You know how."

"Hey, now." Eleanor must have forgotten how the power boost had backfired when I'd tried it. When Olivia had tried to sap my power through sex, the opposite happened. She became so weak she had a hard time recovering. Maybe William had never told Eleanor that story.

"You know, I always had a crush on you, even when I was with William."

"If you think flattery will get you out of this—"

"I'm serious. How can a woman keep from falling for you? Men are my business, and I've never seen one as gorgeous as you. Those blue eyes, that thick black hair, that fabulous physique. What are you, six feet five?"

"Something like that."

"My God, your chest feels like granite."

Her squirming had taken up a hypnotic rhythm. It distracted me enough to cause me to ease up my grip. She took advantage of my momentary lapse and freed her arm enough to reach backward over my belt and into my jeans. She might have lost some of her vampire power, but not her speed. She had me in her hand before I knew what was happening.

"Auggghh!" I said. "No fair. Turn loose."

"You first."

Now, here was a dilemma. If I roughed her up, I'd only be hurting Ginger's body. Besides, those sharp talons were within striking distance of the family jewels. Yet I couldn't give her what she wanted, even to trick her into losing more vampire power. It wouldn't be right to have sex with Ginger's body without Ginger's consent.

What did I do now? I'd bet my last dime that Eleanor wanted my power more than her freedom, so I'd let her think I was going along.

"You want some of this, huh?" I asked, pressing myself into her.

She gasped. "Oh, yeah. Jack—you're huge, just like I knew you'd be. Just like I like them."

"Take down your slacks then."

About two seconds after Eleanor had taken her hand off my Johnson, I had her hands tied behind her back with the shawl. What can I say? I used to rope calves in the rodeo back in the day. Some things are like riding a bicycle. You never forget. Silk is really strong, but Eleanor's struggling proved she didn't have her old strength. At full vampire power, even a fledgling female like her should have been able to break through silk bindings.

"March," I said as Eleanor let go with a stream of curses. Before we got to the door to the tunnels, I looked around for any sign of another vampire. "Where's your smelly friend?"

"Our gramps?" Eleanor laughed bitterly. "Believe me, Reedrek's the least of your problems."

"What do you mean?"

"That bitch Diana and her new boyfriend are in town."

"Ulrich is here?" I asked, stunned. He was the evil blood drinker who had masterminded Renee's kidnapping and was as vicious and sadistic as the old lords themselves.

"Don't look so surprised. You must have known the Council would send someone for the Slayer."

"Yeah. I was afraid of that. But I thought—"

"You thought William killed Ulrich and that Diana

would stay buried under the pile of rubble beneath London. Well, think again. And if you think they only have plans for the Slayer, you can think a third time."

"What do you mean?"

"They have some special plans for you, too, though I don't know what they are." She sniffed.

"How do you know all this?"

"Reedrek told me. He tried to get them to cut him in on a deal."

"Deal? What kind of deal?"

"Diana and Ulrich are bucking for a promotion. They think they can get seats on the old lords' Council."

"So Reedrek wants a promotion, too," I surmised. "What did he agree to do for them?"

"Give them information on you and the Slayer. He told them who she is, where she lives, and that you were hunting down the double-deads together."

I started swearing, calling my grandsire every name in the book. After I'd gotten myself back in control, I demanded, "How do they intend to kill the Slayer?" I knew Mel had been researching ways to kill Connie. I had forced her to promise me she'd tell me if she figured it out so I could use the information to keep Connie alive. So far, she hadn't turned up anything. How much information did the old lords have? With their resources, they'd have lots more than me, that was for sure.

"I have no idea what her Achilles' heel is. My understanding is she can only be killed in the same ways a vampire can. Except for the sun, of course. She's immune to it so far."

"What do you mean 'so far'?"

She shrugged. "Some *dhampir* legends say that eventually, as she takes on more and more traits of the vampire—as her fangs grow, for example—she'll reach the point where she can't go out in the sun."

I considered this, remembering our last demon kill. She was already developing a taste for blood, especially mine. How far would she eventually go toward becoming undead? The question made my head spin, but I didn't have time to think about the implications now. "Why are you being so open with me? I would have thought you would be trying to cut a deal with Diana and Ulrich yourself."

Eleanor swore and spat on the floor in a most unfeminine fashion. "You're forgetting how much I hate Diana. She would double-cross me in a heartbeat."

Eleanor blamed Diana for stealing William's affections, leading to her downfall. "Oh yeah. That. So what happened with Reedrek and his deal?"

She laughed harshly. "They'll screw him over, of course. Ironic. The same old bastard who double-crossed William at every turn expects Ulrich, his own sire, to deal with him in good faith."

"That'll serve him right. Just see that you don't double-cross me in this body-swapping agreement."

"Oh, I won't, Jack," she purred. "Being a bird is the perfect disguise to protect me from the Slayer. At least until Diana and Ulrich kill her." She turned to level a maniacal smile at me.

I vowed to myself again to keep Connie and my baby alive. And to make Eleanor pay if she tried to steal someone else's body.

I would see that Eleanor went into that bird body if it was the last thing I did. It had been a long time since I'd had to eat crow, but I was going to enjoy my next meal of it or my name wasn't Jack McShane.

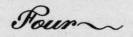

Four

When I frog-marched Eleanor to where Huey hung out behind the garage, Ginger the crow started squawking to beat the band. She was excited at the prospect of getting her body back, but at the same time I could tell she wanted to punish Eleanor. Short of pecking her own eyes out or pooping on her own head, though, she was clean out of options. For now, anyway.

"You traitorous bitch!" Ginger screeched. "What did I ever do to you but help make you piles of money by doing stuff I'm not proud of?"

"Hello? I'm a demon now," Eleanor said with a shrug. That pretty much covered it, I figured. If Ginger expected a demon to show remorse, she was roosting in the wrong tree.

I sent Otis and Rufus into the garage so they wouldn't be in any danger if Eleanor tried to pull off some trick. I started to tell Huey to back off, just in case Eleanor decided to jump into his body instead of the crow's, but then I remembered that Huey's body was ineligible because it was dead—and would be unsatisfactory to Eleanor because it was Huey's.

Hygiene had never been one of Huey's main priorities and he wasn't what you'd call a handsome fellow even when he was alive and kicking. In death, he'd taken on a grayish skin tone, and the wobbly eye he'd acquired made him even harder to look at. No question: he had a face only a mother could love, and Eleanor wasn't the maternal type.

"Do you need anything to get this party started?" I asked Eleanor.

"No, but before I do, I don't suppose I could talk you into letting me go," she speculated. "I could give you a night you'd never forget."

"Pass," I said. "Do your body-swapping thing."

Eleanor sighed and squinched up her face like she'd had some bad Mexican food. "I call on the power of Satan to seat my spirit in the closest living thing," she recited. Then she started to sway on her feet and the crow, perched on the tree branch right above her, beat its wings and squawked some more.

In unison, Ginger's body crumpled to the ground and the crow pitched forward and landed at our feet. I cradled the human body in my arms and shook it gently. "Ginger? Are you in there?" The redhead's eyes flew open and blinked once, twice.

"Oooh! Thank you, Jack! Thank you so much!"

I could tell it was really her. I looked up at Huey and nodded. Huey picked up his shovel and jabbed at the crow on the ground. Zombies aren't blessed with much of anything besides a taste for flesh. Speed and agility are at the top of the list of their shortcomings—

along with low-wattage brain power overall. The crow hopped away just in time to avoid the sharp steel of the spade.

"Stop that, you dead little freak," the Eleanor crow shrieked, darting away from Huey's next stab. She took wing and dive-bombed, pecking at the top of the zombie's head and flying away with some strands of his hair.

"Ouch," Huey said, rubbing his noggin.

"What's wrong with this crow?" Eleanor screeched. "It itches!"

"Those are mites, and I hope they eat you alive!" Ginger called out.

Eleanor circled us a few times, cursing us all and our lineages back to the time of creation. The last thing she said before flying away was "You haven't seen the last of me, McShane. When the time is right, I'll be back. You take good care of that slayer, you hear?"

"What the hell?" I muttered as I watched her disappear into the moonlight. That last part didn't make any sense. Why would Eleanor want me to take care of the Slayer? She'd claimed to be terrified of Connie.

Ginger was so happy she cried. She hugged me hard and even kissed the top of Huey's head where Eleanor had pecked him. "You guys are the best!"

I told her she should probably go into the garage and thank Otis and Rufus for their part in getting her back. Then she should have Rennie drive her to her apartment. I had to go find Connie for our usual nightly demon-hunting session.

I also wanted to see if I could get a sense of whether

she and Seth had done the deed the night before. I was going to dread the answer, whether it was yes or no, for different reasons. Either one was going to tear my heart out in its own extra-special way.

Even more important, I had to warn Connie about Diana and Ulrich. I couldn't remember if she'd ever met Diana and I didn't even know what Ulrich looked like, so a lot of help I'd be. She'd be able to smell them out as vampires, but she might mistake them for double-deads who had taken over other people's bodies.

Oh, crap. The double-deads. What had just taken place between Eleanor and Ginger introduced a whole new wrinkle in the already thorny problem of how to get rid of the vampires who'd stolen human bodies. Connie and I couldn't just kill them like we'd killed the more obvious monsters. If we did, the evil spirits might be able to take up residence in still another host and the body of the human spirit would be lost. Why the hell couldn't anything be *easy*?

I had to reach Connie right away. She was on duty, so I called her on my cell phone.

"Jones," she answered tersely.

"Where are you?"

"At the Lazarus Point Marina," she said. "There's been an attack. A woman went berserk and started stabbing people with a steak knife. One of them is in critical condition."

"Could be one of the double-deads in a human body," I said.

"Just what I was thinking."

"Do you have her in custody?"

"No. She's still at large."

"I'm coming over there. If you catch her, and she smells like a vampire, don't kill her."

"Why the hell not?" I could hear the wildness come back into Connie's voice. She could pretend to be normal in front of the other cops when no vampires were around, but just talking to me was bringing out the monster in her. I could feel the murderous psychic buzz in her head even on the cell phone.

"Because you might be killing an innocent host, that's why. It's complicated. I'll be over there as soon as I can and I'll explain everything then."

I could hear her grumbling even as I hung up. My car was at William's so I headed toward the wrecker. It wasn't as fast as the 'Vette, but it would have to do.

As I turned to climb into the tow truck, I heard a very British, very female voice from behind me. "My, but you look in a hurry."

"Olivia!" I whirled toward the voice and a tall, thin blonde flew into my arms.

"Jack! I came as soon as I could get away. You poor, poor darling."

I held her away from me to get a better look at her. "You're a sight for sore eyes." Olivia was the leader of the good European vampires and had worked closely with William and me in our fight against the old lords. It was the murder of her beloved sire Algernon that set off the renewed war with the Council, which had decided to become active again after having been literally underground for who knew how long. Olivia and I had had our differences, but I knew she loved William almost as much as I did, so she felt like family.

"I can't tell you how heartbroken I am about William." She peered at me soulfully with her wide gray eyes. Her platinum bob shone in the moonlight like a halo. As sweet as she looked, an angel she wasn't.

"Thank you for coming, but you shouldn't have. We're all in danger from the Slayer. What were you thinking?"

"I think I can hold my own."

"She killed William!" I said incredulously.

"He was injured." Olivia sniffed.

"You can't possibly think—"

"Relax, Jack. I'm not going to challenge her or anything. I'll take care to stay out of her way."

"You understand why you can't try to kill her, right?"

"Of course."

"Look, I have to go and talk to her right now. You might as well come along. I don't want you running into each other in some dark alley before I've had a chance to try and talk Connie into giving you a pass—for now."

"For now?"

"Get in. I'll explain on the way."

On the drive to the marina, I caught Olivia up on the hunt for the double-dead vampires and the tenuous truce I had struck with Connie. I also filled her in on my encounter with Eleanor and what she had to say about Diana, Ulrich, Reedrek, and the Council.

"None of that surprises me," she said, her delicate silver brows knit in concern. "I am worried about the plans that Diana and Ulrich have for you, though."

"Yeah, me too. Any ideas?"

"Not really. If I had to guess I'd say they'll probably promise you the moon and the stars to get you to carry out some bit of evil they think will impress the Council. And when you don't comply they'll try to kill you as an offering to the old lords."

I thought about how Reedrek tortured William in an attempt to get his way. By all accounts, Ulrich was even more sadistic than Reedrek was. They might want me dead, but like a cat with a mouse, they'd play with me first. "They won't kill me quick," I muttered.

"If I have anything to say about it, they won't kill you at all. Now, aren't you glad I'm here to help you?"

I reached across the seat and squeezed her hand. "I really appreciate it, but I don't want you to put yourself in danger because of me."

"What are cousins for?" she said, and flashed one of her dazzling smiles. Her sire and mine had both been sired by Reedrek, who was sired by Ulrich.

"Speaking of cousins, have you heard anything from Will?"

Will was Willam and Diana's son. He and Diana had been turned into vampires long ago by one of Reedrek's offspring. I hated that little sonofabitch, but William had insisted that his son had come away from the dark side. I'd believe that when I saw it.

"Unfortunately, I haven't heard from Will. There was some bad blood between him and Donovan, my second in command. I think Will left to give Donovan some time to calm down."

"So as far as you know, Will doesn't know William is dead? Or who killed him?"

Olivia winced. "No, and I dread the moment he finds out. It's so sad! Will had just found his true father after hundreds of years. They were beginning to bond as father and son. You should have seen it, Jack. Will was blossoming under William's attention. He was truly one of us by the time William left Europe. When Will finds out his father is gone, he'll be heartbroken, the poor thing."

"The poor thing?" I ground my fangs to keep from cursing. "If you'd seen that monster rip out my friend Sullivan's throat you wouldn't be so concerned about his tender feelings."

"That was before he changed, Jack. He's a different vampire, a different *man,* believe me. I saw the metamorphosis with my own eyes."

"Bullshit."

"If you'd only seen him risking his life to save my coven members from that fire. He was horribly burned."

"And fully healed within days. So what?"

"Don't forget that he played a crucial role in helping William save Renee."

"Yeah, after he was in on the plot to kidnap her in the first place," I said. "You're a fool if you think he cooperated with you and William for any reason other than to get back at Hugo for torturing him all those years."

Olivia huffed, exasperated with me. "Admit it, Jack. You can't keep an open mind about Will because you were jealous of his relationship with William."

"I had nothing to be jealous of him about," I lied. "I was more of a son to William than that redheaded bastard ever was."

Okay, I admit it: when Will came to Savannah I was in the dog house with William. When I saw William playing host to his true son, I turned as green as River Street beer on Saint Patrick's Day.

Olivia sighed. "You'll never be objective about him."

The subject of Will was just too touchy, so I decided to change it. "What have you found out from all those ancient documents y'all uncovered after Alger died?"

"We've only cracked the surface," Olivia said, staring out the window. "They're being painstakingly cataloged and translated now. It's slow going, I'm afraid."

Algernon's early days as a libertine had given way to scholarship later in his undeath. He'd collected all kinds of vampire history and genealogy, much of which his offspring didn't even know about until after his death. Olivia had taken over his research and added it to her own documentation of female blood drinkers down through time.

"Has your research revealed anything about the Slayer?"

"Nothing you don't already know, I assure you."

I looked at her carefully. "You wouldn't hold back on me, would you?"

She sighed. "I give you my word on the memories

of both of our sires, I am not keeping anything from you."

"See that you don't."

Olivia looked at me thoughtfully. "Melaphia still hasn't figured out how Connie can be destroyed, has she?"

"No, but for starters Eleanor said she can be killed in the same ways as vampires can."

"Wooden stake to the heart, fire, decapitation," Olivia recited. "That makes sense, I guess."

"El also said that one day Connie won't be able to go out into the sun. Is that true?"

"I've seen that in *dhampir* legend, yes."

I sighed. If Connie was going to eventually wind up like us, I wasn't sure I wanted to hear about it. "But both Melaphia and Eleanor believe that Connie has some special weakness that can be used against her. I just hope the old lords haven't figured it out either. Do you think they've kept any records of their own? Like prophecies and stuff?"

"I'd be very surprised if they haven't. There's no telling what Diana and Ulrich know that we don't," Olivia said seriously. "I know what you're concerned about, Jack. I promise that the moment that I or any of my people discover anything about the Slayer or any mention of your child in the documents, I will inform you immediately."

"Thanks," I said and squeezed her hand again. Olivia was aware that Lalee had appeared to us and that she and her old texts had hinted at something important about Connie's and my baby.

"The most recent revelation that we've gotten from the Council came through one of our spies," she said.

"You have vampires spying on the Council?"

"Yes."

"Sounds dangerous. I imagine that anyone who got caught spying by the old lords could count on some special kind of hell."

"Dangerous indeed, but invaluable. The spy was the one who found out the old lords were using their combined power to harness the elemental forces. It's unfortunate we didn't figure out what that meant until the earthquake."

"Do you think they're going to come at us next with one of the other forces?"

"It's possible, but hard to anticipate. I mean, will they use air, fire, water, spirit? If so, *how* will they use it?"

"Good point. I guess we've just got to be on our toes, ready for anything."

"That about sums it up, I'm afraid." Olivia squeezed my hand in return. "At least we're in this together."

"Listen, that reminds me. It'll help me reason with Connie if you promise to help us deal with the rest of the double-deads."

"By all means. I'll stay and help as long as I can." Olivia looked at me for a long moment. "You really love her, don't you, Jack?"

I sighed. "I really do."

"Poor darling." She drew her legs onto the bench seat, snuggled up by my side, and kissed my neck, sending a jolt of lightning down my back. "Did you ever wonder what would have happened if we'd been more . . . sexually compatible? Hmm?"

"Once or twice," I admitted. "Things would certainly be a lot simpler." Simpler than impregnating a Mayan goddess who now would give her eyeteeth to skewer me on her magic sword.

"You know, I went by William's looking for you before I came to the garage. While I was there I had a little chat with Melaphia. Now that you've had to swear off Connie, Mel thinks she might be able to figure out a way for you and me to shag again without you nearly killing me."

That didn't surprise me a bit. Melaphia would do anything to keep me and Connie apart. I couldn't say that I blamed her. "I don't know, Olivia . . ."

"I know you're in love with somebody else, but the Slayer is poison to all of us, you most of all. And I think I could make you forget about her, darling. If only for a night now and then."

Olivia ran her tongue along my neck, and I felt my jeans getting tighter. I thought about the first and only time we did the nasty. It *was* pretty intense. "I tell you what—I'll think about it."

"Good boy."

When Olivia's hands started roaming I nearly drove off the road and into the marsh. Tonight was my night for getting felt up by red-hot lady vampires. "Not now, babe. We've got work to do," I told her.

When we got to the marina, the cops and CSIs were still swarming around the crime scene. Connie stalked over to the wrecker as Olivia and I got out. The

Slayer's nostrils flared and her eyes turned dark as she picked up the scent of vampire on Olivia.

Even though I'd seen it many times while on the hunt with her, it still shocked me how quickly Connie's killer instinct kicked in. She was in Olivia's face in what seemed like a nanosecond, but the willowy vampire stood her ground.

"Jack, how nice of you to have brought me a snack," Connie said.

"I'm a bit peckish myself. Perhaps I'll take a bite out of *you, dhampir*." Olivia smiled widely, revealing her fangs.

I wedged my way between the two beauties—one as slender and light as a moonbeam, the other dark, Latin, and voluptuous.

"Ladies, ladies. Let's not forget we're all on the same side here."

"So this is one of your so-called *good* vampires?" Connie asked mockingly.

"Oh, I'm good all right," Olivia assured her.

"You all smell alike to me. A lot like dead meat." Connie bared her fangs and her body tensed as she prepared to strike.

I grasped her shoulder and gripped it tightly. "Look at your cop pals over there," I said. I tried to be as soothing as possible, but my stomach was doing backflips. "Do you think they'll look at you in the same light after they've seen you tie a young woman's guts in a bow?"

"She could try," muttered Olivia.

Connie glanced over at the policemen and technicians, many of whom were staring her way, wondering what the confrontation was about. She composed her face, shook my hand off her shoulder, and took a step back.

"Now let's start over," I said. "Connie, this is Olivia. Olivia, Connie. You may remember meeting each other at William's party a while back."

"Yeah, I remember," Connie growled.

"Such a pleasure to see you again," Olivia said sarcastically. She made sure to use her most cultured accent.

"I propose a truce," I said. "I can vouch for Olivia. She's peaceful and doesn't kill humans. How about if she helps us find the rest of the double-deads and you don't kill her."

Olivia narrowed her eyes.

"Okay," I corrected. "You won't *try* to kill her."

"Why would I agree to that?" Connie asked. "I'm starting to think I don't even need *you*."

I glanced over at the police personnel to make sure all of them were still out of earshot and told Connie about the body swap I'd witnessed and the implications for our demon hunt. Connie didn't take the news well.

"Okay, let me get this straight. I know that we've killed all the demons that *look* like demons as far as we know, and that what we've got left are demons in human disguise."

"Yeah. Right."

"Now what you're telling me is that these demons in human form will still smell and act like vampires, but we can't kill them because the displaced human spirits are still alive outside of their bodies."

"That's about the size of it."

Connie let fly with a stream of curses that almost made me blush. "How are we supposed to fix this?"

"Even if we could get the vampires to agree to give up their host bodies like Eleanor did, how can we find the people—or animals—into which the human spirits were forced?" Olivia asked.

"And what happened to the people who inhabited *those* bodies, the secondary hosts?"

"And on and on and on," I said with a shudder.

"Wait a minute," Connie said, her eyes widening.

"What?" Olivia and I asked in unison.

"The cop shop has heard from the hospital that there's some kind of local mass psychosis going on. They're calling it dissociative disorder," Connie said.

"What's that?" I asked.

"They said it's when your perception of self breaks down. They're blaming it on the stress caused by the earthquake," Connie explained.

"If this works the way we think it does, it could be spreading exponentially through the human population," Olivia said gravely.

"Which means it's spreading faster than we could stop it even if we could figure out how to match up what body with what spirit," Connie observed grimly, looking from one to the other of us.

Then it hit me. "Oh, my God," I said.

"What?" Connie asked.

"Saint Patrick's Day!"

"What about Saint Patrick's Day?" Olivia wanted to know.

"Don't you see?" I said. "People are coming here to

celebrate from all over the country. If their spirits get cast out of their bodies while they're here and they get shipped home in straitjackets—"

Connie finished my thought. "This—this body-stealing business will spread all over the country until no one's in their right body." She ran one hand through her long black hair and broke out into more curses. With visible effort she pulled herself together and asked, "Do either of you have any ideas for how to head this off?"

"I'll talk to Mel," I said. "Maybe she can figure something out."

"I'll make some calls," Olivia said.

"To who?" Connie said, sounding skeptical.

"To some very wise women back in the old country," Olivia said, reaching into the truck for her bag. "How's the mobile reception out here?"

"Should be fine," I said.

Oliva dialed her cell phone and walked a little way from Connie and me.

"Look," I said to the Slayer, "there's something else I've got to tell you."

"Save it, McShane. You've used up your quota of bad news for one night." Connie waved one hand and started to walk away.

"Wait! You've got to hear this." I took her by the arm and Connie stopped walking. She stared at my hand on her arm for a moment and then she leveled a look on me that could have flash-frozen hot lead.

Before she could tell me again to buzz off, I filled her in on the fact that two of the nastiest vampires I'd ever heard of were gunning for her. When I'd gotten through talking, I could tell that Connie wasn't nearly scared enough. In fact, she wasn't scared at all. Though she was full of concern for the citizenry, she had no concern for her own well-being. That scared me more than anything.

"Have you heard what I just said?"

"Yeah, yeah. A couple of badass bloodsuckers are going to try to bite me."

"Look, they know you're the Slayer, they know your name, and they know where you live."

"Whatever."

"Do you have any idea what a prize your death would be to the vampire who killed you? Whoever could take you out would be looking to get crowned king of the vampires!" I stared at her, exasperated. The light of malevolence was so palpable in her eyes that I was beginning to think of her exactly as I thought of the humans who'd had their bodies stolen by demons. This—this Slayer thing that had taken over Connie wasn't afraid of anything. How could you protect someone, some*thing* that had no fear?

"I get it," she said finally. "But don't tell me; let me guess the rest. A poor slayer can't tell the good vampires from the bad vampires without a program—or rather without *you*, right? Not that I have any particular reason to trust *you* as a judge of character." Connie glanced at Olivia, who was chattering to someone in Gaelic. "Take her, for example. She your girlfriend?"

I had to bite my tongue to keep from saying, *You're my girlfriend.* Then I remembered myself. "Yeah," I finally said. "Something like that. So how's *your* love life? Are you and Seth . . . seeing each other again?"

"Something like that," she mocked. "Not that it's any of your business, vampire. Especially not since you tried to kill me."

She almost had a point there.

"And I *will* kill *you*," Connie said with conviction. "Just as soon as this double-dead mess is cleaned up, the truce is over. I'll kill you like I killed William. No, wait. I killed him quickly. I do believe I'll kill you the way you tried to kill me."

She came closer to me, so close the tips of her breasts touched my chest. Her eyes, blazing with hatred, gazed steadily into mine. "I'm going to sink my fangs into your jugular and suck your blood drop by drop until there's nothing left of you." Then she wheeled and stalked away from me, back to the crime scene.

Feeling like an empty shell already, I walked the few feet to the water's edge and peered into its glasslike surface. The moonlight was bright, but of course I didn't cast a shadow on the ground or a reflection in the water. It was as if I wasn't there at all. How nice that would have been.

I heard Olivia's cell phone snap shut and saw that she was back at my side. "I do believe she means it," she said.

"Oh my, yes," I agreed. "She does."

"And by the misery in your eyes, I'd say you almost want to let her do that to you," she said.

I said nothing, only stooped to pick up a stone from

the spongy patch of ground where the sea grass gave way to the water.

Olivia followed me to the edge of the water. "Promise me something, love. Promise me that when the time comes, you'll fight her as hard as you can to stay alive."

"I'm *not* alive."

"You know what I mean."

"I can't promise you that," I said, and skipped the rock across the surface of the sea. The ripple reassured me that I was really there.

For now anyway.

Five

On the drive back to William's, Olivia explained that she talked to some of her Irish friends who were practitioners of what she called the old magic. William had hinted that in addition to being a vampire, Olivia was also some sort of witch. I didn't care what kind of witch as long as she and her buddies could wave a wand over this body-swapping situation and make it go away.

"So what do they think?" I asked her as I pulled the wrecker into William's driveway.

"They said they'd study the problem and get back to me. While they're doing that, Melaphia and I can put our heads together. She might know something in the voodoo realm that could help."

As it was nearly sunup, Melaphia was at her usual place in the kitchen, drinking coffee and cooking fragrant spiced oatmeal for breakfast. I was glad it wasn't time for Renee to wake up yet. I didn't want her to hear the troubling news I had for her mother.

She'd had to deal with too much evil lately, more than any nine-year-old ever should.

I didn't waste any time in explaining the situation to Melaphia. She responded by covering her face with her hands and moaning. I didn't blame her.

"What do you think, Mel?" Olivia asked. "Is there anything you can do? Chants to call on the gods? Spells? I've contacted some of the practitioners of the Celtic magic tradition, and they're working on it, but in the meantime, I thought perhaps you—"

"It's too much!" Melaphia cried, slamming both fists on the table.

I laid my hand on her arm. "I know it's a lot to ask, especially now, but . . ."

"No! Do you hear me? I can't do it again. I can't save the world. Look at what happened the last time I tried! Because my timing was off by seconds, William died and he's never coming back!"

Olivia leaned in close and said gently, "Darling girl, you did your best. What happened to William wasn't your fault. There is no doubt you saved humanity by closing the portal from hell as quickly as you did. Otherwise, Savannah would have been overrun by demons."

"To hear you tell it, Savannah's going to be overrun with demons anyway! You can't ask me to do this. It's too much!" Melaphia folded her arms on the table, lowered her head, and sobbed.

Over Melaphia's bowed head, I looked helplessly at Olivia. "Liv, why don't you go on to bed. I'll be there soon."

With a parting pat of Mel's shoulder, Olivia nodded and headed downstairs. I sat and stroked Mela-phia's dreadlocks while she cried. She was right, of course. William and I had placed the weight of the world on her shoulders more than once. The pressure we'd put on her to help us fight satanic forces would have stressed out anyone. But Renee's kidnapping had brought Melaphia to the brink of madness and her nerves weren't fully recovered. The last thing she needed now was to feel as if she'd been saddled with the responsibility for the souls of potentially every human on earth.

She stopped crying and sat up, gathering her strength to tell me something I could tell I wouldn't like. "Dex came again yesterday."

Dammit. I had forgotten all about him. "What happened? Did he threaten you again?"

"No, he didn't. We actually had a good talk." Melaphia sniffed and delicately blew her nose with a tissue. "He's taken a professorship in Ireland and he wants Renee and me to go there with him and try to make it as a real family."

"A *real* family," I repeated numbly. Between the lines in Melaphia's words was one inescapable fact. The family she and her daughter had grown up in was composed of two vampires and two mystic, shape-shifting Egyptian sighthounds. Not exactly what you would call the Brady Bunch.

"First he wanted to take Renee and now he wants to take you both," I muttered.

Melaphia abruptly shoved her chair back from the table and stood up. "Take me? I don't belong to you, Jack!"

"Oh, Mel. I know. I just meant—"

"You just meant you think of me as being destined to serve you like all my female ancestors back to colonial times. And you think that Renee has no choice but to serve you when her time comes."

"Surely you know you've always had the right to leave. William and I would never have kept you here against your will. You could have done anything you wanted. Gone anywhere. Made yourself into anything. William would have paid for you to tour the world, further your education however you wanted, whatever."

She sobbed once in frustration, leaning against the cabinet for support. "Don't you see it wasn't as simple as that? He would have made any of those things possible for me, but he *wanted* me *here*. He had the expectation that I would stay. He always talked about the tradition of my foremothers and how ancient and powerful it was.

"Don't you see? I couldn't leave. The ties that bind me to this place might only have existed in here." She pointed to her heart. "But they trapped me all the same. Because of *William*."

I stood up slowly and walked toward the windows, where the curtains had been drawn shut tightly in anticipation of my arrival home—as always barely in time to beat the sun. Just one of the countless little things Melaphia knew to do for William and me without asking, without us even thinking about it. Her assistance was something we just took for granted. Melaphia's words, *because of William,* resonated in my head and weighed on my heart like a gravestone.

"And now that William's gone," I said simply, "there's nothing for you or Renee here anymore."

Melaphia's voice broke on another sob and she ran to me. Wrapping her arms around me, she said, "Don't say that, Jack. You know I love you, too. I always have and I always will. But I can't do this anymore. I can't sit here waiting for dawn and worrying that you won't make it back in time, and even when you do come home, I can't bear knowing that William's not coming home with you.

"I don't want much. Just a normal life and a real family. I've never had that before, not even as a little girl. I want it now, before it's too late. I want it not just for me but for Renee. Don't we deserve that?"

"Of course you do," I murmured. "You deserve every good thing life has to offer." I held her against my chest, her head tucked under my chin. I stroked her back lightly as I had when she was a little girl and I soothed her hurts. How I loved her.

How I'd miss her.

I started to speak, but was so choked up I had to clear my throat and start again. "You know those invisible bonds you talked about? The ones around your heart?"

"Yes," Mel said, her voice muffled against my chest.

"Don't consider them bonds," I said.

"Hmm? What do you mean?"

"Think of them as bungee cords."

Melaphia raised her head and looked up at me. As

she began to laugh I could feel the tension flow from her body. "What do you mean, silly?"

"They're bungee cords from my heart to yours. They'll stretch enough to let you live your own life wherever you want to go. But if you ever need me you can pull on the cords and I'll be at your side in a heartbeat. And if you ever get homesick, they can always lead you and Renee back to me."

"Thank you," Melaphia said, resting her cheek on my chest again. "Thank you. Thank you."

I held her away from me and whisked away the tears on her cheeks with my fingertips. "You and Renee will be right in the heart of the old lords' territory. You have to use all the cloaking spells you know to disguise yourself."

"I've already thought about that, and I have everything we need."

"Otis's fey friends are headquartered in that area, too. I'll get him to talk to them. They can help protect you. Olivia's network of Bonaventures can look out for you and Renee."

"With all that help, we'll be fine," Melaphia agreed.

"All right, then. It's settled. You and Dex make your plans. You can tell me all about them at sundown."

Melaphia nodded, beaming. "I will."

"Oh, and there's one more thing."

"What's that?"

"My superior sense of smell tells me that breakfast is about to burn."

"The oatmeal!"

When Mel turned to run to the stove, I slipped through the open door from the kitchen to the stairway to the vault, closed it, and locked it from the inside. I think I took a couple of steps toward the bottom before sagging onto the stairs. I propped my elbows onto my knees and let my head fall into my hands. A sense of loss overtook me, almost as deep and dark as the void I felt whenever I thought of William and Connie. I was losing everything I'd ever held dear.

William was my rock, Connie was my heart, and Melaphia was my soul. A substitute soul for a creature without one. A beacon of goodness to light the darkness. Soon that light would be out and I'd be left in the shadows with all the other monsters, without knowing which way to turn. The pain I felt would surely break me in two.

Where was a vampire slayer when you really, really needed one?

I felt a hand on my shoulder. Olivia whispered, "The door was open. I heard."

She sank down onto the step above where I sat and took me in her arms. "I'm so sorry, Jackie," she crooned.

"What will I do without them? All of them."

"You'll carry on just like you always have."

"I don't know how to do this alone."

"You can do what I did when I lost Alger. Build a new family of blood drinkers you can trust. William had a whole network of peaceful vampires he kept in touch with. Make yourself part of it."

"I don't want strangers. I want my family back."

"I know. There, there, my sweet. I know just the thing to take your mind off your troubles. At least for a while. You see this?" She produced a scrap of paper covered by what looked like a formula in Melaphia's handwriting.

"What's this? Some kind of recipe?"

"You could say that. Melaphia came up with some incantations for you and me to have . . . safe sex."

"Um. That's great. But, I'm really not in the mood."

"Don't be silly. You're a man and a vampire. You're *always* in the mood."

I thought about our visit with Connie earlier. I'd do most anything to blot out the memory of the hatred in her eyes and her oath to kill me. "Let me think about this," I said. "I need a drink."

Olivia let out a musical little laugh. With her help I got to my feet and staggered to the wet bar. I hadn't fed, and I felt weakened by hunger as well as emotional pain. Squatting down, I opened the mini-refrigerator under the bar. I fumbled for a bag of fresh blood and ripped into one with my teeth, squeezing the liquid directly into my mouth. A stream of blood ran down my neck and onto my chest, but I couldn't bring myself to care about table manners.

I felt better immediately and rose to a standing position, only to be rocked back on my boot heels by the sight that greeted me across the bar. Olivia stood stark naked, holding out a highball glass. "Why don't you chase that blood with some of this? It'll help you relax."

"Sure, why not?" I said to Olivia and her magnificent breasts. "Here's to all three of you."

I swallowed the liquor, or what I thought was liquor, in one gulp and immediately collapsed in a coughing fit. "What's in here?"

"Something to help you relax, just like I said." Olivia looked at me and winked. "Call it a pick-me-up."

It was picking me up all right. In all the good places. "Let me guess. This is Melaphia's recipe?"

"Uh-huh. I guess you could call it a parting gift from her to you. And to me as well, since this formula will keep you from sapping my power."

Vampire sex is a complicated transaction. Normally, females draw power from males through the act. In the cosmic balance of things, it has something to do with making up for the fact that females rarely survive being made into vampires in the first place. That's why female vampires are as rare as hen's teeth.

Now, by the time I met Olivia I'd had sex with too many human women to count, and I'd never had any complaints if I do say so myself. But I'd never even met a female blood drinker before I met her, much less had sex with one, so I didn't know what to expect. I mean, are vampire girl standards for sex higher than human girl standards? Were there any special vampire sex moves that I needed to know?

For Olivia's part, when we first met she figured she'd seduce me and sap my strength while putting another notch on her bedpost. But for some reason, the opposite happened and I got stronger while leaving poor Olivia as limp as a dishrag. It had taken both time and a lot of blood to recover, so naturally where Jackie-boy was concerned, she'd said "Never again," and I could hardly blame her.

"Have another." Olivia poured me a second round from a decanter that I hadn't noticed sitting on the bar. Several different kinds of herbs floated in it, and a little bit of steam rose off the surface.

"Through the fangs and over the gums. Look out stomach, here it comes. Something tells me this is going to give me one hellacious hangover."

"If so, I'll just give you more hair of the dog that bit you." Olivia lightly bit my nipple through my shirt.

"Ow," I said, letting her lead me toward the chaise. "Speaking of dogs, where's Reyha?"

"I banished her. She wasn't happy about it, believe me. The little bitch slunk upstairs to Renee's room with Deylaud."

"Hey."

"No more dog talk. It's not romantic. I'm going to make you forget your troubles."

Olivia took the glass out of my hand and pushed me backward onto the chaise, and I let her. My lady vampire friend was certainly capable of giving me a case of temporary amnesia, but the concoction that Melaphia had brewed up was doing a pretty good job of that all on its own. My upsetting conversation with Mel started to seem like it had happened in another lifetime, and I stared at the ceiling, barely able to remember that the last time I'd made love on this chaise it was with Connie.

Olivia shucked off my clothing and took up the glass again. "You are a very fine specimen of vampire, darling," she said, her gaze taking the full measure of me.

"Right back at ya," I said, waiting.

Olivia straddled the chaise over my crotch, her parted legs long, slender, and athletic.

"Hmm. You *are* a natural blonde," I observed.

Ignoring that remark, she took up the glass again and removed an ice cube. Slowly she ran the cube along her collarbone, its progress leaving a shiny moist trail I wanted to follow with my tongue.

Then she passed the cube in hypnotic circles around her left breast until she got to the nipple. She caught her bottom lip in her teeth as she held it there, letting its coldness harden the blushing bud into pink sapphire.

I watched with fascination as she gave her other nipple the same treatment until they were both standing at lurid attention. I made a little salute and sat up to reach for them. "Come to Jackie," I mumbled. Olivia put her hand flat against my chest and pushed me hard until I was on my back again.

"Not yet."

By this time my swollen member was rubbing against that nest of curls I'd been admiring just a second ago. I wriggled my hips and tried to get closer to my goal.

Olivia twisted away but leaned forward enough for those awesome breasts to touch my chest. Gripping my biceps she propped herself over me and licked at the blood I'd spilt on my neck.

"Mmm-mmm, good," she whispered, letting her silky hair tickle my throat.

I let my fangs graze her neck and felt her shudder in response. Her tongue glided downward toward the center of my chest. "I like this fuzzy little trail," she remarked, "and the treasure it leads to."

She nipped at my flesh, tugging lightly at my chest hair now and then until she reached my cock. I moaned as she grasped it tightly at the base with her fist and ran her tongue around the head. She teased and tasted, applying suction and pressure in just the right places with the skill of a courtesan and the eagerness of a sex nymph. I felt as big and hard as Mount Vesuvius and just as ready to explode.

"Enough teasing, woman," I growled. I sat up and caught her under the arms. She lost her grip on me and tried to squirm away as I lifted her up. "I'm in control now."

"Of course you are." She giggled and flailed her legs in an effort to get the upper hand, but when she tried to put one foot on the floor and make a break for it, I took advantage of the part in her thighs and sat her down onto my throbbing cock astride me, entering her only a little at first.

"Gotcha," I breathed and finally, triumphantly captured one of those distended nipples in my lips like a battle prize.

She arched her back away from me and pushed at my shoulders, but not hard enough to convince me she wanted me to turn her loose. The mewling sounds she made gave her away. I drew more of her into my mouth, working her sweet flesh between my tongue and teeth, demanding that emotional sustenance that only a ripe woman can give.

At the same time, with my arms locked around her waist, I eased her down on me some more. She moaned again, louder this time, her body tensing against mine in an involuntary move to stave off the full invasion.

I switched to the other breast, giving it the same treatment—laving it, sucking it, claiming it for mine. The fists with which she pressed against me opened like flowers and spread eagerly over my back. The push turned to pull as she tried to get me closer.

She raised her legs and all along my shaft I felt her core muscles turn relaxed and welcoming. "Please," I heard her beg. "Do it."

With an upward thrust, I buried myself in her body, causing her to cry out. Once I knew I was seated within her as deeply as she could accommodate, I raised us both and flipped us so that she was underneath me.

With her legs wrapped firmly around my waist, I began to move inside her, slowly at first, my strokes long and firm. Her hips found my rhythm and worked in concert. Her body was warm and responsive, and it was easy to pretend we were warm-blooded creatures driven by the same urge to merge as everyone else. But the mating of vampires was special, unique, mysterious, and I wondered, even as I reveled in the awesome sensations of sex, if using a potion to alter the rules would come back to bite us.

When Olivia came she grasped me to her with all four limbs like she was drowning and I was the only thing in the ocean that could float her boat.

My own convulsive release felt like a river surging

into the sea. I lost myself in her and never wanted to come up for air. We stayed joined for long minutes, using each other's bodies to shut out the world and all its dangers.

But not even mind-blowing sex can shut out the world forever. I raised my head and looked into Olivia's face. "How do you feel? Did the potion work? Are you all right?"

She opened her eyes, then blinked. "More than all right," she said. "You set a new standard."

"Yeah, right."

Olivia punched me lightly on the arm. "I'm serious. I'm positively knackered. But not like I was before. Now I'm knackered in a good way."

I had no idea what *knackered* was, but it didn't sound all that good.

Without saying much more, we showered together and then settled naked into the same coffin. Curled against my side, Olivia said, "See there, I told you I could make you forget your troubles."

I stroked her hair until she settled into the deathlike stillness of all vampires at their rest. Olivia and Mel's magic potion did make me forget for a while, but the effects of both were wearing off.

Had I betrayed Connie? Did it matter anymore? Plagued by the twin demons of guilt and loss, I finally drifted off to sleep.

Six

When I woke up I was alone. Maybe the previous night's roll in the hay was bad for Olivia after all, and she'd decided to get the hell out of Dodge. Reyha was waiting for me, though, looking both put out and heartbroken.

"Come here," I said, and she slunk forward. If she'd been in dog form, her tail would have been between her legs. She put her slender arms around my waist and I hugged her. By now Melaphia would have broken the news to her and Deylaud that she and Renee would be moving overseas.

"They're leaving," she moaned.

"I know," I said, stroking her long pale hair.

"They can't. Can they?"

"Yes. They can." I kissed the top of her head and disentangled myself from her so I could get dressed.

"But they belong here! Melaphia's women have always been here!"

I started to point out that William belonged here and had always been here, too, only now he wasn't, but that would have been cruel. True, but cruel. I didn't meet her sad eyes as I pulled on my jeans. "Things change, darlin'. Mel and Renee think they'll be happier if they go to Ireland and live with Renee's dad. We'll miss them, but we'll have to make the best of it."

Reyha's bottom lip trembled as she handed me my shirt. "Will we ever see them again?"

"Of course we will. They can come and visit any-time they want." I tried to sound upbeat, but I wasn't sure I believed they ever would come back. They'd seen so much evil when living with demons they might just relegate the twins and me to the past like a bad dream. As Mel had said, there was no more William and therefore nothing for her here anymore. I rubbed my chest, trying to get rid of the pinch I felt there.

To change the subject, I asked, "Do you know where Olivia is?"

Reyha gave me a look like she just bit into a pickle. "She's upstairs doing research with Deylaud and talk-ing to people on the phone. Melaphia and Dexter are making moving plans."

I sighed. It was going to be a long few days. At least when Mel and Renee left they'd be out of danger from the crisis *du jour.*

Reyha announced she was going for a walk and I went upstairs to the kitchen. Renee was sitting alone, a large book open on the table in front of her. I paused a moment to memorize how she looked there so I could remember it forever. She was just shy of her tenth birthday, at that gangly all-knees-and-elbows stage. She wore a pair of pink sweats and matching sneakers with pink and purple barrettes at the tips of her braids.

"You finished with your homework?" I asked.

"Mom says I don't have to. We're leaving tomorrow so I won't even be going back to my school."

"So soon." I almost stumbled as I moved forward to take the chair beside her. "What book do you have there?"

"It's about Ireland. Dad bought it for me."

The open page showed a vivid emerald-colored landscape of rolling hills and smiling, freckled children. "Did I ever tell you my father came from there?" I was pretty sure I hadn't. I didn't like to talk to her about unpleasant things, and my father wasn't a pleasant man. I had left home as a teenager before one of us had a chance to kill the other.

Renee shook her head. "I forgot you had a father besides William."

"I almost forgot it, too, it was so long ago."

"Why did he leave Ireland?"

"There wasn't much food to eat over there at the time, so he emigrated to Georgia. He always missed Ireland, though."

She looked up at me with her old-soul eyes. "I don't want to go. I want to stay with you."

That nearly did me in. I paused to get myself under control before I spoke. "Your mom wants you to be part of a real family with your dad. Wouldn't you like that?"

"I've already got a real family."

I looked at the floor for a moment, her words like a

balm to my heart. When I looked up at her, I tried my best to smile. Leaning forward, I said in a conspiratorial whisper, "Something tells me that none of your school friends have a vampire for a godfather and shape shifters for a brother and sister."

My joke failed to get a smile out of her. She only shrugged. I reached out and took her little hand. "I would love for you to stay, sweetheart. But this place is a lot more dangerous without William. Your mom's right. It'll be better for the both of you if you go with your dad."

"But that's why you need me," she insisted. "I can help protect you. I can protect all of us."

I noticed with interest that she said *I* and not *we,* as in both she and her mother. William had lately become convinced that Renee's power would eventually eclipse that of any of her forbears, even Melaphia. Maybe one day she *could* protect us all. That is, if she ever decided to come back once she'd seen the Emerald Isle.

"I know you would, and I appreciate that. But I think you should at least give this family thing a try. Who knows? You might like it."

"I'll come back," she stated flatly.

"Sure. You can come back and visit anytime."

"No. I mean, I'm going to come back to stay. As soon as I'm old enough to leave."

"You know you'll always have a home here if you want it. But you have to promise me something."

"Sure. What?"

"If you do decide to come back, whether it's just

for a visit or for good, come back because you really want to, not because you feel obliged to."

Renee looked at me like she thought I'd just fed on a crack addict. "You're silly, Uncle Jack. Of course I'll really want to. I haven't even left and I want to already."

I brought her little hand to my lips and kissed it. "Promise anyway, okay," I managed to say through my constricted throat.

Renee crossed her heart with her other hand. "Promise."

I used Olivia and Deylaud's research as an excuse to beat it upstairs before the moisture escaped my eyes. Wiping my tears with the back of my sleeve, I walked into the den where they were working and went straight to the wet bar to pour myself some breakfast.

Olivia looked up. "You slept in a bit. Did you get that hangover you were anticipating?"

"Yeah. You might say that. You want anything?"

"Thank you, no. I've fed already."

There was no telling if Olivia meant that she'd polished off a bag from the blood bank, or if she'd gone out and fed on some passing young stud and left him in the shrubbery sleeping off the blood loss and her considerable glamour. As long as she didn't do any permanent harm, and she wouldn't, it was none of my business.

"What are you guys studying?" I asked, and poured myself another round of O positive.

Deylaud looked up from the book open on the coffee table and said, "We're assessing the feasibility of leveraging a specific divinity source to stanch the spirit dislocations."

"What would that be in English?"

Deylaud blushed. "We're trying to figure out if the old Celtic gods can help us get people back into their own bodies and send the double-deads to hell."

Deylaud was what William called *erudite*. He had a photographic memory and could recite reams of old literature, chapter and verse. He seemed to know everything, and what he didn't know, he had a thirst to find out about so he could add it to the vast encyclopedia in his head.

At first glance he looked to be a boy of twenty or so. He shared his blond, wholesome good looks with his sister. You'd never guess these Bobbsey Twins were actually mystical shape-shifting dogs who used to guard the pharaohs. It always amazed me to think that creatures as gentle and harmless-looking as the twins were so potentially deadly.

"Do you think it's going to work?"

Olivia said, "I think it's worth a try."

"Some of Olivia's contacts are neopagan priestesses," Deylaud explained. "They're really high on this ancestral god named Bilé. He's associated with trees and virility."

"No wonder they're high on him." I winked at Olivia, who gave me a smirk. "So you're going to get him over here and have him threaten the double-deads with his big . . . tree until they behave themselves?"

"It's not just virility. He's also considered to be the

god of death," Deylaud continued. "It's his job to escort the dead to the underworld."

"Now I'm starting to follow," I said. "So how are we going to get this god to appear to us on this continent? Do we have to do a bunch of pagan spells? Dance naked around a maypole in the moonlight or something?"

"That rather sounds like fun," Olivia said, "but I think we'll just use Delta."

I knocked back the last of my blood cocktail. "All righty then. Make sure you get him a first-class ticket, since he's a god and all. We don't want to look chintzy."

"I'll go to my desk and make the arrangements," Deylaud said.

"Get him on the next plane smokin'," I said.

"Will do."

When Deylaud had gone I settled myself on the sofa next to Olivia. "How're you feeling?"

"You mean, am I feeling any ill effects from last night?"

"Uh, yeah."

Olivia smiled seductively. "None whatsoever. How about you? Are you feeling anything bad except for that hangover?"

I figured I'd better not tell her the truth—that I was suffering from a major-league case of guilt because of Connie. I had learned a thing or two about women over my extra-long life span, so I decided to keep my mouth shut on that score. Instead, I said, "Oh, no. I feel fine. Just dandy."

"Excellent." Olivia put her arms around me and I

could feel a kiss coming on, but I was saved by the bell when her tiny cell phone rang. "Olivia," she said tersely and listened a long time. "Brilliant! Get in touch with him and get back to me. I'll make all the arrangements from over here." She flipped the phone closed. "Hurrah!"

"Good news?"

"Yes. The other piece of the puzzle just fell into place. We have Bilé to get rid of the double-deads. Now we have Gwydion on board to get all the spirits back into their bodies."

"Who's he?"

"He's a Welsh god who's a trickster—a magician if you will."

"Your witchy friends feel like he can trick the spirits out of the bodies they were forced into and back into their own?"

"Exactly. He's so powerful he once animated an army of trees to fight a battle against the god of the underworld."

"Hmmm. There was a battle with trees in *Lord of the Rings*," I said.

"Where do you think Tolkien got the idea? It's been part of Celtic lore forever."

"Here's what I want to know. What's with all the trees?"

Olivia nudged me in the side. "You know us pagans, Jack. We're always interested in nature. Besides, trees have wonderful symbolism. They're big, hard, upright—"

"I get it, I get it. But sometimes a cigar is just a cigar and a cedar's just a cedar."

Olivia laughed. "I hear you. However, we have a consensus among the practitioners that because of his power, Gwydion's the man for the job."

I laid my head against the back of the sofa and closed my eyes for a moment. "Liv, do you really think all these pagan god shenanigans are going to work?"

I opened my eyes again and Olivia was staring at me earnestly. "Unless we want to live in a mad, mad, world forever . . . they have to." She patted my knee. "Now I'm going upstairs to help Deylaud with the arrangements to get both of those gods here."

She stood to leave and then stopped. "My, I forgot to tell you about a very interesting phone conversation I had before you got up."

"Lay it on me. Who was it?"

"Remember the spy I told you about? He called one of my associates in London and said he'd figured out what those plans are that Diana and Ulrich had for you."

"Do I really want to hear this?"

"Forewarned is forearmed," Olivia said practically. "They know about your powers with the dead."

I thought about the time I raised a whole cemetery of angry wraiths to keep Diana and Hugo under temporary guard. "Yeah, Diana saw it firsthand. So what?"

"They promised the old lords that they'd force you to raise any of Savannah's dead that would threaten the humans."

"How do they aim to make me do that?"

"Probably just the usual—promise you political

clout within the Council and then double-cross you. Since they don't know you like I do, they wouldn't guess that you can't be swayed by such things. They think every vampire is as ruthless and power hungry as they are."

"Raising a few bad guys seems like small potatoes after that earthquake stunt. Why even bother?"

"The spy said he thought Diana and Ulrich were grasping at straws. They'll do anything to curry favor with the Council, and I imagine they didn't want to overpromise and underdeliver again."

"I can understand that," I said. "I'm surprised they didn't get drawn and quartered—or whatever those devils do to punish their own—for failing to deliver Renee and her blood to the Council. I'm still surprised at their limited plan."

"It was probably the only scheme they could think of on short notice."

"If that's all they've got for me, I can handle it. I'm just worried what they might cook up for a plan B. Who were they going to force me to reanimate exactly?"

"All my spy said was it involved serial killers, terrorists, that sort of thing."

I jumped straight up onto my feet. "Wait a minute! There was a creepy little vampire named Velki over at Werm's club the other night questioning us about serial killers and terrorists from Savannah's history."

Olivia's eyes went wide. "I've never heard of anyone called Velki, but I'll wager he's an advance man for Diana and Ulrich."

"Yeah. He said he was researching a book, but it

sounds like the research was for those two infernal bloodsuckers. I've got to get over to Werm's club right away and see if he's been back there. If I can find him, I'll wring out of him everything he knows about Diana, Ulrich, the Council—everything."

"Do you need my help?" Olivia wanted to know.

"No, I can handle him. You just get those pagan gods over here." I started for the door.

"Call me on my cell if you need me. If I don't hear from you, I'll head over to the garage after this to talk to Otis and see if he can contact his Sidhe supervisors. They might have some input that would be helpful in getting the body-swapping problem fixed."

"Good idea." I bounded out of the house and hopped in my Stingray. I'd felt so powerless the last couple of days. At least now I had something concrete to focus on.

There was nothing like a good, old-fashioned ass-kicking to make old Smilin' Jack feel alive again.

Seven

I was glad Velki was a petite little man. He fit easily into the trunk of the 'Vette, which was handy. Most grown men didn't, unless you flattened them like a fritter, and I hated to ask Huey to clean up that kind of mess. Not that he would have minded. He once was a dead body stuffed into my trunk as well, but that's ancient history.

Presently I was dangling Velki by the ankles over the Bull River Bridge out toward Fort Pulaski.

"The fall won't hurt you," I told him, "but it'll be unpleasant. So will slogging yourself out of the river and finding your way back to town before sunup. Or you could burrow into the mud like a frog and wait for the next sunset."

"Noooo," Velki wailed. "I don't know anything about any Diana and Ulrich. And I don't want to have to burrow like an amphibian!"

I shook him until change fell out of his pockets. "You're strange-looking enough when you aren't dripping with mud and marsh grass. The folks at the

Bull River Yacht Club back yonder will probably call the police and have you locked up in a nice, sunny cell."

"Pleeease! Nooo!"

About that time, I saw Olivia running toward us. "Hey, Jack! How could you go a'torturing and not take me along?"

"Be my guest," I offered as I prepared to transfer Velki's ankles into Olivia's fiendishly capable hands.

She reached out eagerly and then got a good look at the blood drinker in my grip. "Oh, my goddess! It's Mole!"

"Miss Olivia! Praise Brigid you're here!"

"Wait a minute," I said. "This guy's the one who's been helping Diana and Ulrich."

"I've been *pretending* to help Diana and Ulrich while I've been spying for Olivia," Mole finally 'fessed up, now that he had an advocate on the scene.

"It's true, Jack," Olivia said. "I know him as Mole. I had no idea he was the Velki you spoke of."

"Velki's my real name," he said. "Mole is the code name I gave myself so your London associates would have some way to refer to me without knowing my real name."

"Why 'Mole'?" I asked.

"I've been underground for so long, serving the Council without going to the surface of the earth, that's what I feel like, really."

Now that was just sad, but the time he'd spent with the Council accounted for his sometimes odd, old-fashioned way of speaking. I raised him back up and over the side of the bridge, letting him drop gently onto the pavement. "Sorry, man," I said. "Why didn't you tell me who you were?"

"I didn't know if I could trust you," he said, sitting cross-legged, rubbing his ankles. "I'd rather fall from this bridge into the river than be revealed as a spy to someone who might tell those bloodthirsty blood drinkers about my treachery."

"Let's get off this bridge before a car comes along," Olivia said.

Once Mole was on his feet I marched him back to the Savannah side of the bridge where I'd parked the car. Olivia had borrowed William's Escalade and parked it beside my convertible.

"How'd you find me?" I asked Olivia, who was following us.

"Werm guessed where you were. He said this was your favorite dangling bridge for when you're interrogating reluctant informants."

I was getting too predictable.

The little vampire had lost his fedora and sunglasses into the river. All six of his hairs were standing on end and he squinted, even in the dark. Every time I looked at this guy, he just kept getting more unsightly. "Start talking," I told him.

He looked at Olivia. "Can I trust him?"

"With your life," she said. "I do."

He shrugged. "Diana and Ulrich brought me here from England with them as their assistant."

"And you were supposed to scout out dead trouble-makers for me to raise," I said.

"That's right. But the plan was abandoned."

"Let me guess. It was because Werm and I couldn't give you any names."

Velki looked insulted. "Believe me, I came up with more than enough material on my own to make the plan a success. I'm quite a talented researcher, if I do say so. And as you indicated the other night, your city has a quite fascinating history of violence."

"It sounds like you're playing both sides against the middle," I accused.

"If I hadn't tried to gather information for them, they would have done it themselves. At least I was able to report on what they were up to."

"Why *did* Diana and Ulrich give up on this plan?" Olivia asked.

"Unfortunately for the good citizens of fair Savannah, they've come up with a much more diabolical plot. If it's successful, it will endear Diana and Ulrich to the Council much more than raising a handful of evildoers."

"I was afraid of that," I said bitterly. A chill shook its way through me as I exchanged worried glances with Olivia. I thought maybe we didn't want to hear this, but of course we had to. "Go on."

"You're familiar with the Savannah River Nuclear Site?"

I groaned. Now I *knew* I didn't want to hear this. "Yeah. It was built in the fifties to produce nuclear weapons materials, mostly tritium and plutonium. Now they mostly process nuclear waste. What about it?" I asked.

"Well, now the facility is extracting tritium from materials the Tennessee Valley Authority irradiated in their commercial nuclear reactors. Diana, Ulrich, and Reedrek think they know how to get some of that material as it comes into the plant."

"And do what with it?"

Mole looked apologetic. "Put it in Savannah's drinking water supply. And poison the river for good measure."

"How do they plan to do that?" Olivia asked, her eyes wide with alarm.

Mole shrugged. "I don't know yet."

"Why am I only now hearing about this?" Olivia complained. "I just this morning found out about the reanimation plan."

"The information has to work its way through channels," Mole whined. "I can't take a chance that word will get back to the Council that I'm a double agent, so there have to be checks in place. You—you can't imagine what they *do* to vampires who dare to cross them." I wouldn't have thought it possible for the guy to get whiter, but he blanched at the thought of the Council's capacity for cruelty.

"Why *are* you crossing them?" I asked. "I would have thought a cushy Council job would be a plum assignment for an ambitious blood drinker."

Mole stared at me and his mouth worked like a beached grouper's for a second before he spoke again. "Are you mad? They're hideous! Now that I'm out of there, no matter what happens I'm not going back!"

"But your spying is invaluable to us," Olivia said.

"I'm never going back, I tell you," he insisted. "If I survive long enough to escape from Diana and Ulrich,

I'm not even going back to Europe. I'm staying in Savannah. I like it here."

I didn't know what to say. It was kind of flattering, but damn! Why did I get saddled with all the weak sisters? Werm couldn't fight his way out of a wet paper sack, but Mole made him look like a ninja master. I looked down at his sad and wizened little face blinking up at me with rheumy eyes, expecting me to say some words of welcome, and sighed. At least the guy had guts.

"The more the merrier," I said wanly. "Why don't you let me buy you a new hat?"

He beamed.

Olivia blinked at the high beams of a passing car. "Now that we're all on the same page, let's go somewhere we can talk. I have news of my own."

Since we were so close to Tybee, we met up at a bar on the lighthouse side of the island and got a table in a dark corner. Olivia drew plenty of appreciative glances from the few late-night drinkers. Mole drew just as many revolted ones. When I went to the bar to order drinks, the barmaid asked me what the deal was with my friend.

"He has a condition," I said sadly. "It's fatal." Hey, it wasn't a lie.

"Aww, poor thing," she said. A jolly woman of fifty or so hard years, her vermilion lipstick had bled into the laugh lines around her mouth, making her look almost like a sloppy vampire who'd just fed. Her hair was dyed matte black, piled on top of her head in a neat stovepipe stack, and lacquered into place with some space-age polymer.

"Yeah," I sighed. "Pitcher of margaritas, please. Three glasses, extra salt. Salt's good for my friend's low blood pressure."

When I returned to the table Olivia began explaining what she'd learned from Otis. "Huey has uncovered a nemeton! Can you believe it?"

"Brilliant!" Mole said enthusiastically. "How extraordinary."

"I thought he uncovered a Chevy Corsica," I said.

"After he kept digging, silly. He felt something calling to him, and before you know it—"

"Oh, right, I remember now. He said there was something else down there."

The barmaid came over with the pitcher and glasses on a tray. She poured our drinks and then leaned over to give Mole a little hug with her right arm. Her height was such that she effectively trapped the side of Mole's face against her ample bosom and laid her cheek on the top of his head for a couple of seconds. "There you are, you poor little thing. You enjoy that extra salt. My name is Sharona. Just give me a shout if you need anything else."

As she tottered back to the bar on her high heels, it occurred to me that the barmaid had been spending her tips on toddies. Either that, or going the efficient route and guzzling directly from the beer taps.

Mole had frozen in place long enough to make me wonder if he had died of happiness. Those bodacious ta-tas were past their prime but pleasing enough. A man who had been underground with demons for gods knew how long must have felt he'd just achieved nirvana.

"She's an angel," he finally murmured, confirming he was still animated.

"You're a man of questionable taste," Olivia remarked. "You're not even drunk yet."

"Don't be mean," I said. "What's a nemeton?"

Olivia took a sip of her margarita and continued. "It means 'sacred place' or 'sanctuary.' I'm telling you, I could feel the magic. Otis could feel it, too. And along with this particular nemeton is some sort of spring."

"So Huey struck water. That's not unusual, especially this close to the ocean. What's so special about it?"

"I think it might be a holy well. Wells were sacred in the ancient Celtic world. Mostly in Ireland, Scotland, and Wales. A well represents two of the major elements coming together—land and sea."

"I'm still not following."

"I think it's the ideal place to have the gods do their magic. Otis agrees."

"So you think this nemeton will give—whatever it is those guys are going to do—more umph?"

"What do you think, Mole?" Olivia asked.

"Hmm?" Mole asked dreamily, staring at the barmaid as she winked a blue-shadowed eye at him and pulled the lever of a beer tap suggestively.

"Never mind," Olivia said.

"So this is all going down as soon as those two god guys get here?"

Olivia nodded. "And they should be here by sundown tomorrow."

"Saint Patrick's Day. Not a minute too soon."

"What are we going to do about the nuclear threat?" Olivia asked.

"There's nothing much we *can* do without knowing more about how they plan to pull the caper off," I said wearily. I snapped my fingers in front of Mole's face. "Buddy, you need to report back as soon as you know what Diana and Ulrich plan, all right?"

"Absolutely," he promised, shaking off the trance. "I shall stay as close to them as possible until I learn something of use. Then I'll contact you at the club." He licked salt off the side of the frosted glass. "The libations here are really most enjoyable."

"I'm glad you like them," I said. "Why don't you go talk to the lady bartender until Olivia is ready to give you a lift back to town."

Grinning, Mole topped off his drink from the pitcher and sauntered over to do just that.

"Where are *you* going?" Olivia asked.

"I should touch base with Connie."

"Are you going to tell her what Diana and Ulrich are planning?"

"No. She's got enough on her plate. Besides, she can't do anything about it without knowing more either. If she calls the authorities at this point, what's she going to tell them? That she has it on good authority from one bunch of vampires that another bunch of vampires plan to hijack some nuclear material?"

"Good point," Olivia said. "On the other hand, it would make me feel more secure if Homeland Security locked Connie away in the loony bin for a while."

"No straitjacket is strong enough to hold her," I said. "Besides, I thought you weren't afraid of her."

"I'm not. I'm just jealous of how she looks at you."

"What are you talking about?" I said incredulously. "She looks at me like she wants to kill me."

"Oh, she still wants you, all right."

I almost tossed my tequila when Olivia's foot slid between my thighs. "Hey, now."

"Are you going to tell her about last night?" she teased.

"Absolutely not," I said. I was getting uncomfortable with this subject. To my way of thinking, last night had been just fun and games. But was it Olivia's way of staking her claim on me? Pardon the expression.

I thought about the possibilities. Say for the sake of argument, Connie did still desire me on some level. Could you imagine the catfight between a powerful femme fatale vampire and a demigoddess vampire slayer? And me caught right in the middle.

How hot would *that* be?

When I called her, Connie told me to meet her at the city jail. She signed me in and took me back to see the soccer-mom steak-knife stabber, as she was being called. The woman was lurching around her cell, cursing and throwing herself against the bars.

"That's a double-dead, all right," I said to Connie.

"Ya think?" Connie said.

"Why must I be trapped in this frail and pitiful shell?" it wailed.

"Who are you?" I asked.

"I am Victor von Abendroth. I was the most feared fiend in the sixteenth century."

"Uh-huh," Connie said, unimpressed.

"Not anymore, you ain't," I said. "You look more like a suburban Savannah housewife in a heap of trouble. Who killed you? As a vampire, I mean," I asked him out of curiosity.

"The Bard himself!" the demon declared. "He staked me while I fed on the lily white flesh of a highborn lady. How was I to know she was a patron of his?"

You couldn't miss the irony: a drama queen like this being killed off by a playwright. "Good for him," I said. "So Shakespeare was a vampire killer."

"Who knew?" Connie asked.

"How did this come to pass?" snarled the vampire in the blond lady's body. She would have looked cute in that little golf skirt and polo shirt if she hadn't been possessed by a nasty demon with a murderous gleam in its eye.

The thing thrust its pink manicured nails through the bars toward my throat, but overestimated its reach, staring with horror at its own exfoliated and emolliated flesh. "This is not to be borne!" it screeched.

"Are you sure I can't kill it?" Connie asked.

"We may be able to get this woman's spirit back together with her body. Walk with me."

As Connie walked me back out of the building, I told her the plan for the next night. When we were on the street, she said, "That sounds like a lot of hokum to me."

"You have any better ideas?"

"You and your polytheism," she said, scowling. "I'm a Catholic." She reached into the neck of her shirt and drew out a Saint Patrick medal on its chain. "Saint Patrick is my patron now. He drove the snakes out of Ireland with his staff, just like I'm going to drive the vampires off this planet with my sword. I'll pray to *him* while your pagans are—are—doing whatever it is they do."

I ignored the threat, instead concentrating on what she said about the saint. "It can't hurt. It *is* Saint Patrick's Day and all."

Her delicate little nose twitched. She stared at me hard, with that flinty, hateful look in her eyes again, and I sensed she wasn't thinking about saints anymore.

"What is it?" I asked tentatively.

"You've had sex with that bloodsucking bitch," Connie accused. "I can smell her on you."

Busted! I started to stammer some lame denial, but it was no use.

Connie jabbed me in the chest with her index finger. "I hope your little scheme works like a charm. The faster we get those double-dead vampires back in hell where they belong, the faster I can send you there with them."

Talk about a woman scorned. Connie stalked away as I put my hand against the place where she'd touched me in anger. Was it the last time she'd ever touch me except to kill me? Would the next time I saw her really be the last?

I closed my eyes and imagined her killing me the way she had killed William and thought it might not be such a bad way to go. I turned to go, humming that old tune, "Dust in the Wind." Maybe I really had inherited William's death wish.

Eight

I woke up feeling disoriented. There was something significant about this date, but I couldn't remember what it was. When I lifted the lid of my coffin to the sounds of Reyha and Deylaud's mournful howls, I remembered. Part of me wanted to climb back into my box. The coward part. But I had to be strong for all of them.

I dressed quickly and took the stairs two at a time. My family was in the kitchen. Reyha and Deylaud were huddled together in their human form, making a keening sound that was between a human wail of grief and a dog's mournful howl. It always made the hair on the back of my neck stand up.

Melaphia, afraid of what Dex would think, was trying to calm them down. Renee stoically stared out the window, waiting for William's driver.

Dex came downstairs just as Mel had gotten the dogs under control. "What in heaven's name was that racket?" he demanded. Who was he to demand anything in this house? I had to bite my tongue to keep from telling him what he and the horse he rode in on could do.

Dexter Culhane had always been the scholarly type as long as I'd known him. He was tall, thin, attractive, and smart. They said he could be charming when he wanted to. Around me he must never have wanted to.

Melaphia had fallen hard for him when she was a freshman and he was a junior at Savannah State University. William had offered to send her anywhere in the world she wanted to study, but she'd chosen the nearby university so she could live at home with us.

Despite Melaphia's beauty, intellect, and charm, Dex treated her from day one like he was too good for her. I can't imagine why. It wasn't as if he knew William and I were vampires. His tidy worldview didn't make allowances for blood drinkers. She still adored him. There's no accounting for taste, I guess. When Mel got pregnant, William prevailed on the young man to marry her over the objections of his equally snooty family. His signature wasn't dry on Renee's birth certificate before he'd left Melaphia and gotten a quickie divorce.

He'd never had more than a cursory interest in his little girl until the last couple of days. I smelled a rat, but there wasn't anything I could do about it. Besides, the more I thought about it, the more I actually wanted them to go. They'd been through hell in the last few months because they lived with monsters. If either of them became disembodied by the crisis we now faced, I'd never forgive myself.

The magic would start in a few hours, and I wanted

them on a plane headed far away from Savannah as fast as it could fly.

When Dex saw me, he cleared his throat and adjusted his glasses. In the old days I'd threatened to take him out back a time or two for the way he treated Melaphia, and judging from the panic in his eyes, he hadn't forgotten.

"Hello, Jack," he said.

"Dex, come with me a second." I stepped forward and put an arm around his shoulder.

"Jack—" Mel warned.

"Relax. I'm just going to say good-bye, man to man." I walked him out into the foyer where the luggage was stacked. "You know how important Melaphia and Renee's happiness is to me, don't you, Dex?"

"I remember," Dex said. His glare spoke volumes.

"I figured you did. You take care of them now, you hear?" I released his shoulders with a pat that was half punch. It was a good thing Dex never dreamed how dangerous I *really* could be. That would have sent him running off screaming into the night.

I saw through the panes on each side of the front door that Chandler had pulled up in William's limo. He had instructions to wait for the pagans' plane and fetch them to the garage after he dropped off Melaphia's family at their terminal.

I hugged Melaphia and kissed her cheek. "Be happy," I whispered. She hugged me back and nodded, tears spilling down her cheeks, not able to say anything. It had all been said anyway, hadn't it?

As Chandler began to move the luggage into the

limo, I kneeled down beside Renee and she threw her skinny arms around my neck. "Good-bye, Uncle Jack. I'll see you soon," she said pointedly.

"Take care of them," I said, holding her gently, reminding myself that leaving me was the best thing for her. "And remember your promise."

The three of them walked to the car. Reyha and Deyland moved forward from where they'd been cowering, and I took each of them under one arm. As the doors closed, the twins clung to me and began to howl in earnest. Only once or twice in my existence had I heard that plaintive, primal sound coming from them in their human forms, and it always meant profound sorrow and loss. I walked them both upstairs, turned down Melaphia's bed for them, and tucked them in.

They cradled a stuffed dog between their bodies. Renee had left it behind so that they'd have something with her scent to remember her by. "It's just the three of us now," Reyha said as I turned out the light.

"Don't worry. We'll be fine," I said, wishing that I believed it.

As soon as Mel's family had left, Olivia and I rushed to the tourist district where all hell was breaking loose. People who had been bumped out of their own bodies and into others were staggering around bewildered and incoherent.

Usually I don't pick up on psychic vibes from live humans. But I could feel the human confusion and panic in the air like someone had overturned a fruit basket of souls.

It was a good thing it was Saint Patrick's Day. The mass bewitchment came off as the result of excess alcohol consumption. By tomorrow we wouldn't have the cover of the holiday, and then all this strange behavior would go from appearing natural to being completely weird and *un*natural. Then it would only be a short step from unnatural to supernatural, and the *real* panic in the human population would spread.

The main thing we vampires, shape shifters, faeries, and other denizens of the dark have going for us is the element of disbelief. Most humans don't believe in us, so they tend to deny the little ways in which we can be recognized—the unnatural pallor of a blood drinker's skin, and the way shape shifters disappear on the nights of the full moon.

Werm had made me for a vampire the night he failed to see my reflection as I carelessly towed a car in front of a store window. But free thinkers like him were few and far between. Most people would have written off that moment as a matter of poor eyesight or a trick of the street lamps.

Olivia and I had a couple of hours to kill before the Celtic gods were to arrive at the garage, so we walked along River Street looking for signs of real trouble. The Red Hat ladies who now found themselves stuck in the bodies of frat boys were bad enough, but the main threat still came from the double-deads who walked around in their new stolen bodies.

We'd made it about a block and a half when a tall, willowy woman stepped out from one of the stone-lined alleyways. She was a gorgeous redhead, well dressed and classy-looking. Tall and thin like Olivia, she sauntered toward us with an unmistakable twinkle in her eye.

"Olivia, darling, imagine meeting you here," the woman said.

"Do I know you?" Olivia asked, approaching her.

"Why, it's me, Algernon. Do you like my new look? I've often felt I was a man trapped in a woman's body." The woman's body in question issued a maniacal high-pitched laugh.

"Alger!" Olivia began to run forward, her arms raised up to embrace the woman. I caught her arm and hauled her back toward me.

"Olivia," I hissed, "This is not the Alger you know. Remember, he's been to hell as a twice-killed vampire, and he's evil now. He's not the good, gentle sire that you knew and loved."

"Don't listen to him, my dear." Algernon put his arms out and Olivia shook me off and went to him.

"Oh, Alger, I've missed you," Olivia cried.

Ignoring me, Algernon said, "And I you, darling. But I'm back now, and we can be together as always, but I need your help to stay alive."

"How? How can I help you?"

"A blood exchange. This body is not truly the body of a blood drinker. It's weak. You simply must do me the honor and courtesy I did you some eighty-odd years ago and . . . turn me."

"You can't, Liv. This woman's spirit is out there somewhere, and she needs her body back. If you turn it, what then?" Looking at Algernon now, I said, "And Alger has to go back to hell. There's nothing we can do for him now. It's too late. He is lost to you."

Olivia wheeled and got in my face, and I could see up close the desperation in her eyes. "Are you saying that if it were William standing here instead of Algernon, you wouldn't help him? You wouldn't take whatever body he was in and make it into the body of a true vampire so that he could come back to you?"

"That's exactly what I'm saying. Because it wouldn't really be William. Alger has *changed,* and there's no turning him back to what he was before. The Devil turned him into a demon. This isn't the real Algernon and won't be, even if you try to turn his new body."

"Damn you, Jack!" Olivia hauled off to hit me, but I grabbed her arm before the blow could land.

A young guy passing by misinterpreted the situation and decided that I was mistreating Olivia. "Do you need any help, lady?" he asked with a challenging look toward me.

I looked into his eyes and laid some calming glamour on him. "Move along, junior," I said, and he did.

When I returned my attention to Olivia, she was looking around wildly. "Where'd Alger go?"

In the moment of distraction, Algernon had fled. "Come on," I said.

We searched the narrow park area between the street and the river, dodging drunks, partiers, and vehicles, but didn't find him. We combed the dark places behind the row of buildings fronting River Street. The buildings had been warehouses and exchanges back when cotton was king in the south. The streets and alleys were paved with large stones that were brought over on sailing ships as ballast. The stones had been dumped out in favor of bales of cotton bound for the factories of England's industrial revolution.

We scrambled up the steep stone steps that led from the back alleyways up to the Bay Street level. The street was lined with another strip of small parks. It was from one of these that we heard a scream. We followed the sound until we saw two figures struggling on the grass. Together we pulled Algernon off a young woman who was clutching at her own neck. "What kind of crazy attack lesbian are you?" she demanded.

I pinned Alger to the ground while Olivia checked the younger woman's neck. "You'll be okay," she said. "Put some antiseptic on it."

"What's wrong with her?" the woman asked, brushing off her jeans. "And for that matter, what's wrong with me? Why am I wearing someone else's clothes?"

I pointed to the woman I had pinned to the ground. "She's criminally insane. You're just drunk."

"I am not," the girl insisted.

"Yes, you are. I know drunk when I see it." I narrowed my eyes and used glamour to convince her.

"Okay," she agreed. "I guess I am."

"Run along now," Olivia said. "Off with you." The girl walked away meekly as I continued to struggle with Alger.

"What are we going to do with him?" Olivia asked.

"Let's take him back to the garage. It's almost time for the holy guys to arrive. We'll use Alger as a test case. If the transformation works on him, it's going to work on everybody."

"What transformation?" Alger wanted to know.

Olivia ignored him. "Good idea."

Olivia helped me get Alger back on his—or her—feet and we marched him toward William's Escalade.

I peered into the hole Huey had dug behind the garage. Water from the spring he'd struck earlier had turned the whole thing into a giant mud puddle.

"Can't you just feel the magic?" Olivia asked with a little shiver.

"Not so much," I admitted. "What is it about this Benetton that's supposed to help us out, anyway?"

"That's *nemeton*," Olivia corrected. "It's usually a grove or glade. This is the first time I've felt one in a—a—"

"Mud puddle?" I supplied.

"Never mind, Jack. It's impossible to explain to someone who's not in tune with Celtic mysticism. You'll just have to take my word for it. This is a holy . . . mud puddle."

I was beginning to think that this whole scheme was just wishful thinking, but I hoped I was wrong. Algernon was tied to the nearby pine tree that had been Ginger's perch until Eleanor had flown off in the bird body.

We'd assembled the whole garage gang plus Werm. Right now they were helping by standing around and swilling my beer—the same way they usually helped whenever their assistance was needed in a crisis.

"Where are the gods?" I asked Olivia.

"Close. I can feel them."

Sure enough, in the next few minutes the limo

glided down the street and pulled up beside the garage. Chandler got out and opened the door for two very unimpressive specimens of godhood, who looked at the rest of us like *we* were the weird ones. Chandler opened the trunk and set their bags on the curb.

"Shall I wait, Mr. McShane?" Chandler asked.

"Yeah, why don't you stick around for a while."

"Very good, sir. I'll be in the vehicle."

I figured if the conjuring didn't work, I would have Chandler get the Celts back to the airport as soon as possible. There was no telling what kind of trouble two foreign deities could get into. I had enough to deal with already.

The taller of the gods looked at Olivia. "You the bird what sent for us, then?"

"That's right," Olivia said, shaking his hand. "You must be Bilé."

"Yeah, but you can call me Billy. Everyone does," said the Irish god of virility and whatnot. Lanky and sallow, dressed in a floppy raincoat, Doc Martens, and jeans rolled up at the hem, he didn't look like a guy who'd have any special way with the ladies, but who knew what he was packing? His limp, sandy hair was combed into a poofy attempt at a pompadour. He actually looked like he could have been the bastard son of Brian Setzer.

"And I'm Gwyn," said the short one. He was the Welsh god of something else I couldn't remember, but he was the one who was supposed to put the bodies and souls back together. He had darker, greasier hair and wore a leather bomber jacket and motorcycle boots. I started to point out to these two that the punk scene had gone out in what—the eighties? But there stood Werm in his high-heeled boots with every spare inch of his visible flesh pierced to make a liar out of me.

Olivia shook Gwyn's hand as well and introduced the rest of us. The two foreigners didn't look any more impressed with us than I was with them. In fairness, though, I must admit the eclectic collection of vamps, shifters, faerie, and zombie was a fairly odd lot.

"How was your trip over?" Olivia asked.

"You can have your modern air travel," Billy said. "Give me an old-fashioned passenger liner any day. I remember the old days when the Irish would come over in steerage with immigrants from all over Britain. The singing, the dancing, the camaraderie. Of course some blokes don't go in for all that." He gave Gwyn a look.

"The Welsh clergy weren't much fun on a voyage," Gwyn admitted. "They didn't approve of the dancing and drinking, much less the fighting, so they tried to ruin the fun for all my lot. But they couldn't be everywhere at once." He grinned, showing off a gold tooth.

"What did y'all fight about?" I asked.

"Who had the most consonants in our names," Billy said and brayed with laughter.

"We Welsh won that one, ya old sod," Gwyn said, doubling over.

I looked at the two of them laughing like hyenas and was sorry I asked. "I guess you had to be there."

"Seriously," Billy said. "Do you know how hard it is to get people to dance on an airplane? First, there's no room. Then, no music."

"They could use a good reel on the stereo," Gwyn said.

"Or a hornpipe," Billy agreed. "And then there's those women with the scarves who boss you around. No sense of humor, I tell ya. None a'tall."

I got a mental picture of these two boys going all *Riverdance* in the aisle of a Boeing 757 while the flight attendants beat at them with those little pillows. "Uh, why don't y'all get started?" I suggested.

When they went to the edge of Huey's hole, I noticed that neither of the gods could walk a straight line. I drew Olivia to one side. "Hey, these guys are soused. I don't have to tell you what happened the last time I tried to perform a ritual at this same spot while I was knee-walking drunk."

Olivia looked at Huey the zombie, who was trying to focus both eyes on the proceedings. His bad eye kept wandering away like it was searching for something more interesting to look at.

"Relax, Jack. You're looking at an Irishman and a Welshman. *They* can hold their liquor."

I must admit that remark stung the pride of my southern manhood. "Hmmph. We'll see."

"Do you need anything before you start?" Werm asked them.

"Do you have any Guinness?" Gwyn asked.

"All we have is Budweiser," Jerry replied.

The gods agreed to try one, but when they tasted it,

they found it disagreeable. "Och!" Billy said. "This is awful."

"It's the king of beers!" Rufus insisted. You don't insult a man's brand.

"It's not a fit offering," Gwyn said, after spitting out a mouthful.

"Rennie, get the Scotch," I said. "The good stuff."

Rennie returned with my good single malt and two glasses on a tray.

"You been holding out on us, Jack," Otis said accusingly.

Annoyed, I threatened, "Quiet or it's strictly BYOB from now on."

The two gods knocked back a couple of shots of whiskey. Billy pointed at Alger and asked, "Who's that, then?"

"Test subject," I said.

Gwyn sighed. "Oh, ye of little faith."

Olivia said, "My sire, Algernon, passed into that woman's body. When we found him . . ."

"No need to explain, is there, Gwynnie?" Billy said. "We know we're out of fashion with the general public. We don't mind a test now and then, unlike some gods we know."

Gwyn burped. "Who shall remain nameless."

"Bring 'im over," Billy said.

The guys untied Algernon and dragged him to the hole kicking and swearing. When they didn't let him go, he begged. "Olivia! Olivia, you must help me, my child!"

When Olivia began to sob I put my arm around her.

"We're going in," Billy announced.

"Godspeed," Olivia whispered, more for Algernon than for Billy and Gwyn, I figured.

Each of the gods took one of the woman's hands and they jumped into the hole, dragging her along with them. The rest of us spread out in a circle along the rim and watched.

What happened next looked like a cross between a holy roller revival baptism and a mud-wrestling match. Make that a holy roller baptism on a reluctant baptizee. Now there's something you don't see every day.

The two gods dunked each other and the woman who was Alger over and over again while taking turns yelling incantations in languages I could only assume were Gaelic and Welsh. It sounded like dueling gibberish to me but Olivia looked enthralled. I could tell it was speaking Otis's language, too, him being a genuine Irish faerie and all. His eyes kind of lit up and he swayed back and forth.

The rest of us just stared. "Can you feel anything?" I asked Werm.

He nodded slowly. "I actually think I can. I can't describe it, but I can feel something strange is happening all around us."

All of a sudden a loud buzzing whine filled the air, as if a million angry bees had just been turned loose. Then the water in the mud hole began to boil, and the woman's screams took on a higher pitch.

"Where am I? What's happening?"

Billy and Gwyn each grabbed her by an arm and hoisted her out of the pit right into the arms of me and Werm. Olivia wiped the mud from the woman's face and looked carefully into her eyes. "Alger's gone," she said with certainty. "Come with me, you poor dear. Let's get you cleaned up and into fresh clothes. I'll explain everything."

And by *explain everything*, Olivia meant she'd put enough glamour on the lady to make her forget her misadventure. Later her spell of temporary amnesia would explain how she wandered away from her family.

I closed my eyes and opened my mind to the vibes from the city. The disorientation, stress, and fear I had felt earlier were gone. All gone. It had worked. The magic from that mud pit was spreading out to free people who'd been taken over by demons. I sighed with relief, thinking about all the humans who were saved and all the demons they were saved *from*, none worse than that unholy bitch Eleanor.

"Oh, man, that was great!" Werm said as he and the others helped Billy and Gwyn climb out of the slippery hole. "I want you guys to come over to my club to celebrate. Since the lady's using Jack's facilities to get cleaned up, I'll take you to my apartment underneath the club and you can shower and change there."

"Drinks are on me," I added. "That includes everybody. This is really something to celebrate. Happy Saint Patty's Day!" The lot of them piled happily into the limo and drove off, but not before I got Chandler aside and told him to take the newcomers straight to the airport when they'd drunk their fill.

Talk about a load off my mind. Now all I had to do was head off a nuclear catastrophe and defend myself from a vampire slayer with a grudge and I'd be home free. By the time I finished picking up beer cans and tidying up the back forty, Olivia had Jean, the lady we'd just rescued, cleaned up and dressed in a fresh pair of Rennie's coveralls. Then Olivia put Jean in a cab and pressed a wad of cash as big as a softball into her hand.

"Not bad for a night's work," I said to Olivia as she waved good-bye. "Are you okay about Alger?"

Olivia sighed and I saw that she'd been crying. "I'm okay," she said. "At least Alger's no worse off than he was after Reedrek staked and burned him. You were right, though. The vampire who spoke to us from that woman's body wasn't the Alger who made me."

We embraced then, holding each other like a lifeline. We'd just come through a major crisis and had more to do before we could rest. Without William, stripped of Connie's love, and just having lost Mel and Renee, I'd have felt all alone in the world if not for Olivia. She, like me, had lost her soul mate and sire and was the only other creature on earth who understood what that loss was like. I held on to her like she was the only thing anchoring me down to a world spinning so violently out of control it was about to sling me into space through centrifugal force.

"Well, isn't this nice?"

The venom in Connie's voice was as thick and dark as sorghum syrup.

Olivia and I stood apart. I stared hard at the Slayer, searching again for any spark of my old Connie in her eyes. There was nothing but malevolence.

From a scabbard on her back, Connie drew the

magic sword that had helped her make the transition from half-human goddess to vampire slayer.

"Oh, don't break it up on my account," she said. "Go ahead and hug each other again. In fact, get as close as you can."

She swung the sword in two graceful arcs, first on one side of her body and then the other, as if she were born with that blade in her hand.

"That way," she continued, "I can kill you both with one blow."

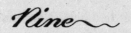

Nine

"But we just sent the double-deads back to hell," I said. "And got all the humans into their right bodies. Don't we deserve some snaps for that?"

Connie gave us the triple snap with her free hand. "I'd applaud," she said. "But then I'd have to put down my sword, and I'm not doing that."

"After all we've done, you're still going to kill us?" Olivia asked. I tried to put myself between her and Connie, but she stepped out beside me. "Even after we've proved we're benevolent to humans?"

"We had a deal," Connie said, taking a step toward us. "I agreed to let Jack live until the double-dead threat was gone. Now it is. Vampire time is up."

The sword caught the moonlight and put off a weird, silvery glow. Connie's skintight black leather suit, the blue-black highlights in her hair, and her cat-like athleticism made her look like a comic book action heroine. But she was real, and she was coming for my head if I didn't think fast.

"Hey. Listen," I said. "There's a new threat out there you need our help with."

"You wish," Connie said. She continued to swing the blade, first over one shoulder and then the other, making it sing with a metallic twang as it sliced through the air.

"Jack's right," Olivia said as we backed away from the advancing Slayer.

"Talk," Connie said, still coming at us.

I started talking fast. "That vampire who was William's wife, Diana—she and this dude she's hanging with now are planning to steal some tritium on its way from a TVA plant to the Savannah River site and make a dirty bomb or something."

"That's a great story," Connie said. "I give you an A for creativity. Tell me another one."

"Oh, goddess, why doesn't she believe you, Jack?" Olivia asked.

By this time, Olivia and I had backed all the way behind the garage.

"I think it has to do with that little matter of me trying to kill her," I said.

"Bingo," Connie confirmed.

"What do we do now?" Olivia asked.

"I'm open to suggestions," I said.

Olivia's eyes widened. "I think you should tell her everything. Maybe she would let you live."

"Tell me what?" Connie asked suspiciously.

"About the—"

I clapped my hand over Olivia's mouth before she could finish. "No. Not that."

Olivia slapped my hand away. "You're a fool, Jack."

Connie narrowed her eyes. She might not have believed the terrorist story—although it was true—but for some reason she sensed we weren't bluffing now. Maybe it was the look of desperation I could feel on my face. "Out with it," she said. "Whatever it is."

"Look, uh," I said, "I need time to get more information. Then I'll be able to tell you all about it."

"Okay, but it better be good," Connie said. She sheathed the sword and frowned. "You've got twenty-four hours to get the information—and your affairs—together. Or, if you'd rather use the time for a head start, go ahead and run. It doesn't matter to me. I'll find you wherever you go. I'm beginning to understand how to sense where you are."

She turned her back. I couldn't help but watch her leather-clad derriere in motion as she walked away. Olivia followed the direction of my gaze and punched me hard in the arm.

"Ow," I said, rubbing my biceps.

"What are we going to do?"

I sighed and thought for a moment. "You're going back to England. Tonight."

"Oh no. If you think I'm going to leave you here to face her alone—not to mention whatever Diana and Ulrich have in store—you're daft."

I took her hand. "Olivia, you've already saved the day by bringing those god guys over to take care of the double-deads and body swappers. You've done enough. It's not safe here. Go to your own people. They need you."

"*You* need me."

"Think what will happen to our cause if we both die," I said. "Alger and William, the two original leaders of the good vampires, are gone. Now there's me here in America and you in Europe. Having us both in the place the Slayer calls home is like—like the president and the vice president flying on the same plane. One of us has to survive to carry on. Besides, this is my fight more than yours."

Olivia looked pained, but I could tell she knew I was talking sense. She pursed her lips and stared at the ground. "I suppose you're right," she finally said.

"You know I am. Now, let's go back to William's so you can make your travel arrangements and get a good day's sleep before you have to go."

Olivia squeezed my hand and brought it to her lips. "All right," she said at last. "I'll ask you again, though, to promise me that you'll do everything, and I mean everything, in your power to stay alive—even if that means killing the vampire Slayer."

"I promise." It's hard to lie to a master vampire, but I tried. I knew by the sad look in Olivia's eyes that she didn't believe me, but she had the good grace to let it go.

"Come with me while I lock up," I said.

Olivia followed me inside the garage. I turned off the coffeepot and the lights in the kitchen. Then I locked the front and back entrances and closed the bay doors except for the one where the Corvette was parked. We'd back out and I'd close that door from the outside.

Olivia grabbed the chain and closed the door behind the Stingray.

"Hey, how're we going to drive out?" I asked.

"We're not," she purred. "Not for a while, anyway. And I don't want your policewoman to come back and arrest us for indecent acts in public."

I looked at her standing there under the one overhead light that I'd left on. She put a high-heeled foot on the 'Vette's chrome bumper and gave me a come-hither look.

Twenty-four hours, Connie had said. And then she would come for me. If I was going to be double-dead by this time tomorrow, I might as well have a nice time tonight.

Olivia reached under her pink wool miniskirt and wriggled her hips. A scrap of black lace fell to the floor and she stepped out of it. She hopped onto the trunk of the 'Vette, arched her back, and drew up one leg, looking like a pinup girl in an auto calendar.

"Eat, drink, be merry, and fuck my brains out, for tomorrow we may die," she said.

"That's very poetic." I sauntered toward her, undoing my belt as I went. "But somehow I don't think that's how it's worded in Ecclesiastes."

"No?" Olivia whipped off her top, leaving her wearing only a wispy pink bra and the skirt. "I never claimed to be a biblical scholar."

I hopped along on one foot, then the other, taking off my boots. "I won't hold it against you." By the time I reached her I was naked.

"That's not what I want you to hold against me

anyway." She reached down, grabbed my Johnson, and tugged me toward her open legs.

I almost said *Ask and ye shall receive,* but I didn't want to take the Bible thing too far. If I was going to hell in less than twenty-four hours, I didn't want to piss off God any more than I already had by willingly giving up my soul to be a bloodsucker so long ago. Who knows, maybe I could do something to get a last-minute reprieve. Anything's possible, right?

"Whatever the lady wants," I said. "But not right now." I eased out of her grip and raised the little skirt. "First, while you're on the trunk, let's see what you've got under the hood."

I stuck my head under the fabric and pressed my face between her thighs. "I love the way your engine smells." I teased the swirly curls with my nose and worked my tongue into her opening, exploring her dewey girl petals. I could feel that she was plump with need down there, so I massaged her little hood ornament with my thumb while inserting one finger into her opening. "My thumb feels the little man in the convertible raising his head," I teased.

"If you say I'm a quart low, I'm going to kick you," Olivia said breathily.

"You don't need a lube. In fact, I think you're as ready as you're going to get."

"Stop talking and get to it then."

I raised up and spread her skirt all the way back, braced myself over her, and rammed into her full length.

Olivia gave a little shout of pleasure and locked her long legs around my waist. I braced my feet against the concrete floor and leaned close, pistoning in and out of her warm wet length.

"I think you should adjust my front end while you're at it," she said from between gritted teeth, and captured my head between her breasts.

"Whatever you say." I bit the front closure of her bra apart with my fangs, freeing her breasts, their nipples already standing at attention.

I lapped at her breasts, sucking first one hardened nub and then the other while she clawed at my back with her nails. She dug her high heels into my hips the way a cowboy sinks his boot heels to keep his feet in the stirrups while hanging on to a bucking bronc.

We rode each other hard enough to have bruised flesh and broken bones if we'd been human, but we weren't. So we went at each other like the crazed, souped-up immortal predators we were, driven only by animal need. Somewhere in my lizard brain I realized this was the first time I'd ever had sex where I didn't hold anything back. I wasn't trying to keep from hurting a human woman, and I knew now I couldn't hurt Olivia's vampire powers. So if this was going to be my last time, I was going to make the most of it.

I put my hands under her buttocks and lifted her off the car, driving her body down onto mine over and over until she screamed out her release and I saw exploding orbs of light behind my eyeballs. I came in a blast of pleasure that weakened my knees almost enough to make me drop us both. I laid her back down on the car's trunk and rested on top of her until my strength and my vision returned to normal.

"That was . . . beyond anything I ever thought possible," Olivia said. She wriggled a little. "I can't believe it, but I think you're still hard. Want to go 'round again?"

"Anything that cranks your camshaft," I said.

I woke up the next night to the feel of Reyha's tongue lapping at one of my quickly healing wounds. I think it was a hole over my hip bone where Liv speared me with the heel of one of those crazy shoes. They didn't call them stilettos for nothing.

I climbed out of the coffin, showered, and dressed while Reyha changed into her nightly human form. Olivia was nowhere in sight.

When Reyha was a biped again, she went to William's desk and handed me a note. "*She* said to give you this." My shape-shifting pal didn't like to speak the name of the woman who had kicked her out of what she saw as her rightful place in my coffin.

Jack, forgive me for leaving without saying farewell in person. I've grown so fond of you, I don't trust myself not to break down and disgrace myself. So while a note is cowardly, at least it's dignified. I feel ashamed for leaving you alone and in danger, but I can't deny the wisdom of what you said last night. Let this be so long and not goodbye.

All my love, Olivia.

I crumpled the note and told myself I was glad that she was gone. Now that she was out of danger from the Slayer, I only had to concentrate on keeping myself, Werm, and Mole alive. But at the same time I felt almost as bereft as I did when I considered that Connie and I would be separated forever. It felt like Olivia was the only one on earth who had a clue what it was like to be me.

I wished her well. Maybe someday the old lords would go back into hibernation and she could find happiness. Maybe even with Billy and his big tree.

I tossed the note in the wastebasket by the desk. I didn't have time for a pity party. I needed to go and warn Werm that the Slayer was on the warpath.

The patrons of the Portal looked a little wrung out, as did the proprietor.

"You look like you've been rode hard and put up wet," I said to Werm as I sat down at the bar.

"I guess I had too much to drink last night," he admitted. "Those gods can really put it away." Werm slapped a coaster on the bar and handed me a draft.

"Please tell me you didn't try to keep up with two Brits in the drinking department. Those people can out-drink an elephant." I took a sip of beer and added, "An elephant who can really hold his liquor."

"Now you tell me," Werm said. "But I gotta say, you don't look so hot yourself, my friend. You must have had a hard night after we left."

"Yeah, you could say that. But listen, I've got some bad news."

"Ugh," Werm said, struggling with the top on a bottle of aspirin. We vampires are immune to almost everything, but not hangovers. "We just got rid of the double-deads. What's happening now?"

"Dude, you're a vampire and you can't even open a child-proof aspirin bottle?" I asked with disgust. When Werm went at it with his teeth, I took the bottle from him and opened it myself. "Not with your *fangs*. You *need* those, and going to the dentist to get broken ones bonded before they have a chance to grow back will be hard to explain."

I looked at what—in the vampire world—was the equivalent of my little brother, as we had the same sire. How in the hell could he protect himself if Connie killed me? That both depressed me and made what I came here to tell him even harder.

"Look, Werm, Connie came by the garage last night right after you guys left. She says now that the double-dead threat is over, it's open season on vampires. I sent Olivia back to England for her own protection."

"Oh, crap!" Werm said, and shook a few more aspirin out of the bottle.

"Maybe you ought to let Seth run the bar for a while. Lie low, maybe go back to crashing in your parents' wine cellar until I get some idea of how to convince Connie that we can be useful enough to keep alive."

Werm sighed. "Okay. I'll think about it."

"Don't think about it too long. She said she was going to give me a twenty-four-hour head start." I looked at my watch. "And that was twenty hours ago."

Werm and I smelled vampire and looked up in unison to see Mole, a.k.a. Velki, come through the door. The little vampire hurried up to me and said, "Jack, I hoped I'd find you here. Diana and Ulrich are about to make their move. Reedrek's with them. You've got to come with me!"

"What's happening now?" Werm said, holding his head with one hand.

"It's just a potential nuclear disaster I've got to stop, that's all. Another reason for you to go underground for a while."

"Well, just . . . crap!" Werm moaned as Mole dragged me toward the door by my jacket sleeve.

I tried to get the details out of Mole as I drove us down to William's dock on the river, but he didn't seem to know any specifics. He kept insisting that if we got to a particular boat in time we could stop Diana and Ulrich from stealing the tritium. The boat in question was one of the cabin cruisers that William had equipped with a specially tinted windshield and windows so that, if he was very careful, he could walk around in the bridge during the daytime.

"They must be aiming to cruise up the river to Augusta and then go from there on land to the site in Aiken," I said.

"Yes, I think so," Mole said.

"Do you have a plan?" I asked.

"Plan?" Mole asked.

"Yeah, you know—an idea of how to stop them. You do know how Diana and Ulrich operate, right?"

"Um . . ."

The little guy had seemed a lot sharper the first day

I met him. I guess he must have figured he'd done his bit as the tipster and the rest was up to me. I'd have to play the dual role of brain and brawn to get us out of this mess. On the other hand, it occurred to me that he could be leading me into a trap.

Considering all the angles first, before going off all half-cocked, was what William would have done. Shooting from the hip had always been my style. Maybe I was learning after all. Still, I was pretty sure that Mole had been sincere about helping us. As terrified as he was of the old lords, I couldn't figure a reason why he would switch his allegiance again. Besides, I didn't figure I had much choice but to go along.

"Okay," I said. "I'm going to stop by William's warehouse on the way and get some things to work with."

"What things?" Mole wanted to know.

"Never you mind. The less you know the better. Stay in the car."

I sneaked into William's warehouse and unlocked the small workshop I maintained there. No one had the key to the place except William and me . . . now only me. In addition to all my other responsibilities, I had also been William's demolition man. The workshop was packed with everything I needed to make bombs, including meticulously wrapped and preserved explosive material.

Over the years William had called on me now and then to make something go boom. The most recent time was when he asked me to blow up one of his yachts, the *Alabaster*. It had been a big and luxurious oceangoing craft that William used to import European vampires. Although an ocean voyage took a long time, it was a much safer and more comfortable way for blood drinkers to travel than by air. It was a shame we had to blow up that beautiful ship.

Explosions are useful for more than just destroying evidence, though. They're a good way to murder multiple vampires: the fires that ensue can kill vampires if they're hot enough and the victims have been blown into enough tiny pieces. So a nice conventional bomb seemed just the ticket for the situation at hand. I usually liked to build my incendiary devices carefully and painstakingly, but time was a luxury I didn't have. I would have to put this one together on the fly.

I grabbed a burlap bag and began selecting the components as quickly as I could. Fuse, alternator, gag rod, detonator, battery, housing all went in the bag. Newfangled bombs are all electronic and fully programmable with no moving parts. But I'm old school.

As soon as I had what I needed I got back into the convertible with Mole and drove to the nearby dock. Mole eyed the bag with curiosity but must have instinctively known not to ask questions. I parked far enough away so that we could sneak up on the boat without making any noise. Diana and Reedrek's scent was everywhere, along with a powerful vampire stench I didn't recognize. *Eau de Ulrich,* no doubt.

We crouched beside a repair shed right next to the dock. The shed was tall enough to tow a sailboat underneath and repair its rigging from the rafters. From where we were I could see a slight glow from the cabin of one of the cruisers tied up nearby.

"They're already on that boat," Mole whispered, all six of the hairs on his head swirling in the breeze. "I saw them board."

"How did you slip away from them, anyway? You're supposed to be helping them, right?"

"He did help us, Jack. He brought you right where we want you."

Oh, shit.

Ten

At the same moment I heard Reedrek's voice from somewhere above me, a net made of chains heavy enough to tow battleships fell over me, knocking me flat. The blow would have killed a human at once. From the corner of my eye, I saw that Mole had stepped neatly away from the trap.

Three vampires jumped down from the roof of the shed. I lay on the dock, unable to move.

"Hello, child," Reedrek said.

"Hey, Grandpa," I said.

"You remember Diana, I'm sure. May I introduce you to your great-grandsire, Ulrich."

I raised my head as best I could manage and looked at the tall vampire standing between Reedrek and Diana. He had a livid scar across his throat where William had almost cut his head off back in the day. The fact that he'd survived those wounds boggled my mind and proved just how freakin' powerful he was.

I remembered what else William had told me about my great-grandsire. Ulrich went by another name in the late 1800s—Jack the Ripper. Even by vampire standards this creature was a savage. I could remember reading accounts of the murders in the newspaper at the time. It still made me ill as I thought about it.

Ulrich had longish salt-and-pepper hair and a matching beard. He was much better groomed and dressed than Reedrek, who always seemed to have some dirt clinging to him from whatever tomb he'd last slept in. Ulrich was about forty when he was made; all he needed was one of those blazers with elbow patches, and he could pass for your average college professor.

"So this is the estimable Jack McShane," Ulrich said.

I just loved being mocked. "Pardon me if I don't get up," I said.

"You do seem to have quite a weight on your shoulders," he remarked. Reedrek and Diana both laughed uproariously at his stupid joke. The toadies.

"Do let us help you with that, dear Jack," Diana cooed. "In fact, we have a proposition for you."

"I'm listening," I said to buy myself time. I braced my palms against the surface of the wooden dock and pushed with everything I had, but I couldn't even get onto my knees. *Hell.*

"We want you to help us wreak havoc among the human population," Reedrek said.

"What would be the point? Is it just for shits and grins, or is there more to it?"

"My, he is as colorful as you said, Diana," Ulrich said. "Our plan is to create so much terror in the world of the living that they will eventually be happy to join the world of the undead."

"You want people to *volunteer* to become vampires?"

"Of course."

"So where do I fit in?"

Diana said, "We want you to come with us to the nuclear site. There are a variety of things we can do there. Ulrich, Reedrek, and I will intercept bomb-making material on its way from other sites. Your role is to divert the atomic waste from one of the containment canyons into the groundwater. The water table is so low because of the drought in the southeast that any nuclear material that makes it into the drinking water will be ultraconcentrated."

I was so horrified I couldn't even pretend to go along anymore. "Do you *know* what radiation poisoning looks like in humans?"

"Why of course, you silly man," Diana said. "The three of us have been around for hundreds of years. We remember everything that happened during the birth of the atomic bomb just as you do."

I shuddered. These bloodsuckers were just as evil as William had said. "So, just for the sake of argument, let's say I do what you're asking. What's in it for me?"

"Why, power, of course," Ulrich said. "There are two seats available on the Council of old lords. After our plan succeeds, I will have one of them."

"And I will have the other," Reedrek announced. He looked at me with a self-satisfied grin and made a preening gesture against his straggly hair.

While he was looking at me, I saw Ulrich and Diana exchange a look meant only for each other. That look spoke volumes, and it didn't take a genius to figure out what it meant. Reedrek would never get that other seat on the Council. They would kill him after they used him to achieve their dirty work, and Diana would take the other position. Even if Reedrek had seen the look that passed between them, he was so full of himself and sure of his own importance that he would never have been able to interpret it for what it was.

"So you'll have seats on the Council. What's that supposed to mean to me?"

"We'll be in a position to make you our lieutenant," Ulrich said. "We will have the wherewithal to show you great favoritism."

"Perks," Diana clarified.

"What kind of perks?"

"You can martial hundreds of vampires to do your bidding," Reedrek said excitedly.

"Uh-huh," I said. "To do what, for instance?"

"Whatever you want," Ulrich said. "You can bid them lay waste to the land."

"Why would I want to lay waste to the land?"

The three of them looked at one another and back at me, confounded. "Because it's fun?" suggested Reedrek.

"I can have fun shooting rats at the dump," I pointed out. "What else?"

"With the glamour we can wield, you'll have access to the most beautiful women in the world," Diana said, stroking her long blond hair suggestively.

I gave her my special look, the one that made the most of the cleft in my chin, my dimples, and my cheekbones, or so I've been told. In any case, it was the look that had gotten me laid by thousands of women. Her hand fluttered from her hair to her bosom. "Oh," she murmured.

"What else you got?" I asked.

Sensing that he was now the one being mocked, Ulrich raised his foot and stomped on my lower leg so hard the bone should have broken. But the splintering sound I heard over my own roar of pain was the wood giving way underneath my leg.

"You insolent bastard," Ulrich growled. "How dare you toy with us."

"Don't be a fool, boy," Reedrek said.

"What is your answer?" Diana demanded.

"What happens if I refuse?" I asked, although I figured I already knew.

"The sun will be up in a few hours," Ulrich said. "We'll let you burn slowly." In a move so quick I could barely see it, he reached into one of the openings in the metal net, removed the cell phone from my pocket, and tossed it into the river.

"Even if the regular workmen show up before daylight and you manage to call them to your aid, no human or group of humans will ever be able to free you in time. The three of us were barely able to hoist the net over you, and there's no heavy equipment at hand that could remove it."

"It looks like you've thought of everything," I said bitterly.

"We try to be thorough," Ulrich said. "Now, what is your answer?"

"Hmm. Let me think," I said. "I remember reading an article about those nuclear canyons. If I understood it right, they heat the atomic waste at temperatures so high it turns to glass and that's how it's stored. So my choices are to try and mess with that process and get burned to a crispy crunch by heated up spent fuel rods or stay here and wait for the sun to burn me to a crackly crunch right here on the docks. Does that about sum up the situation?"

"We think that with time and care, any burns you sustain at the nuclear site will heal nicely," Reedrek said cheerily.

"Uh-huh," I said. "Thanks for the opportunity, but I'll pass."

Ulrich sighed. "You make me sad. Very well, then, have it your way. Our friend Velki will have to do the honors in your stead."

"Huh?" said Velki.

"Come along," Ulrich said. "We must away."

"Farewell, my child," Reedrek said airily. "Soon you will be joining William in everlasting torment. May he rot in hell for all eternity."

I shot my hand through an opening in the chain and grabbed Reedrek's leg. I yanked it toward me, throwing him onto his back, and sank my fangs into his ankle as hard as I could. I heard his head bounce off the lumber as he fell. He screamed loud and long, and as Ulrich and Diana pulled him away from me I spat out a mouthful of sinew and bone. "God, gross!"

I muttered, spitting out bits of my flesh and blood's flesh and blood.

"Come, we have work to do," Ulrich said, dragging Reedrek away by one arm. Reedrek cursed me, clutching his ankle with his free hand. Diana had to drag a reluctant Velki along with her. They boarded the boat and were quickly off down the river in the direction of Augusta.

I strained with all my strength against the chains, but I couldn't budge them or move myself in the direction of the shed for shelter. The bag with the bomb components was gone. One of them must have taken it while I was struggling to get to my feet. There was nothing else I could see within reach that would help me out of the jam I was in. Where was that MacGyver guy when you needed him?

I forced myself to relax. I tamped down the panic, tried to rest and think. I found myself wondering first why Mole had decided to double-cross me. He had provided valuable information to Olivia at considerable risk to himself. The last thing he'd wanted was to remain at the beck and call of the old lords, and now he was in more potential trouble than before. And all for what?

Hell, what did it matter at this point? What did anything matter? I opened my mind to Werm, but his psychic porch light was out. I should have reminded him to be on the listen, but I hadn't thought about it. William would have. William would have spent the previous night planning instead of screwing around. Typical for me, I'd followed my cock instead of my brain, and look where it had gotten me.

There was one thing I did right, though. I thought about Melaphia and Renee and how much better off they were now than they would have been had they stayed. I was glad I'd encouraged them to go. By the time they learned I was dead, they'd be starting their new life. In time, they would relegate me to the distant past. I would just be a creature that populated some half-remembered nightmare. Isn't that where vampires belong anyway?

That thought made me sad for a minute, but I wanted more than anything for my daughters to lead normal, happy lives, and to my way of thinking forgetting me would be a step in the right direction.

The twins would be fine without me. Deylaud knew enough about William's business matters to keep himself and Reyha in kibble for the rest of their lives, even if they lived until the end of time.

I didn't even want to think about poor Werm. I hoped he would be clever enough to stay out of Connie's reach. Maybe he could go and join the western clans and together they could defend themselves. For her part, maybe she would come back into some sense of reason. Eventually, she might learn to tell the difference between the good guys and the bad before it was too late.

As I resigned myself to my fate, I faced the most unbearable thought of all. I would never meet my child. Maybe that was for the best, though. At least my child would never know its father was a monster.

I couldn't help wondering what William would do if he was in this situation.

"William!" I yelled. "Father, if you're out there, give me a sign! What should I do now?"

A minute passed, then two. Just as I was about to give up hope, I heard the wood underneath my injured leg splinter again. Instead of struggling upward against the chains, I pushed my knee experimentally down on the surface of the dock. A whole chunk of wood gave way and fell into the water.

"Thank you, William!" I said. My sire had come through for me, even in death. Invoking his name would help me see that I lived to bite another day.

Although my leg hurt like a sonofabitch where Ulrich had stomped it, I managed to work a bigger and bigger hole in the dock. Eventually I made enough of an opening to go at it with both arms and both legs. The dock was several layers of timber thick, but thanks to the voodoo blood, I had the power to break it bit by bit.

I could feel the sun rising, but my spirits were rising, too. Even if I didn't free myself in time to get home, I could probably get to that shed. If worse came to worst, I could just dive down into the river and burrow into the mud until the sun went down.

I kicked, pushed, and pulled until the last of the wood came free. I lowered myself through the opening in the dock and hung there with one hand. Freedom was within reach. I wasn't going to slow-roast in the sun and I wasn't going to make a spectacle of myself for the humans in the process. All I had to do was let go with my left hand and—

A lightning bolt of pain shot through my hand as I dangled above the river. What the hell? It felt like—

I peered up over the surface of the dock, and now I could see what had hurt so badly and stopped me on my way to freedom. My hand was pinned to the lumber with a sword.

"Hello there, lover boy," Connie said. "Tick-tock. Your twenty-four hours is up."

Eleven

William had tried to save me. There was no doubt in my mind about it, but he was also the one who told me the day would come when Connie tried to kill me. This was that day.

"Boy, is this rich," Connie said.

"How's that?" I tried to keep the agony out of my voice as I dangled over the river.

She kneeled down and looked across the dock at me. From where I was hanging, she looked like a golfer surveying the lie of a ball on a putting green. Then she started speaking: "It looks like your head is literally being served to me on a platter. How funny is that?"

"Yeah, funny," I agreed. And it was. Looking back on it, me thinking I was going to make it out of this jam with my undeath intact was hilarious even to me. At this point, Connie could kill me any number of ways. It was all up to her now. I just hoped she would make it quick.

She relaxed from a kneeling position into a cross-legged sit. All the time she kept one hand on top of that vampire-killing sword that was stuck in my hand. She had all the time in the world and all the savagery of her birthright as the Slayer to enjoy the kill. I had a feeling that by the time she got through with me I would wish I was back with Ulrich and the others.

She drummed her fingertips on her lips, thinking. "I know I said I would kill you like you tried to kill me, but maybe I can think of something more . . . entertaining."

Her face was only a few feet away from mine now. Once again, I searched her eyes for some sign of my old Connie, the woman I loved more than any other in my long existence. There was none of the warmth, the kindness, the love of justice. Connie Jones was gone, and this vicious killer was in her place.

"You're the cat. I'm the mouse. I get it," I said. "Do your thing."

"Don't rush me." She took a deep breath. "I like the smell of your blood, vampire." She pushed the sword further into my pinioned hand, causing my blood to flow faster. I could not move as she reached down with both hands to touch the flowing blood.

I yelped in pain as she brought her fingers to her lips and licked them clean. "Not bad," she said. "Maybe I'll drink your blood after all."

Before I could brace myself, she'd lain on her belly on the dock and encircled my head in the crook of one elbow. She put the heel of her other hand under my chin and pressed my head back, exposing my throat. This was it, then. It was over. I always used to think that the best way to die would be in Connie

Jones's arms. And that was just what was going to happen. I relaxed and let myself be . . . happy.

"Good-bye, Jackie," she said. "Any last words?"

I thought about that. At this point, was there any advantage in not telling her all of it? Wouldn't there be some benefit to her knowing everything I had left to tell? Surely there was something to be said for knowing the truth just for truth's sake. Besides, call it selfish but I didn't want to die with her hating me if I could help it.

"Yes," I said. "There are some things I need to tell you before you kill me."

"Make it snappy," she said, and released her hold on me. She folded her arms on the dock and looked at me, eyeball to eyeball.

"First, when I followed you to the underworld that time, more happened that I didn't tell you."

Connie's delicate brows arched inward. "What?" she asked warily.

"You didn't kick your ex-husband's ass for killing your kid."

"You bastard! You kept me from getting my revenge, didn't you? You stopped me because you wanted to get me back here!" Connie drew back her fist to hit me.

"No! The angel stopped you!"

Connie's arm froze before she landed the blow and she composed herself. "Tell me everything from the beginning. And you'd better hurry. The sun's almost up."

"The angel said you could stay and do battle with your ex-husband's spirit in hell, or you could fulfill your destiny on earth as the Slayer. It didn't look like much of a choice."

Connie's eyes turned hard as she let this sink in. "So you've known since the first that I was the Slayer. I guess I don't have to ask why you lied to me."

"It's more complicated than just trying to keep you from killing us," I insisted. "Remember, you weren't activated as the Slayer until the night of the earthquake."

"How much more complicated can it be?"

"I was afraid you might try to get yourself killed so you could return to heaven with your little boy while you still could—even if that meant defying the angel and circumventing your destiny as the Slayer."

"*Still* could? What are you talking about?"

"You're immortal now. Nothing can kill you besides things that kill vampires. The old lords fear you because of it. For all we know, you don't have any weaknesses."

"You mean there was a window of opportunity for me to—" Connie's face registered the anguish of what I'd just told her.

"We think there might have been a period of time when you could have returned to the underworld and spent eternity in paradise with your little boy, despite what the angel said."

"Why did you stop me? It doesn't make any sense. You and the other vampires could have gotten rid of me easily before the sword turned me into the Slayer! Why didn't you just kill me?"

She stopped in mid-sentence as realization dawned. It wasn't the only thing that was dawning. The sun was creeping toward the horizon and I was trapped, facing it. My eyes had already started to water and burn.

"You *did* want to send me back to the underworld that night when you tried to drain my blood!"

"I didn't want to kill you. You have to believe me. I tried to figure out a way to keep you alive. William had a big meeting with all the other vampires— Olivia, Travis, Werm, Iban, who loves you almost as much as I do. I argued with them all. They insisted that to die and be with your son in paradise for all eternity was exactly what you would want."

"And they were right!" Connie cried.

"I was selfish," I said, talking even faster now that the crowning sun was burning my arm, forehead, and cheeks. "I wanted to keep you with me, but William finally convinced me that it was the right thing to do. So I came to you, held you, used my glamour to make you fall asleep in my arms, and then I sucked your blood."

"But you didn't finish me off!" Connie said, sobbing. "Why?"

"Because when it was near the end and your life was almost gone, I—I couldn't kill you." My words disappeared in a scream as the dawn broke and my flesh sizzled. As smoke rose from my face and arm, Connie leapt to her feet and pulled the sword out of the timber.

My body slid into the river and I felt the immediate relief of the cold water on my wounds. I let myself sink deeper and deeper until I hit the muddy bottom. Peace settled over me and I could feel my burns and the gash in my hand begin to heal. I let myself lie back among the underwater plants that grew near the edge of the riverbank. They swayed gently with the rhythm of the moving water and caressed my injured cheek lightly.

Then I felt strong arms around my waist, lifting me upward. Legs kicked powerfully; I could feel them against mine. I was rising again, and I didn't want to.

My head broke the surface of the water right beside Connie's face. We were under the part of the repair shed that was suspended over the water. A narrow shaft of sunlight made its way between the two-by-fours in the wall, but the ceiling let nothing through. Connie had dragged me to a place where the light couldn't find me.

I was safe—for now—but exhausted. A vampire forced to stay up beyond daylight now and then won't suffer much harm, but a gravely injured one needs his sleep to heal. My body was demanding that rest. I sagged limply against Connie, forcing her to tread water for the both of us.

She used one hand to splash cold water on my face. "Why didn't you kill me?"

I heard her but couldn't answer. I was in another world again, the underwater world of comfort and peace. And sleep. I drifted in the soothing fluid. Was this what it was like for my baby as it was growing inside Connie? I had never allowed myself to think mushy thoughts about my baby before, but now that my mind was completely relaxed it allowed itself that luxury. I pictured myself in a human world, bouncing a blue-eyed baby on my knee in the sunshine.

Then I could feel the burning again. Harsh sounds assaulted my ears, and the smell of diesel nauseated me. Worst of all, I lost the healing water. A hard surface was at my back and I was racing forward to the gap in an open-ended tunnel. I burst through the surface of consciousness, gasping and blinking. When I could see again, I realized I was in the bridge of William's other custom cabin cruiser.

Connie knelt over me, holding my head in her lap. I looked deeply into her eyes and I saw it. It was faint, like the beating of my baby's heart, but it was there and growing.

The spark of Connie's humanity was back.

"Why didn't you kill me?"

"I . . ." I started to tell her that I heard our baby's heartbeat, but something stopped me. I guess it was the return of that unmistakable glimmer of the old Connie. It told me that my plan to have Seth save her and the baby could still work after all.

"I couldn't kill you because I love you," I said.

Twelve

Connie cradled my head in her hands. On her face I could see a whole parade of emotions. The power of my love had gotten through to her, just as it had drawn her out of the underworld against her will.

"You should have killed me," she said.

"I know."

"I ought to be furious with you right now because you didn't have the guts to finish me off."

"But you're not furious, and I know why. You're the old Connie again and you value life, including your own. You know it's true, don't you?" I said. "You can feel it now that you're . . . back."

Connie's eyes grew wide. "I *am* back."

I felt myself drifting off again, but something in the back of my mind nagged at me. There was a reason I should stay awake. What was it?

"The nuclear site! Diana and the others are on their way there now."

"You mean you were telling the truth about that?" Connie asked.

I told her what the other vampires had threatened to do. Before I'd finished the story, Connie had the boat backed out of the slip and headed upriver. Although I wished we were in one of William's speedboats, I happened to know we were on the faster of the two cabin cruisers. I knew because I'd just tuned this one up myself.

Connie set the boat on the right course and put it on autopilot. Then she kneeled down next to me again.

"You're injured. You need this." She pushed up the sleeve of her Savannah PD sweatshirt.

"No," I said. "I just need sleep. Just go up the river full throttle. If you see that other Thorne cabin cruiser before we get to Augusta, wake me."

"All right," she agreed.

The last thing I felt was Connie's warm lips pressed to my cold ones.

I dreamed about a toddler with my eyes and Connie's cheekbones and chin. "Come to Papa," I said to the child. I bent over and held out my hands, ready to swing the tyke up into my arms. I didn't know whether it was a boy or a girl, but it was beautiful. It toddled over to me and threw its plump little arms around my knee.

And bit me in the leg with its tiny fangs.

I woke up shouting and immediately felt a hand across my mouth.

"Shh!" Connie whispered. "I think they're just up ahead. What should we do?"

I roused myself and got to my feet. The sun had just

set, and the photochromic tinting on the windshield and windows had turned almost clear. "You're right. That's them," I said.

"Should we cut the running lights?" Connie asked.

"That won't help. Blood drinkers can see in the dark, remember?"

"Oh, yeah. I'm still pretty new at this. How do you feel?" Connie gave me a smile that was completely lucid and completely human. If I didn't know better I would have sworn that my own heart had started beating again.

"I feel great," I said. "Never better."

"Look," Connie said. "They're out of the cabin."

I took the wheel and steered it toward the other cruiser. "It looks like they've broken down," I said. Their boat was dead in the water. All four vampires were now walking around the cabin and scrambling around the deck. I saw Reedrek open the hatch to the engine compartment.

"We're going to take them on hand to hand, aren't we?" The sparkle in her eye told me that while Connie the human was back, Connie the Slayer was still just under the surface. As happy as I was to have the real Connie in the house I was also really glad to see that she still had her killer instinct. It would help keep her and the baby alive.

"You up for a fight?"

"Oh yeah," she said.

"Let's do it. Whatever happens, don't let them take over this boat."

"Wouldn't dream of it."

"Get ready. I'm going to aim the boat at them and

cut the motor only after we've got the momentum to ram them," I said. "And don't forget your sword."

"Aye-aye."

As soon as I cut the motor, Connie and I climbed onto the sundeck and grabbed the handrail. "Hang on," I said. There was no possibility of a sneak attack. All four of the vampires on the other cruiser saw us coming, and I saw them brace themselves for a fight. All except Mole.

"It's the Slayer!" Diana cried.

"No!" yelled Mole. "Don't come any closer!"

"It's not like this thing has brakes," I explained.

Ulrich looked at Mole. "Buck up, you mongrel. It's four against two."

But Mole was already over the side, dog-paddling for our boat and in grave danger of getting crushed between the two crafts.

"Looks more like three against three," I called out, although if I had my pick of fighters to come over to the light side, Mole would have been my last choice.

As we pulled closer I extended a hand to Mole, plucked him out of the water, and set him on the boat between Connie and me. I guess the little guy had just been pretending to go along with the bad guys after all. He picked a nifty time to switch allegiances again. I would have to watch my back since he helped leave me to die.

As soon as his feet hit the deck, Mole spit out a mouthful of river water and croaked, "Start up that engine and get us out of here now!" He jerked his head in the direction of the other craft's engine compartment and I suddenly remembered the missing bag of bomb components.

"Get inside," I yelled to Connie.

But the Slayer had drawn her sword and had blood in her eye. I caught her by the waist, slung her over my shoulder, and hoped she wouldn't cut my ass off with that blade. "Hey!" she protested.

"We've got to get inside. Trust me on this," I said.

By the time I'd set Connie on her feet on the bridge, Mole had gotten the engine started and it was damn the torpedoes, full steam ahead. The three vampires on the deck of the other cruiser looked perplexed until Ulrich decided to take charge. "Board their boat!" he commanded.

The bow of our boat rammed theirs and kept going, knocking Diana, Reedrek, and Ulrich to the deck.

The explosion on the other cruiser rocked our own craft and knocked Connie and me to the floor of the bridge. Mole stayed on his feet by hanging onto the throttle for dear undeath.

"Connie, are you all right?" I asked, scrambling to my feet and taking her hand.

"I'm fine." She joined me at the window just in time to see a fireball consuming the boat the other vampires had been on.

"Did you see if they got away?" I asked Mole, who was bringing the boat around in a wide arc.

"I didn't see anybody make it off the boat," he said.

We turned our boat around and circled the smoking wreckage three times. I retrieved a couple of flashlights from belowdecks, but we saw not a sign of a vampire break the surface. "We should get out of here before somebody sees the smoke and calls the authorities," I said.

"Anything you say," said Mole, steering the vessel back toward Savannah.

"Can we assume they burned to death?" Connie asked.

"Those immortals haven't lived hundreds of years for nothing," I said, remembering how Ulrich had survived more than one attempt at a beheading. "We can't assume anything."

"So what do we do now?" Connie asked.

"Maybe you could find a way to anonymously tip off the authorities that attempts are going to be made to sabotage the nuclear site. Maybe that way they'd double down on security for a while."

"I'll take care of it," she said. "Is that all we can do? If they're not dead, I mean."

"Until such time as they decide to show themselves, yeah, I guess."

"They're dead!" Mole shouted vehemently. "Dammit, they have to be."

I studied the little vampire, surprised at his outburst. Olivia had said he was a minion of the old lords for ages. Surely with everything he knew about those three vampires the idea that they might have survived couldn't come as a shock to him. Something about the gleam of hatred in his eye struck me as strange. The change in his formal manner of speaking was weird, too.

"What happened back there?" I asked him.

"They told me to steer the boat while they slept.

While they were dead to the world, I set the cruiser on auto, put together the bomb, then took it back to the engine compartment and set it up."

"I see," I said. Something about his story bothered me. "How'd you know how to build a bomb?"

He shrugged. "The Internet. After I placed the explosive device, I ripped out wires from the engine until the motor stopped."

"Nice going," I said.

"Thanks."

"I don't believe we've been introduced," Connie said, extending her hand to Mole.

I made the introductions, explaining Mole's background to Connie and vice versa. Mole looked her up and down. "Wow. So you're the Slayer," he said.

"That's what they tell me."

"Listen, I'm sorry for yelling before. It's just that Diana, Ulrich, and Reedrek treated me like dirt, you know? Like their flunky or something. I'd really like to believe that they burned up back there."

"Me too," I agreed. "Until we know different, let's assume that they did, but keep one eye open all the same. We can't afford to let our guard down."

"Sure," he said. "Speaking of keeping your eyes open, you guys must be really tired. Why don't you go below and get some rest. I'll steer us back to Savannah."

"I got some sleep earlier," I said.

"I couldn't close my eyes if my life depended on it," Connie said, rubbing her arms. "Too much has happened tonight."

"You're the one who's gone without sleep the

most," I told Mole. "We can steer while you go below."

"No. I insist," he said. "I couldn't sleep for the death of me. I'll stay right here. I expect you two could use some time alone even if you don't have to sleep."

"We do have a lot to talk about," Connie said.

"You're on," I said to Mole. "Just call us if you need us."

Before I'd had time to turn my back, I heard an awful avian screeching from outside the boat. Connie and I scrambled back on deck with Mole at our heels. A crow was circling the boat, squawking its lungs out. It tried to dive-bomb Mole, but the vampire ducked out of its way. The bird turned in mid-air and came back for him, this time spreading its tail feathers and crapping on the blood drinker's head.

Mole let loose with a string of curses as he swiped at his head.

"Jack! It's me, Mole!" the bird shrieked.

"What the—" Connie began.

The vampire on board with us—whoever it was—made a move to grab Connie's sword out of the scabbard on her back, but the Slayer was too quick. By the time it occurred to me what was going on, Connie had knocked the creature's feet out from under it, had one foot on its chest, and was holding the tip of the blade against its chin.

"Eleanor!" I said. "It's you, isn't it? You're supposed to be in hell, bitch!"

"Will somebody tell me what's going on?" Connie demanded, not taking her eyes off Mole's body.

"If you let me up I'll explain," Eleanor said.

"Watch her," I told Connie.

"I'm watching," she said.

The Slayer allowed Eleanor, who was now obviously inside Mole's body, to get to her feet slowly, but she never let the tip of the sword move farther than a few inches from Eleanor's throat. The crow lit on my shoulder like one of those parrots in the pirate pictures.

"How did you do it?" I asked Eleanor, trying to reconcile the fact that the ugly, bird-poop-covered bloodsucker standing before me had only recently been one of the most beautiful and desirable women I'd ever met. "How did you manage to save yourself from being zapped back to hell with the other double-deads?"

"How dense can you be, McShane? I'm a child of the voodoo blood, remember?"

Dammit. She was right. I *was* dense. I should have anticipated that the spell the Celtic gods cast might not work on her. Maman Lalee's powerful life force protected us Savannah vampires from all kinds of bad mojo. "When did she switch bodies with you?" I asked, addressing the crow.

"Just after the last time I saw you," it croaked. "I've been watching her every movement since then. I didn't know who or what she was."

"Why'd you do it?" I asked Eleanor. "Why didn't you just fly off to some happy hunting ground, switch bodies one last time with some hot young chick somewhere, and feed off unsuspecting victims to your evil little heart's content?"

"Because of *her*!" Eleanor gestured back in the direction from where we had come. "I hate Diana so much, I had to destroy her. Even if it meant swapping bodies with the most disgusting creature I've ever met outside of hell itself."

"Oy!" the crow said and flapped its wings against the side of my head. "That is most unkind."

"Settle down," I told the poor little guy. Then I turned back to Eleanor. "You still blame Diana for coming between you and William."

"Shut up!" Eleanor screamed. "It was her fault—all of it! I wasn't about to let her live after she took everything from me. I observed them from the air and took over their toady's body. When I realized what they were up to, I went along, keeping alert for any way I could step in and thwart their plans. I would have done anything to keep Diana from getting that—that *promotion,* for lack of a better word."

"And you saved Georgia and South Carolina in the process," Connie observed.

"I couldn't care less about the humans," Eleanor spat. "I just wanted to see Diana burn. And I did!"

"So, what now?" Connie asked, lowering the sword slightly. "Are you going to Disney World?"

"I'm going any damn place I please," Eleanor said. "During the split second I was switching bodies with that nauseating little vampire, I tapped into all his knowledge. I now know everything he knew about the old lords and what Olivia and her coven intend. Knowledge is power, but I'm not finished arming myself yet. There's only one more thing left to make myself unconquerable and get back the beauty I am so accustomed to possessing."

Suddenly two things occurred to me. First, I was troubled by the fact that Connie had let her guard down by lowering the sword, if only a little. Second, something that had been bothering the back of my mind had worked its way to the brain's front burner. What had Eleanor said when she had first taken the body of the crow, right after swapping bodies with Ginger? *When the time is right, I'll be back. You take good care of that Slayer, you hear?*

Even as I was realizing Eleanor's next move, I was lunging at her. But she was quicker. She drew a gun from the folds of Mole's strange clothing and shot me in the chest.

Thirteen

"I know that won't kill you," Eleanor said. "But all I have to do is slow you down while I steal the body of the Slayer. *That* will be my final move. Oh, and incidentally, I was lying about getting weaker each time I switched bodies. That happened to the others, but not to me. I kept my strength because of the voodoo blood. When I'm in the Slayer's body, I'll be invincible."

"Stop her," I ground out, trying to get to my feet, hoping my injury wouldn't fatally distract Connie.

Connie looked down at me and I saw the Slayer take over. "You bitch!" Connie said, returning her attention to Eleanor.

Eleanor squinched up her face again, just as she'd done when she body-swapped into the bird. "I call on the power of Satan to seat my spirit in the closest living thing!"

"Like hell!" Connie yelled and took a back swing with the sword just as the crow flew at Eleanor's head. "Take that, whore!"

I saw Mole's sad old expression return to his own face as Connie sliced the bird in two. The bird's beady, dead eyes froze into a silent stare.

"Jack!" Connie was at my side at once, helping me to my feet. "Are you going to be all right?"

"Yeah. Just help me get below and get this bullet out of me. It feels like silver. She thought of almost everything." I looked at Mole, who had sagged against the handrail in relief. "But she didn't count on our quick-thinking friend."

"How do we know he's really Mole?" Connie asked.

"Mole," I asked him, "what's the name of the barmaid on Tybee?"

Mole got a sappy look on his face. "Sharona," he murmured.

"It's him," I assured Connie.

"But Eleanor would know the name of the barmaid," Connie insisted. "She searched his mind."

I walked over and placed my hand on Mole's shoulder. "Yeah, but he wouldn't have had that dumb look on his face if he wasn't the real Mole."

Mole agreed to steer the boat back to Savannah while Connie and I went down into the cabin.

"When we get back to dry land, burn that bird carcass," I ordered.

"Yes, sir," he agreed.

I sat on an ottoman in the cabin's plush living area and let Connie strip off my shirt. "What will a silver bullet do to you, Jack?"

"It could weaken me enough to make me a lot easier to kill if it stays in long enough and it's close enough to my heart. You've got to take it out. Are there any steak knives in that drawer over there in the galley?"

"Steak knives?" Connie gasped in alarm. "You expect me to take a bullet out of your chest with a steak knife? What am I, a surgeon? A really bad, like, steak knife surgeon?"

"Just stay calm. It'll be fine. Go see what you can find to work with and I'll just lie on the sofa until you get back."

Connie returned with an oyster knife and two fondue forks. "I feel like I'm throwing a really grisly cocktail party," she said fretfully.

"Speaking of cocktails," I said, "it might make this a little less unpleasant if I was plastered."

"Oh, yeah. I'll be right back." Connie went to the small bar and came back with a large bottle of William's better whiskey.

"Should I pour some on the wound before I start?"

"Nah," I said, and took a drink. "It would just be a waste. I'm pretty impervious to infections."

"What should I do first?"

I took another drink. "Stick your finger in the wound and see if you can feel the bullet."

"Thank God it was a small-caliber pistol," Connie said, tentatively placing one index finger into the hole in my chest and wincing.

"I guess this might be a good time to ask you if there's still a part of you that's in love with the idea of killing me," I said. "And, ouch."

"Of course not." She looked at me sorrowfully. "I

should have known you'd never want to hurt me. I wasn't myself. You know that."

The liquor burned as I more or less poured it down my throat. I closed my eyes, trying not to remember the awful night Connie was talking about. "I tried to kill you," I said.

"You tried to save me. Save me from what I've become," she said.

A monster like me. I felt a warm tear fall onto my chest but didn't open my eyes. "I did try," I said through gritted teeth as she probed deeper into my chest. "I'm sorry it didn't work out. No, that's a lie. I'm not sorry. I'm glad you're here with me."

"But now I've—I've matured, just like my father Travis said I would. I can work with the good vampires. I mean, if you want me to."

"Of course I want you to." I opened my eyes and started to sit up before I remembered what was going on. "Ow!"

"I feel the bullet!"

"So do I," I said, lying back down. "Connie, it's not as easy as all that. Iban, Tobey, Werm, Olivia and her people—you're safe from all of us because of that prophecy I told you about. All the others—they're mostly in Europe, but only a plane ride away—will be coming for you. You'll spend your life hiding, looking over one shoulder."

"So what am I supposed to do?"

The liquor was hitting me fast and I could hear the slur in my own words. "My plan was for Seth to take you away. I should have known you wouldn't leave Savannah right after the earthquake, even for your own safety. You're a good cop. Seth could still take you up into the mountains, and he and his werewolf family would hide you and protect you from the vampires."

What I didn't tell her was that I hoped Seth would seduce her into thinking the baby was his. While she wouldn't leave Savannah or give up her duties as the Slayer for her own sake, she might for the sake of her unborn child.

"You were going to give me to Seth?"

"Well, yeah. For your own good."

So there I was, flat on my back shot and flat on my ass drunk, telling the vampire Slayer, her fingers two knuckles deep in my chest, that I was trying to give her away to another man. I fully expected her to ram the bullet right into my heart.

"I see," Connie said, her mouth a straight line. "So Seth's coming on to me was your idea?"

"Yes, uh, no. I mean, he loves you. He always has." I swallowed hard. The words were difficult for me to say. "I knew he'd protect you in ways I can't. Bad vampires are always going to be coming for me, too."

"Do you know anything about Seth and his clan? His pack in north Georgia, I mean?" Connie's voice was hard.

"Not specifically, no. I know about werewolves and shape shifters in general. Why?"

"Nothing. It doesn't matter now. Lie still."

I opened my eyes and looked around. I was still undead, as far as I could tell. "It could still work," I said. "You could go off with Seth and let his werewolf pack protect you."

"You should know me well enough by now to know I won't run."

"So are you up for the two of us fighting off the old lords and their little helpers?"

"We have to," Connie said. "It's the only way. I'm not going to go anywhere and hide."

I felt like I'd come full circle, and not just because my head was swimming. Connie was back and she knew everything. Well, almost everything. She would go forward at my side, no matter what the future held.

I looked into her eyes. "Okay, then, babe. It's you and me against the world. Let's go get 'em."

Connie gave me an odd look. "And we will. Right after I pry this silver bullet out of your chest with this fondue fork."

It was a great moment, fondue fork notwithstanding, and I wanted it to be perfect, but guilt nagged at my conscience. If I was going to make a clean start with Connie, it had to be just that—clean. She'd accused me of having sex with Olivia, but I had to confirm it. I stilled her wrist in my hand and forced her to look into my eyes.

"Wait," I said. "If we're going to be working together from here on out, there's something I have to tell you—something I have to get off my chest."

"The only thing you've got to get off your chest is that bullet and this fondue fork," she assured me.

"But I have to tell you—"

She bent forward so that we were eye to eye and gave me a look that was troubled, but firm—a look that stilled my tongue and unburdened my heart. "No, Jack," she said with conviction. "You don't."

I nodded, hoping that she meant what I thought she meant—that whatever had transpired before this moment didn't matter. I let myself relax completely and closed my eyes again. When the metal fondue fork struck the silver bullet, pain shot through me and I almost passed out from shock.

"I can't get it out with just the one," Connie said through gritted teeth. "I've got to get the other one in there so I can use them like pincers."

Since relaxing didn't seem to make me feel better, I steeled myself for the next probe. After a couple of misses, Connie got a grip on the bullet and dragged it out. I could tell the minute the silver was out of my body. I went from feeling like I was being poisoned to feeling like I'd been hit by a truck. It doesn't sound like much of an improvement, but somehow it was.

Connie cleaned the area after she removed the bullet, and no more blood seeped from the wound. There was no need for her to stitch the hole closed because I heal so fast. It was already beginning to disappear, and the aftereffects of the silver were gone. The aftereffects of the whiskey were bothering me a little, but that would be over soon, too.

I gingerly turned onto my side and beckoned her to lie down beside me. She put her cheek against my bare chest and we held each other.

"I can't believe you're really in my arms again," I said, stroking her back. "I had accepted the fact that you were eventually going to kill me."

Connie shivered and I held her closer. "What are we going to do now, Jack?"

"We're not in this fight alone," I began, thinking. "We already have a network of good vampires we can depend on. Throw in some shape shifter and faerie friends who can help us in a pinch, and we take it one day at a time."

"We'll have to be vigilant, proactive," Connie said.

"Right," I agreed. "Maybe you should move into William's mansion with me and the twins. Melaphia and Renee don't live there anymore," I said, hating the sound of that. I explained to Connie what had happened.

"I can't move into the mansion. But leaving may be the best thing for Mel and Renee," Connie said. "It'll be good for them to get away after what . . . happened to William."

I felt her body tense. "Oh, my God, Jack. I'm so sorry about William."

If I had any doubts that Connie had come to her senses, I didn't now. It was as if the reality of William's death at her hands was sinking in for the first time. I held her tighter as she began to sob.

"It couldn't be helped," I said. "Everyone who loved him is aware that you couldn't have stopped yourself, even if you'd known how. What's done is done. There's no going back."

"That's true about a lot of things. You're right. There's no going back."

I loved the feel of her cheek pressed hard into my injured chest. The pain reinforced that I was still alive, after a fashion, and that my love was really back, no longer an unhuman killing machine.

I stroked Connie's hair, she turned her face up to me, and I kissed her gently, then harder. Something like a spark ignited between us and we both pulled back and looked at each other. The feeling was similar to when we first kissed and were repelled by an electric shock that burned me. Except that this time I felt only pleasure. What had been a burn was now a powerful magnetism.

"What was that?" Connie asked.

"I don't know. Let's try it again."

I kissed her again, rolling onto my back and bringing her on top of me. The draw we felt to each other was even stronger this time. We couldn't get our clothes off fast enough. The look in Connie's eyes was wild, now not with murderous intent, but with desire.

She straddled me and wrapped her hands around my already hard cock. When she sheathed me in her warm, wet body, we connected like light and dark halves of the same whole. I was rocked by a wave of sensation that almost made me lose control, but I hung on, not wanting to miss what I knew was going to be the ride of my life.

Connie's body, with its warmth and growing life, accepted my darkness but countered it. As she thrust her hips against me, it was like the dance of death that slayers and vampires are destined to do, only in reverse. The life I'd put inside her had changed the polarity of the kinds of creatures we were. Instead of repelling her, I could feel myself being drawn in by her. It was the best thing I'd ever experienced.

She looked every bit the goddess, powerful and in command, as she rose and fell on my throbbing shaft. Her long hair fell like a black veil across her face as if she was performing some dark pagan rite.

If I had thought I was letting go with Olivia, I didn't know what letting go was. Every fiber of my being was alert, alive, in tune with the silent song of Connie's lovemaking. Her rhythm controlled me like the moon controls the tides. Closing my eyes, I kneaded her thighs with both hands, then slid them upward, caressing her breasts.

She lowered herself closer to me and I teased her nipples with my thumbs. She flattened her hands against my chest for support and increased her movements. I was soaring upward toward a climax like I'd never felt before.

"What's happening?" Connie cried, gasping.

"I don't know," I said. I looked down and saw that we were levitating off the sofa, floating in mid-air.

The opposition between the Slayer and blood drinker had turned inside out, and we were more desperately drawn to each other than ever. Nothing in the universe existed for me but her.

I leaned into a sitting position and held her closer. She arched her back, and I circled the delicate skin around each nipple with my lips and tongue. Her breath came in long deep waves as she clasped her arms around my neck, and I felt her lips against my hair.

I sat up fully with her still astride my lap; I raised my head and we kissed again. I felt like we were back floating together in the healing river as we had been earlier, only this time I was healed, stronger than I've ever been, thanks to her. We stayed there in that place, in that sea of emotion until we were swept away in a powerful surge of racking, mind-numbing pleasure.

We clung to each other as wave after wave of climactic joy rolled through us, unwilling to separate until we had wrung from each other every possible ripple of sensation.

Connie collapsed against me and we were on the sofa again, spent. I gently stroked her back, enjoying the weight of her lithe, athletic body resting on mine. For the first time in weeks I had hope. And it occurred to me that together Connie and I might actually be able to protect the baby and build a life.

My hand slid down her side. I longed to turn her on her back and place my palms against her abdomen, maybe even put my ear to her belly and see if I could hear my baby's heartbeat again.

Suddenly I was struck by the conviction that I should go ahead and tell her she carried my child. It had felt so good to tell her the truth about what happened in the underworld. I closed my eyes and imagined her face when I gave her the news about the baby. I knew she would be happy. *By the gods, I'm going to tell her.*

"Connie," I said, at the same moment she said, "Jack."

"You first," I said.

"There's something I have to tell you."

"What's that?"

"This is really hard to say. Especially after what we

just shared." I felt her body, which had been so relaxed after sex, fill with tension.

"Go ahead," I said. The faster she got whatever she wanted to say over with, the quicker I could tell her the wonderful news and could see the look on her face when she realized she was going to be a mother again.

"I shouldn't have made love to you, but I couldn't resist being with you one last time."

"What?" I asked dumbly.

"That was my way of saying good-bye to the idea of you and me as anything but allies in the struggle against the old lords. We can't ever do it again."

That made no sense to me. "Huh?"

"Remember when you said earlier that you had given me to Seth? Well . . . he took me. I belong to him now. There can never be any going back."

I finally had the answer to the question I'd been trying to figure out for days. She and Seth had sex, just like I had hoped they would. It hurt knowing my best friend had made love to my woman, but I deserved the pain.

I realized now why Connie hadn't been madder when I confirmed that I'd slept with Olivia. I guess she figured we were even. "Look," I said, "it doesn't matter to me that you had sex with Seth."

"What do you mean, 'It doesn't matter'?"

"That didn't come out right," I said hastily. "What I mean is, we can put behind us everything we've done since we were last together. We can start over fresh."

"We can, can we?" she said. "And what about Seth?"

"I'm really sorry about hurting him. But this thing between you and me is bigger than all three of us put together. Seth will have to get over it."

"And what if he doesn't?" she asked. "What if there's something in his makeup that won't let him?"

"What are you talking about?"

"I'm not sure I can explain."

"Look. I feel really bad for Seth. I take full responsibility for hurting him, and I'm willing to do whatever it takes for however long it takes to make it up to him."

"And what if you can't?"

"I have to. There isn't any other way."

Connie got up and turned her back on me to dress. "Jack, I understand that we'll be fighting bad vampires together until one of us dies. But that's going to be the extent of our relationship. The lovemaking—" She paused, choking on her words. When I came toward her, she held her hand out to stop me. "It's over between you and me."

"But—but after what just happened between us . . . Surely you can't throw that away."

"You threw it away when you came up with that scheme of yours," she said bitterly.

"I don't understand," I said. "Explain to me what it is about Seth that makes you think he couldn't get over you leaving him. You left him once before."

"That was before we had sex."

Exasperated, I said, "The important thing is that

you've refused to go away with him after all, so you might as well stay with me so *I* can help protect you."

"I don't *need* your protection. This bullheaded macho thing you have going has screwed up all our lives."

"Look, I know Seth will be hurt, but eventually he'll understand."

"No! It's you who still doesn't understand what you're dealing with. Me leaving Seth now will hurt him in ways that you can't even fathom—ways that he could never recover from."

She turned to go topside, but I grasped her arm and turned her back to me. "I love you," I said.

Throwing my words back at me, she said, "It doesn't matter anymore."

Fourteen

The next night I decided to get good and drunk. I figured I deserved it. The double-dead and nuclear threats were over, the real Connie was back, Mel and Renee were safe, and I'd thoroughly screwed up my life. If that didn't call for a good bender, I couldn't imagine what did.

I also figured I could call olly-olly-oxen-free to Werm to let him know he could come out of hiding. I walked into the Portal in anticipation of getting good and liquored up and ran right into the fist of a pissed-off werewolf.

As I sailed through the air, a number of things occurred to me simultaneously. One: The guy had a helluva long reach. Two: I couldn't believe I was too slow to avoid a haymaker, especially after such a big windup. Three: I was about to get my ass kicked like it had never been kicked before. Connie had evidently decided to embark on her new life with Seth with a clean conscience.

When I crashed against the wall, the club completely cleared out. Werm's patrons might be a weird bunch, but they were not stupid. It was a good thing they ran, because I had the awful feeling that my friend—or my former friend, more like it—was about to go all four-footed and furry on my sorry ass. That would have been quite a spectacle for the humans.

By the time I'd gotten to my feet, Seth had vaulted over the bar and seized me by my shoulders, bringing me eye to eye with him.

"You bastard," he began.

It was as good a place to start as any.

"You set me up," he continued. "I ought to kill you for what you've done to me."

Seth and I had spent many a night drinking and debating the most important questions of the universe. Babe Ruth or Hank Aaron? Ginger or Mary Ann? And the most important issue of all—who were the baddest of the badasses—vampires or werewolves? It had all been academic until now.

Now it was real.

"Connie told you," I said.

"Everything," he growled.

"I'm sorry."

"You're *sorry*?" Seth's whole body vibrated with rage. His gold-green eyes blazed with it, his voice oozed it. And I deserved every bit of it. "You gave me back the woman I love. The woman I thought was lost to me forever. You gave her to me not just for safekeeping but for good and always. You swore you and she were finished."

"I thought we were—"

Seth cut me off and went on, still clutching me in a

death grip. "But then, early this morning, she came to me. I was so happy. Then she said she had to tell me something. She told me about your little tryst."

"I lost control," I began. "I was just so happy to have the real Connie back."

Seth shook me again. "You lost control," he mocked. He slammed me against the wall hard enough to pulverize the sheetrock. But I barely felt it as the pain of my shame overwhelmed me.

"I didn't mean for it to happen. I thought she was going to kill me last night, so I wanted her to know the truth about why I tried to kill *her*."

"You wanted to save your own miserable existence, you sorry piece of dead meat."

"No. I swear I didn't know she would spare me. She was in slayer mode. I thought she would kill me anyway. I just . . . didn't want to die with her hating me."

"So you told her you had her best interests at heart. Then she comes out of her *dhampir* trance and the two of you have supersonic slayer sex. Is that about it?" Seth punched me in the gut with such force it felt like his fist was going to go clean through me and come out the other side.

I doubled over and when I could talk again, I said, "That's about it. But look on the bright side."

He caught me with an uppercut that just about separated my head from my body. "What bright side?"

I shook my head to clear it of the stars I was seeing. "You won, didn't you? She said it was over between her and me for good. Last night was—good-bye sex."

Like he had before, Seth grabbed me and brought

my face to his. I could see his eyes take on a decidedly unhuman shape, and his mouth gaped open to reveal daggerlike teeth. He was about to shift on me.

"Oh, yeah, I won. You fool! Do you have any idea what you might have done to me?" He changed without warning and with a speed I'd never witnessed before. The display of raw power stopped me in my tracks. When he'd finished shifting into animal form, he stood before me with hackles raised, ears back, and muzzle dripping. He was huge. A monster.

He flew at me, going for the throat as any good predator will. Even though I knew Seth was the injured party and that I deserved a beating—even a biting—the monster in *me* kicked in. Before I knew it I had a mouthful of his flesh in my fangs. I'd missed his throat, but I was close. So was he. A chunk of tissue from over my right eye came away in his teeth. We backed off, both bleeding badly, and circled each other.

I felt the bloodlust seep into me through whatever orifice my reason had just left by. The taste of the sweet, sticky, coppery juice was a turn-on when it came from a living thing. Blood stored in a bottle or plastic bag didn't come close. Living blood came with an intoxicating kick. Life's blood came with a heartbeat, but also with the promise of death. Werewolf blood was a wild vintage that fed my inner fiend.

We flew at each other again. This time our collision knocked us to the floor, and we locked in a death roll. I'd gotten closer to the jugular, but so had he. His fangs sank into my jaw and forced me to release my bite. When I wrenched away, some of the flesh under my chin was gone. I felt the ultimate primal fear. I was about to be devoured by a wild animal. There was no describing the terror.

I rolled away clutching at my jaw, trying to stanch the spurting blood. I managed to make it to my knees, readying for his next move—a killing bite to one of two spots favored by canines and cats both big and small. Either he'd go for my jugular or he'd try to sever my spinal cord at the back of the neck. I had to be quick enough to avoid him.

But then Seth's body twitched and he began to change back into a human as blood trickled from underneath his neck. I leaned against the wall to catch my breath while he completed the transformation. When he was through he put both hands to his throat to stop the bleeding.

The sight of him with all that blood should have made me even crazier with bloodlust, but it didn't. It returned me to my senses. I was not a monster anymore, but an ordinary man watching his best friend bleed. "Why did you change? You can heal better as a wolf."

"I can't hold this wound together with my paws, Sherlock," he said.

Our wounds were bloody messes. Luckily, werewolves heal as fast as vampires do. As long as we didn't do any more damage to each other we'd be all right.

"I can't believe I did that to you," I muttered, horrified.

"What? Take back the woman you gave me or try to tear my throat out?"

"Both," I answered miserably. "Will we ever get past this, Seth?"

"Don't you understand what you've done to me, Jack?" He looked at me in wonderment, like I should be getting something I wasn't.

"Look, it's not so bad," I lied. "Just forget what happened between Connie and me, and take her away from here until I'm just a distant memory."

"It's not that easy. You don't understand," he said.

I didn't understand. That's what Connie had said. And she'd said she couldn't explain. "What is it I don't get, man?"

He took a deep, rattling breath and said, "Wolves mate for life. Once someone comes between a wolf and his mate, it can never be the same."

"I don't understand," I said. "You've been with lots of women."

"Human women. They don't count."

"But you were in love with Connie when you thought she was human."

"It's like this," he said. "Werewolves are supposed to mate for life with other werewolves. But we can mate for life with humans if we choose to. That usually doesn't happen, because it's bound to result in tragedy. The human only lives a fraction of the lifetime of a werewolf, so the werewolf is always left alone. Unless he's killed before his mate dies.

"But Connie's immortal, so you don't have to worry about that," I said.

"It's different for me," he said.

"How?"

"This is hard to explain. I need a drink."

As we both staggered back to the bar, I noticed his wound had stopped bleeding. Mine was healing now, too. He poured us both a shot of Werm's best bourbon, and started the hard explanation.

"In the werewolf world, I'm kind of like . . . royalty."

"No shit," I said, and downed the shot. "How did that happen?"

"It's a long story. It has to do with werewolf legend going back to when the first man was cursed to walk on four legs and change during the full moon."

"Why have you never told me this?"

"A man doesn't like to brag. Besides, how would you have reacted?"

"I probably would have laughed my ass off," I said honestly. But there was nothing funny about it now.

"Yeah. Just like I would have laughed at you if you'd told me you were king of the vampires." Seth downed his own shot.

"So are you tougher than the other werewolves?"

Seth gave me a sidelong glance. "You knew that already."

"What I mean is, are you tougher because you're, like—what are you, a prince or something?"

"Yeah, I'm a prince or something, and long story short—yes, that's *one* reason I'm tougher."

"That's why you were so sure of yourself in that fight with Thrasher awhile back."

"Yep," he said. He poured us each another shot.

"So what does your being a . . . prince among werewolves mean as far as you and Connie are concerned?"

Seth closed his eyes and rubbed his temples. "In my heart and soul I bound myself to her for life. I felt it when the bond kicked in. It's a physical thing you have to experience to understand. It happens to regular werewolves, but when somebody from my special lineage commits himself, it's an even stronger bond."

"How does that work?" I asked. I didn't like how all this was shaping up. I felt guilty enough for doing the deed with Connie, but now things were getting really complicated.

"It's like this," Seth said. "If Connie was a werewolf, after she had sex with you, she would have been lost to me. As it is—" Seth abandoned the shot glass and took a swig of whiskey straight from the bottle.

"Since she's the vampire Slayer and not a werewolf?" I prompted.

"She chose to come back to me. As far as I can tell, I am still bonded to her."

"How do you know?"

"I can feel it." Seth thumped himself on the chest. "In here."

"Good," I lied. "Then I guess there's no harm done after all."

Seth's powerful hand was on my throat before I knew it. "Let me tell you something, hoss," he hissed. "If your shenanigans had succeeded in breaking my bond with Connie, I would have been smart to let you kill me just now. Without the woman I'm bonded to I'd be only half a person, or half a wolf."

I'd known he loved her. I'd counted on it. But I'd never realized how much until now. I opened my mouth to ask for forgiveness, but the words died on my lips. If he was going to forgive me I'd have to earn it. And I had no idea how to start. So all I said was, "I'm sorry, Seth. I'll make it up to you. I don't know how and I don't know when, but as God is my witness, I'll make it up to you somehow."

Fifteen

"Where is everybody?" someone said.

I looked up to see Werm come through the door. He turned even whiter than normal when he saw Seth and me.

Seth glanced at me, but I couldn't read his expression. "I'm taking the night off," he announced. With as much whiskey as he'd just guzzled I was surprised he was able to walk a straight line, but he did—right out the door.

"We had to close up," I said to Werm.

"What happened?"

"We fought over Connie. It's a long story."

Werm knew better than to ask me for details. He was getting pretty good at reading my moods. It was a good survival skill for a fledgling.

Werm went into the back room and returned with a mop and bucket. A goth couple walked in sporting spiky black hair and matching eyeliner. They took one look at the blood and busted walls and walked right out. "Come again," Werm called out to them.

He sighed and took the bucket to the sink behind the bar to fill it. "Whatever happened, at least it looks like you guys got it out of your systems."

"For now." I picked up the bottle Seth left behind and took a long drink.

Werm began mopping up the blood. "Oh, man, remind me not to piss you off—at least, any more than usual." He looked at me closely for the first time. "Or Seth for that matter. You look like shit. Half your chin's gone."

"It'll grow back. You should have seen the other guy."

"I did. He wasn't as bad."

"I guess he was more motivated." I finished off the bottle and gritted my teeth. "I thought I told you to lie low."

"I was about to. I had to stock up on supplies first. I was low on blood. Um, without getting into what you guys fought about, can I ask you if your plan is still on the table?"

"Yeah, it's coming along just dandy. Oh, incidentally, you don't have to hide now. Connie snapped out of the slayer trance. She's as sober as a judge."

"Thank God," Werm said.

I caught him up on all that had happened since I'd talked to him. Almost all, that is.

"Shit, Jack, that was close. Do you think Diana, Reedrek, and Ulrich are really dead?"

"It's hard to say. We still have to keep our guard up."

"And Eleanor's really gone back to the under-world?"

"Yeah. That I'm sure of."

Werm grinned as he mopped. "So if the double-deads and bad vamps are gone and the nuclear threat is over, maybe we can relax a little."

"Knock wood when you say that, man." I belched, propped my elbow on the bar, and rested the good side of my chin in my hand. Drinking too much sometimes made me melancholy. This would be one of those nights. "We can't ever relax again."

"Jack, I've been thinking." Werm wrung out the mop and took a swipe at the last of the blood.

"Good on you. What about?"

"Tobey and Iban have a whole coven of vampires, but they're too far away to help us."

"You missed a spot." I pointed out a bit of gore, probably part of my missing chunk of chin, that was stuck to the wall.

"Bro, are you listening?"

"Yeah, yeah, go on."

Werm dabbed at the wall with a rag. "There's a whole bunch of bad vampires in Europe just waiting for the old lords to decide how to come at us next, right?"

"Yeah. Right." I could tell that Werm had been formulating what he thought was a cunning plan. "Go on," I said.

"Um, well, don't you think it's time we reevaluate our policy of not making any more vampires?"

I sighed. I couldn't honestly say that I hadn't considered that myself, but I'd always been bound by William's philosophy. "Werm, the whole point of being a good vampire is not to impose our undeath on human beings."

"But what if a person *wanted* to be a vampire? Like me." Werm put away his mop and bucket and came to sit beside me at the bar.

"I thought you were having second thoughts yourself. Not that they'll do you any good. What's done is done."

"I do sometimes, but if I had it to do all over again, I'd still choose this life, er, existence."

"What are you getting at, exactly?"

"I know people who—"

"Wait. Wait. Wait." My head began to throb. Werm was giving me a hangover already and I was still drunk. "Don't tell me you've been lining up volunteers. If I hear you've gone and revealed us to some of your goth pals I'm going to have to bite you."

"No, Jack, I wouldn't do that. But I do know three people who would make perfect vampires."

I wasn't sure I wanted to know what Werm's idea of a perfect vampire was. "What do you mean?"

"They've got *skills*," he said enthusiastically. "They're good with computers; they know a lot about engineering, physics, all kinds of things that could come in handy."

"I'm listening," I said. "What else?"

"They don't have any family. Nobody would delve into their business or question why they only come out at night. They're looking for a place to *belong,* Jack."

"Hmmm. Are they tough? Would they make good fighters?"

Werm looked at me for a moment and blinked. "They're *really* smart."

"Give me another drink," I moaned. Werm's statement was the equivalent of being told a girl had a good personality when you'd asked if she was pretty.

"You've overserved yourself already," Werm stated. "Will you promise to at least think about what I've said? We need to build a team."

"Listen, buddy, I know you mean well," I began carefully. I would have to choose my words with caution so I wouldn't hurt the little guy's feelings. "I need people who are strong fighters. If we get attacked I want to be able to score some clean kills without having to look over my shoulder and worry about protecting people."

"Is that how you feel about me, Jack? Do you think I'm someone who's more of a liability than an asset?" Werm kept a stiff upper lip, but I knew he was wounded.

I patted his shoulder and nearly missed. The alcohol and the fight had taken their toll. "No. You've made up for your . . . physical limitations with your smarts."

"That's exactly what I'm talking about. We can use more smart vampires. We can't ever match the evil vampires in numbers. If we're going to beat them, we've got to outsmart them to outfight them."

I had to admit he had a point. For decades William had drummed into my head the importance of not creating more creatures of the night, but he hadn't had to face a direct attack by the Council until recently. And the last attack had killed him. His philosophy was noble, but in the final analysis it hadn't served him very well. The bottom line was this: *not* making vampires had been William's value system, but as I again painfully reminded myself, he was gone. It might just be time for a change. And we might not have any choice in the matter.

"I'll think about it," I told Werm.

He smiled. "Thanks, Jack."

The phone behind the bar rang and Werm answered. "He lost his cell. Put her through, Deylaud." He handed the phone to me. "It's Olivia."

Even before I could get the phone to my ear I could sense that something was badly wrong. "What's happening?" I demanded when Olivia came on the line.

"Jack, we've been attacked!"

"Are you all right?"

"I'm fine, physically. But several of my family members were slaughtered."

I considered what William had told me about the vampires in Olivia's coven. He said they were smart, quick, good fighters. They were a tight group who had been together for a long time. "How many have you lost?"

"Five." Olivia choked on the word. "Almost half of our group."

"William said you moved to a safe location after the fire. How did they find you?"

"We don't know."

Olivia's voice was shaking. I could tell it was all she could do to hold it together. "Liv, tell me what happened from the beginning."

"An attack force of the Council's operatives stormed

in at sunset. They swarmed up from the sewers where they'd been waiting for darkness. There were about twenty of them. Some went after my blood drinkers. Others went straight for our archives—the ancient writings that Alger had gathered over his lifetime."

"Did they carry away the scrolls and tablets you were hiding?"

"Some of them. Luckily they were the ones that had already been transcribed, translated, and archived onto our computers, so we didn't totally lose that information, only the originals."

"Did they take anything else?"

"No. I think they were just after the scrolls. The ones they took were only under light security since they'd already been captured on disc. I'm hoping they think they've got them all. Maybe they won't come back for the rest."

"How did they know you had that stuff?" I asked. "And how did they know where to find you in the first place?"

"I know what you're thinking," Olivia said. "But I simply can't believe there's a traitor in our midst."

"Do you have any new coven members?"

"No. They're all my trusted . . ." Here Olivia broke down. Her group really was like a family. William told me once that some of her vampires had been with her since she was turned.

"What about that Donovan guy? Isn't he a newbie?"

"Yes, but he wasn't involved. In fact, he was badly injured fighting off the attackers, but he'll recover.

Poor dear was only just recovered from having been burned in the fire. Now this."

As I thought about this, my thoughts turned to Eleanor. "Wait! Liv, I think I may know what happened." I explained how Eleanor had overtaken Mole's body. I also told her that Connie had come over to our side to help us.

"Thank goodness Connie's come back to her senses," Olivia said. "When I couldn't reach you on your cell phone, I was so afraid that—that—" Liv broke down into sobs.

"It's okay, baby. I'm fine. That part's over." When she had gotten a grip on herself, I said, "Eleanor told me that when she switched into Mole's body, she gained access to all his memories and knowledge."

Olivia picked up on my line of reasoning at once. "That means she could have used that information to tell Diana, Reedrek, and Ulrich about where we live and what we were up to."

"That's what I'm thinking. The timing works out, too."

"But how could she have done that while still masquerading as Mole? Mole only knew that information because he was working for me. Eleanor couldn't have divulged what she knew without putting herself— in Mole's body, that is—in even more danger from Ulrich, Diana, and Reedrek."

"Maybe there's some other way she could have given them the information. She could have told *them* she was spying on *you,* for example."

"That's possible. She certainly could have ingratiated herself with the evil ones that way."

"I've got an idea," I said. "I'll talk to Mole and ask him what he thinks about that theory."

"That sounds worthwhile," Olivia agreed. "Let me know what you find out."

Olivia sounded knackered, as she would put it. I really felt bad for her and the losses she'd suffered. "I guess it's selfish, but I'm just glad you were over here with me when the attack happened."

Olivia said on a sob, "I'm not. I wish I'd been at home. I should have been here fighting at their side."

I felt kind of guilty myself, and I'd thought I had enough guilt for one day. While Olivia and I were bumping uglies on the trunk of my convertible, her enemies were busy plotting the demise of her and her family.

"I can't tell you how sorry I am," I said. "But at least you know that there's an explanation besides one of your own turning on you."

"You're right, Jack. Thanks."

"What are you going to do now?"

"We'll find a more secure location and move again," she said wearily. "Perhaps more toward the country this time. Donovan's even trying to persuade us to go to Ireland."

"Why Ireland?"

"A number of reasons. For one, the Council would never expect us to move out of the country, but there's a practical reason as well. That's where our translators are. Ireland is a center for translation and what they call localization, mostly for computer programs that are sold in many different languages."

I thought about the possibility of Olivia being

closer to Melaphia and Renee and wondered if that was a good or bad thing. On the one hand, if Olivia's coven was tracked there, it might bring that part of the world to the attention of the Council. On the other hand, maybe Olivia could look out for Melaphia and Renee and vice versa. I had been hoping that Mel and Renee could put the world of vampires behind them, but I had no right to object to Olivia's moving her coven to a safer locale.

"Liv, if you do decide to move there, I'd like you to touch base with Mel—discreetly, that is."

"Of course," she agreed.

"Is there anything I can do for you? I feel pretty helpless with an ocean between us."

"Take care of yourself, Jack."

"Don't worry about me. Just keep me posted," I said. As I was about to hang up, I thought of something important that had almost slipped my mind among all the other bad news. "Wait, Liv. There's something I might be missing here. I had the impression that you and William thought the Council had their own information, stuff on vampire history and prophecies and what it all meant. If that is true, why would they have bothered to steal your records?"

There was a pause while Olivia considered. "We always assumed they had their own archives, their own historians, even. After all, they are the most ancient vampires in existence. But maybe they don't. Or maybe they felt their own records were incomplete."

I was struck by a wave of nausea as I pondered the meaning of the raid's timing. "We both know why they picked this moment to go looking for information after all these . . . millennia."

"The Slayer. They know she's been activated. Reedrek would have told them—he was there when it happened."

"So now they're looking for pointers on how to deal with her. Do you know what was in those scrolls the Council's goons took? I mean, was there any information there that might give them something to use against Connie or provide any kind of leverage over us?"

"I haven't had a chance to review the information yet," Olivia said. "It came back from the translation service right after I left for Savannah. A couple of the others were reviewing it, but—they were among those we lost. Now that I think of it, though, Donovan might have read the material."

"Could you call him to the phone?"

"He's much too badly injured, Jack. I let him feed on me to strengthen him and then put him back in his coffin to recover. He was barely conscious. It could be days before he's lucid enough to remember what he read, if he got the opportunity to read it at all."

"Liv, I know you're dealing with a lot right now, what with the murders and having to relocate before any more of the bad guys show up—"

"Not to mention trying to get the injured ones healed enough to move," Olivia added.

"But as soon as you can," I said, "I really need to know what was in those documents."

"I understand how important that is, but I don't know when I can get to it. We're five hours ahead of you here, so we have to get secured before nightfall. I haven't slept since I've been back."

"I know," I said. "Your safety comes first. Just do the best you can. And good luck."

"Thank you, dearest Jack. And just know how glad I am that the real Connie's back. For all of our sakes, but especially for yours."

"Thank you," I said. "That means a lot to me." I hung up, closed my eyes, and tried to rub the ache out of my temples. And here I'd always thought vampires couldn't get headaches, aside from an occasional hangover. Now I had a bad feeling my headaches were just beginning.

Sixteen

The news from Olivia sobered me right up. I headed to the Escalade. I was intending to take the short drive to Tybee to see Mole when Connie appeared out of the darkness. "Hey," I said. Lately, it seemed like every time I saw her I had to figure out a different way of relating to her. After a brief moment of thinking she was mine again, it was a painful adjustment to realize she was really and truly Seth's woman.

"I just talked to Seth, so I had to come and see how you were."

The SUV was parked under a streetlight. When she could see me better, she gasped. "Oh my God, Jack. Your face."

She reached out to touch me and I flinched away from her, not so much from her physical touch but from the emotional pain that touch would cause me. "It's nothing. It'll heal."

"Where are you going?"

"I have to talk to Mole and find out what Eleanor may have passed on to the bad vamps."

"I'm going with you," she said.

"Help yourself."

We climbed into the Escalade and she buckled up. I didn't bother with such safety precautions. Why should I? I've been through more than one windshield and lived to tell about it. Once we were headed toward the island, I gunned the engine.

"You do know I'm still a cop, right?" Connie asked. "So much has been going on, I called my supervisor and arranged for an extended leave of absence, but I'm still a cop."

"Sure. Why?"

She pointed to the speedometer. "I should arrest you right here and now."

"Not that again. How many tickets do you reckon you've given me?"

"Probably enough to fund a new station house," she said.

"Maybe you could let it slide just this once."

"I'll think about it," Connie said.

Our lighthearted banter was strained. We both knew we were thinking about the same thing. "I guess you know now why things with Seth and me are . . . complicated," she said, staring out the passenger-side window.

"Yeah. He explained everything." I wanted to ask her whether, if things were different, she would have stayed with me after last night. I wanted to ask her who she loved more—me or him. But I was afraid of what her answers would be. She'd made her choice, and I had to live with it.

"Probably the best thing to do is to never speak of it again. I guess we should just be friends. Can we do that?" she asked, her voice a monotone.

"Yeah, yeah. Let's be friends." I didn't want to hurt Seth more than I already had. But I didn't trust myself to be close to Connie if she gave me any encouragement whatsoever. I just wasn't that strong.

"Good. Because, I mean, we'll have to work together against the bad vamps from now on, right? I'd hate to think that things would be . . . awkward between us."

"Right, right," I said. "We're coworkers now. We're on the same team, huh?"

"All for one, and one for all," Connie agreed.

I hoped our conversation didn't sound as phony to her as it did to me. In the interest of changing the subject, I decided to run Werm's idea past her. "Listen, speaking of teamwork, Werm thinks we should make a few more vampires to help us."

"What? I thought all you good guys were against that."

I recounted my conversation with Werm, highlighting the pros and cons. "So, what do you think?"

"Jack, I'm the Slayer. Am I really the person to ask?"

"Oh, yeah. Right."

"Have you told Iban, Tobey, and Olivia what you're thinking?"

"Oh, geez, Olivia. I nearly forgot to tell you what she found when she got back to England."

"What?"

I filled her in on everything Liv had told me. "So that's why I need to talk to Mole," I explained.

Connie groaned. "Poor Olivia," she said. She was silent for a moment.

"What are you thinking about?" I asked.

"I still can't get over . . . how do I say it? Getting myself back, I guess you could say. I don't feel like a wild animal anymore. I'm actually sad that Olivia's vampires were murdered. Before last night I would have been cheering their deaths."

"I saw it in your eyes the second you came back. Just in time to let me live."

"I can't believe how close I came to killing you." Connie shuddered. "Now that I'm in my right mind, I've been thinking about things more clearly."

I nodded warily. "Like what?"

"Well, I was wondering if you'd heard anything from Travis, my father."

Travis Rubio was the ancient Mayan vampire who had discovered Connie was his daughter the night he came to kill her. We'd known that a vampire had to have fathered Connie, but we had no way of knowing who until Travis saw that Connie was a dead ringer for her long-lost birth mother. Long story short, Travis had left Connie's mother for what he believed to be her own good, assuming she was happily married to a human. Instead, she had borne his daughter, Connie, abandoned her to a group of nuns, and disappeared.

When Travis learned all this, he left immediately

for Mexico City to find Connie's mother and set things straight with her. Naturally, Connie was very interested in all this until she was activated as the Slayer. When her bloodlust kicked in it seemed all she could think about was her calling.

"I'm sorry, darlin'. I haven't heard a word from him. But I promise to tell you the minute I do."

She nodded, staring out the window. "I can't stop thinking about my mother. I wonder if she married and had children. It's possible she's still alive. Maybe I have brothers and sisters out there somewhere."

"Did you ever think about looking for her, the way some adopted kids search for their birth mothers?"

"I thought about it, but I didn't want to hurt my mom and dad—the ones who raised me. And it just seemed impossible, given the circumstances. Nobody saw her abandon me at that shrine. It would be like looking for a needle in a foreign haystack."

"I have a feeling if anybody can find a needle in a haystack, it's a very motivated Travis Rubio."

"Tell me everything you know about my father."

"There's not much to tell. You already know that he was an ancient Mayan priest. I'm not sure what he has been up to since the time the Maya died out."

"Aside from getting my mother pregnant," Connie pointed out.

"Right. From what I understand, he just roams around the southwest. He doesn't stay anywhere for very long."

"When he finally gets in touch with you, tell him to

come back here whether he finds my mother or not. I have some questions for him."

"I imagine you do," I said. "I'll tell him."

"I've been worried about something else, too," Connie said. "Do Deylaud and Reyha hate me after witnessing me kill William? My God, it must have been so awful for them."

I thought about that. "They're very loving creatures. They've been badly hurt, but they respond deeply to kindness and consistency. They'll forgive you in time. I guess you got to know them all those times you came over to the house to study with Melaphia, huh?"

"Melaphia and Renee," Connie moaned, covering her eyes with her hands. "I stabbed William right in front of their eyes. How will they ever get over it, especially that sweet little girl?"

I reached over and took her hand, pulling it gently from her face. "Listen. Melaphia and Renee understand the forces that made you do what you did. They'll be happy to know that you're the old Connie again and that you're back on our side."

Connie looked at me, her eyes glistening. "Thank you, Jack."

"What for?"

"For forgiving me yourself. I can't imagine how you've done it."

I fought the urge to bring Connie's hand to my lips. Instead I gave her fingers a friendly squeeze and let them go. "I imagine that wherever he is, William has forgiven you, too. How could I do any less? What happened wasn't your fault. If Eleanor, Reedrek, and Damien hadn't been there, it probably wouldn't have happened at all. It's not like you asked to be the vampire Slayer."

Besides that, I love you, I wanted to say. Instead, I went on. "I can't wait to get on the phone with Iban and Tobey and tell them you're back." I had to develop a habit of touching base with the key players in the network of good vampires. William spent so many decades maintaining those connections.

"Tell them I'm sorry," Connie said softly, looking out the window again.

"What are you thinking about?"

"I was just wondering about Olivia's archives. What could be in those old scrolls that has you so worried?"

"Could be anything," I muttered.

"Jack, I know you well enough to know that you're fretting about something specific. What is it?"

I sighed. Connie could read me almost as well as William could. "I'm worried that there might be something in those ancient documents that might give the old lords a clue as to how to get rid of a vampire slayer."

"Hmm. That would not be good," she agreed. "I'm sure Olivia will get back to us as soon as she can."

"I just hope they don't get hit again."

"You know what I wish?"

"What?" I asked.

"I wish we could take the fight right to them."

The gleam in her eye made me shiver instinctively, but that didn't make the thought less attractive. "You know what? I'm beginning to wish the same thing," I admitted.

"I just wish I could . . . cut loose, you know? Against some real bad-guy vampires."

"You got to do that already with the double-deads," I pointed out.

"And it was—was—" She gestured excitedly, searching for the right word.

"Exhilarating?" I suggested.

She cocked her head to the side and waved her hands.

"Thrilling?"

She shook her head but flashed a brilliant smile. "It was *fun*!"

"Okay. Now I'm really scared. I don't know if I should let you hang out with me or not. You might just drive a stake in my heart for entertainment's sake."

It was the wrong thing to say. Connie had just begun to shake off her guilt about William, but now she frowned again. "Don't even kid about that. I came way too close to killing you last night."

"Last night's over and done with," I said. "What happened then will never happen again."

Now it was my turn to be depressed. Connie was on my wavelength, and she quickly changed the subject. "What makes you so sure you know how to find Mole?" Connie asked.

"The last time I saw him, before he showed up on

the boat the other night, was in a bar he had taken a shine to."

"What was so special about this bar?"

"It wasn't the bar so much as the bartender. She took a liking to our little friend."

"My gosh," Connie said. "I hate to be mean, but Mole isn't much to look at. I wonder what she saw in him."

"I told her he had a fatal condition."

"Why'd you tell her that?"

"I had to explain his, um, odd appearance. Besides, it's kind of true."

Connie made a face. "His condition isn't fatal; it's undead."

"Close enough. Anyway, I sensed Sharona was the protective type."

"Ah, that's the Sharona he mentioned last night. I'm glad you think she's a good woman."

"She seemed fairly sweet on him. If he's not at the bar, dollars to doughnuts the fair Sharona will know where he is."

"For future reference, don't say 'doughnut' to a cop unless you're prepared to stop at a Krispy Kreme store within the next five minutes."

"I'll keep that in mind."

When we pulled up at the bar and got out of the Escalade, we immediately knew something was wrong. The air reeked of old vampires. With a shared glance toward each other, we ran for the steps. I got to the door before Connie and burst inside with her right behind me.

There was no one behind the bar, but four humans huddled under a table in the corner, cowering. One of them pointed toward the back room. The gesture was an unnecessary one, since that's where the screams were coming from.

"The front is clear," I said. "Get out of here." They scrambled on wobbly legs to do just that.

"Watch yourself," I told Connie. "The double-deads you fought are nothing compared to these guys. These vamps are as smart as they are deadly."

"I get it."

I was glad Connie had decided to take her sword with her most everywhere nowadays. It was easily hidden by her long black leather coat.

I couldn't imagine what she was going to do with it come summertime, though.

"Ready?" I unsheathed my fangs and grimaced widely to show them off.

Connie nodded and drew her sword.

I knocked down the door to the back room with one kick. Diana had poor Sharona by the throat. She had pushed her up against the wall, while Mole had been stripped to the waist and laid out on a pool table. He screamed in pain as Ulrich and Reedrek applied the broken end of a pool cue to his oozing chest. "It wasn't I who tried to kill you!" he cried. "It was Eleanor!"

Reedrek looked shaken when he saw me, but when he glanced at the Slayer, his skin tone assumed the color of talcum powder. I was more than a little miffed, to be honest. I mean, what was I? Chopped liver?

"Why, if it isn't the Slayer," he said with his usual bravado. "How lovely to see you again. We barely got to meet you last night."

Ulrich straightened and Diana blanched as white as Reedrek, but they recovered quickly. "I am Ulrich, Jack's great-grandsire. And this is Diana."

I didn't want to take my eyes off the three evil vampires in case they made a sudden move, but a feeling made me glance at Connie beside me. She seemed to be vibrating with an unseen force. The whites of her eyes had turned almost red and her pupils were dilated. Her lips parted, revealing fangs that had grown longer and sharper than they were the last time I'd seen them. The recovery of her reason hadn't been the last of her evolution into the full-grown Slayer. I realized that she was growing and changing even as I watched. She thrummed with power.

The other vampires could feel it as well. Even Mole had quit screaming and was staring at her. Although I was a little jealous of the effect she was having on them, I must admit it was way cool to see it—not to mention unbelievably hot. I waited silently, as they did, anxious to hear what she would say.

Connie raised the sword over her head and waved it around a few times. "Thanks for the introduction. So good to know who I'm about to kill. Who wants to go first?"

Unaccustomed to her brand-new adult set of fangs, she lisped slightly, causing that last phrase to come out sounding like *Who wantth to go firtht*. Her speech impediment didn't make her words any less frightening. If any of the bloodsuckers found the lisp amusing, they knew better than to laugh.

"Looks like it's on, folks," I said, and started moving forward.

Seventeen

Diana released Sharona and came to stand at Ulrich's right hand. Reedrek took his other side. But Ulrich, instead of meeting us with a united front, took another tack. He seized his offspring Reedrek by the shoulders and heaved him like a missile toward Connie. She sidestepped Reedrek's body and let it sail past her and slam against the wall at our backs. He bounced and landed on the speckled linoleum floor.

Reedrek looked like he was down for the count. "What the hell?" I said. "Using a vampire as a bowling ball is just . . . lame." Diana evidently took offense at my insult to her man. She flew at me so quickly her hair looked like a cascading golden blur. With one eye out for Connie, I caught Diana by the shoulders—right before her fangs reached my throat.

I grabbed her by the hair and tried to wrench her head around. Breaking her neck would not kill her, but it would weaken her enough to let me tear her throat out. She ripped herself free, leaving me with a handful of her blond crowning glory. She backed off to re-group, enraged that I'd torn out some of her lustrous locks. "You bastard!" she hissed, circling me.

Slowly, Connie advanced on Ulrich with her sword. He faked first one way and then the other, but he couldn't fool her. She was locked onto him like a fighter jet's laser-guided rocket. He pulled back his lips and thrust out his chin to bare the most awesome set of fangs I'd ever seen. His eyes glowed red as his entire face became monstrous. A glance at Connie told me she was intimidated by the show. Would she let it throw her off her game? Suddenly fighting at Connie's side stopped sounding like fun. I was terri-fied for her and the baby.

I made a move to get between Connie and Ulrich, but Diana cut me off. Taking advantage of my mo-mentary diversion, she went for my throat again. I raised my forearm to block her, and she sank her teeth into my biceps instead. I gritted my teeth to keep from crying out. Connie didn't need any distractions.

I shook Diana off, but the move cost me a chunk of my arm. As my blood and flesh flew, the Slayer's nose twitched. The scent of my blood had gotten her atten-tion. She looked at Diana, then at Ulrich, with a level of fury I'd never seen on her face before, not even when she was in her unreachably inhuman phase.

Her eyes dilated and she held the sword high. Her fangs, her savage beauty, and her black leather outfit made her look like a female panther about to spring. She charged Ulrich and slashed diagonally with the blade. He jumped backward but not in time. His midsection became striped with blood. He roared with rage and pain and made a grab for Connie's wrist. She couldn't shake him off, but she didn't lose her grip on her weapon either. It was almost as if the sword was part of her.

She reached out with her other hand and slapped Ulrich so hard across the face that his head snapped backward.

Sharona gasped. She had managed to stay out of the battle and make her way to Mole, helping him to sit up on the pool table. He clasped both hands to the wound on his chest.

The slap was not just any blow. It was a contemptuous, open-handed smack that was demeaning, even emasculating, in any language. To Ulrich, who was used to commanding respect wherever he went, it was maddening. I could see it on his face. He trembled with wrath.

"Prepare to die, *woman*!" He said the word as if it was a slur.

Connie grinned fiendishly. "I am the *Slayer*. Hear me roar." And she did. Her shriek bounced off the walls and reverberated in my ears like marbles rattling in a tin can. Her sword arm still in Ulrich's grasp, she thrust her boot against his bleeding torso so hard that it sent him crashing through the back door and down the concrete steps into the alley. Still she never let go of the blade.

Connie raced out the back door with Diana and me close behind. A quick glance toward Reedrek told me he was still senseless on the floor. Ulrich landed hard on his back and tried to get to his feet.

He was at that awkward crab stage of righting himself, with his feet planted, trying to raise himself on his arms, when Connie launched herself off the top step like a flying she-devil, her sword pointed downward. Ulrich's upward momentum only worked against him. His body met the sword in midair.

The blade entered his chest, piercing his heart with an awful sluicing sound, and came out the other side, pinning him to the earth like a bug in a specimen box. Ulrich had only a moment to register a look of utter surprise. This woman had bested him after a thousand mortal lifetimes of being the most savage killer on the face of the earth. Then he exploded into dust.

Ordinarily, a steel blade to the heart wouldn't kill a vampire—only a wooden stake would. But this was no ordinary sword. It was a souped-up, slayerfied, vampire-killing sword. And in Connie's hands it was magic.

Diana shrieked, but her instincts for self-preservation didn't desert her. She shook off her shock and ran as Connie pulled the sword out of the ground and turned her way. Stunned by Connie's display of killing power, I'd completely forgotten about Reedrek until I heard Sharona scream and Mole shout, "Behind you, Jack!"

He jumped on me from the top step. In the nanosecond between Mole's warning and Reedrek's leap, I had just enough time to dodge his fangs, which were aimed at my throat. He still connected with me hard enough to knock me to the ground. I twisted around to face him as he grappled for another strike at my neck.

Connie plucked him off of me like he was no more than a pesky skeeter and threw him back to the ground. Before you could say Jack Robinson, her fangs were at his throat and the point of her sword at his chest. He tried to shove her away, but she had a vise grip on his shoulder. Now she would close in for the kill.

"Wait," I said, kneeling beside him.

"Why?" Connie demanded.

"I want to get some information out of him first."

Connie grimaced, backed off, and sheathed her sword but not her fangs. "Whatever."

"Oh, and thanks."

"Don't mention it."

"I'm sorry Diana got away."

"We'll get her next time."

"Hang on a second." I looked at Sharona, who had come to the doorway and was working her mouth soundlessly like a beached guppy, in shock from what she'd witnessed.

Mole joined me at the barmaid's side. "Are you going to be all right?" I asked him.

He was holding his hand over the wound in his chest. "I'll be fine in a bit. What shall we do about poor Sharona? I put her under glamour, but I must confess I've never been too good at it."

"I'll take it from here," I told him.

He looked at me skeptically. "But you're a relative youngster. It takes hundreds of years of practice to use glamour effectively."

"What can I tell you? I'm a quick study." I shrugged and gently took Sharona's chin in my hand.

She looked in my direction with unfocused eyes, her beehive hairdo listing to one side and her lipstick smeared. Her ample chest rose and fell so fast I was afraid she might faint.

I looked her in the eye and said, "Sharona, you've had a nightmare. You didn't really see any bad people in here tonight, and, uh, definitely nobody with fangs or anything. Everything's fine. Mole, er, Velki here is going to take you back to work now."

The barmaid blinked her mascara-coated eyelashes and focused in on me. "Oh, hello," she said. "Can I get you another pitcher of margaritas?"

"Yeah. Sure," I said.

"Extra salt?"

"How sweet. You remembered," I said. "I'll be in there in a minute."

Mole gave me a look of astonished respect and helped me get Sharona to her feet. She tottered on her high heels for a moment before smoothing down her skirt and hair and following him back into the bar, oblivious to the rest of us. Holy crap, I *was* good.

Connie still had Reedrek pinned to the ground by his shoulders. "It looks like your little friend Ulrich threw you to the wolves," Connie said, and executed a very convincing animalistic snarl.

In response, Reedrek quaked in her grip, but he still managed to curse the name of his sire. "Damned despotic demon," he muttered. "I should have known I couldn't trust him. I'm glad you killed him, my dear."

"Yeah, I'll just bet you are, Pops," I observed. "Even Eleanor was savvy enough to figure out that they were going to screw you over in that Council promotion deal, and she was just a fledgling. Incidentally, it *was* Eleanor who blew up the boat you were on, not Mole. She had swapped bodies with him against his will."

"I'll kill her," he spat. "I'll kill Diana. And then I'll kill that Eleanor for good measure."

"I'm afraid I've robbed you of the pleasure of killing her," Connie told him, and shrugged in mock apology. "Been there. Done that. Got blood all over the T-shirt. I cut her right in two with my trusty sword." She reached behind her shoulder to tap the glittering hilt.

Reedrek stared at the Slayer with renewed awe and horror. "Well—well done," he stammered.

I had to laugh. "You can't toady up to the Slayer," I said. "Your goose is as good as cooked. But I want that four-one-one I mentioned first."

"Ah. Information," he interpreted for himself. "By all means. What do you wish to know?"

"How did you survive the explosion?" I asked him, partially because I was curious and partially to give him more time to be psyched out by Connie's menacing presence. His usual bluster was gone. As scared as he was of Connie, there was no telling what kind of knowledge we might drag out of him.

But I had to be careful here. If I was an expert at glamour, Reedrek was even better at intercepting the thoughts of his offspring, his offspring's offspring, and so on. Call it the old Vulcan mind meld, vampire style. I concentrated really hard on closing my mind to my grandsire and locking the outgoing thoughts as tightly as I could.

"We—we were thrown into the water so forcibly by the explosion that the fire that ignited us was extinguished before we had time to burn," he said. He licked his lips nervously and added, "I always knew you were special, my boy. You are indeed a prodigy at glamour."

"Save it," I replied. "Flattering me won't work any better than sucking up to her."

"Can I drink his blood?" Connie asked.

"Do you want to?" I asked, surprised, although I shouldn't have been. She was half-vampire, after all.

"I think so," she said. "Am I supposed to want to?"

"We're in uncharted territory here, babe," I said. "Say, Granddad, what do you know about vampire slayers?" I was tipping him off to our ignorance, but I figured we still held the upper hand. Besides, after we'd wrung out all the information he was good for, Connie could always just kill him. I couldn't do it myself because a vampire couldn't kill his sire without dying in the process. Killing a grandsire was almost as bad. Good thing Connie was chomping at the bit to do the job.

"I . . . um . . ." Reedrek hem-hawed. I could practically see the devious little wheels turning in his evil brain. Should he lie or tell us the truth? Eenie, meenie, miney, moe. Catch a vampire by the toe.

"Make yourself useful, old man, or I'll turn her loose on you. She was just getting warmed up on Ulrich. She doesn't even know her own strength yet, but we can find out real quick. You can be our guinea pig.

Oh, and don't even think about lying to me. You saw how I put glamour on that woman? That's not the extent of my talents."

Reedrek nodded. "Indeed. As I pointed out, it was an impressive display, my boy. I couldn't have done better myself. In fact—"

"Stop blathering. I can smell a lie from anyone no matter how far off in my bloodline," I bluffed, wondering if he could smell mine.

"What would you like to know?" he hedged, giving no indication that he didn't believe me.

"Have you people figured out how to kill the Slayer yet?"

He looked back and forth from me to Connie. "It can only be done by decapitation," he said quickly.

I made a show of leaning close to him and inhaling deeply. All I smelled was old, fetid vampire. Eau de Reedrek. "Why is that?"

"It has to do with the sword mythos," he said. "She can be killed by any blade strong enough to decapitate her. The gods have a certain sense of symmetry. Since one sword is needed to activate the Slayer and serve as her personal weapon, only a sword or something similar can kill her."

"Let me get this straight," Connie said. "Any cutting weapon that can take my head could kill me."

Connie and I exchanged looks. "So you're saying that the other ways of killing regular old vampires don't apply?" I asked.

"That is correct," he said.

"No wooden stake to the heart?"

"No."

"No flame thrower?"

"Not as such."

"No getting caught out in the sun?"

"Negative."

"Do you think he's telling the truth?" Connie asked.

Watching Reedrek's face carefully, I said, "Yes." Reedrek sighed in relief.

"How do you know this about the Slayer?" I asked him.

"From my communication with the Council. The old lords dusted off their ancient texts when they became convinced that the Slayer was among us. And they shared some of that information with me."

"How do you communicate with the Council?" I demanded. All vampires had their own special powers. I knew Reedrek's psychic ability was impressive. If he could communicate with the Council across the Atlantic, the implications were pretty scary.

"Um, we talk by cell phone," he admitted sheepishly.

Oh, man, that was a relief. I was glad he hadn't tried to bluff. Evidently he bought it when I said I could suddenly tell if he was lying. While I had him on the ropes I decided to test out my theory about what happened at Olivia's. "What do you know about the vamp-on-vamp violence that just happened in London?"

"There was to be a raid on Olivia's coven house," he said. "The Council desired some old scrolls and tablets they were missing from their collection."

"How did the Council's goons know where to find the goods?"

"The information came from Mole—er, Eleanor. He, uh, she claimed to have come upon the knowledge by accident. We relayed it to the Council, who acted on it immediately."

"What else did Eleanor tell the Council through you?" I asked.

"That was all. I swear it."

"And have you heard back from them about any new information they might have found in those documents?"

"No, there hasn't been time for them to interpret it yet. But if you keep me alive, perhaps I can find out what the material reveals."

Reedrek had some nerve trying to strike a deal with us. Every time William had tried to bargain with his sire, the old bloodsucker had screwed him over. Did he think I didn't know that? While wondering how stupid he thought I was, it occurred to me how gullible *he* was. I had him believing he couldn't lie to me.

I was reminded of an old human buddy of mine, an underwriter who worked with insurance salesmen day in and day out for forty years. "They lie like rugs," he said to me. "But liars are themselves the most gullible people in the world. They'll believe anything you tell them." Vampires, insurance salesmen— one bloodsucker was much like another, I decided.

I was suddenly struck with a new idea. "Come with us, Grandpa. This is your lucky day." I looked at Reedrek with the satisfaction of knowing that I was going to be able to avenge his part in William's death. "I've got plans for you."

I let my guard down and allowed Reedrek to read my mind so that he'd know what I had in store for him. His face contorted into true terror. "No! Not that! Not again!"

Eighteen

I couldn't help but congratulate myself on my fore-thought. I'd given Rennie an assignment and he had completed it to the letter. He'd reinstalled Reedrek's concrete and steel tomb, the one that served as the cornerstone for the new hospital that William's phil-anthropic foundation had built. All we had to do was stuff the old buzzard in the end of the box, weld it shut, and smear a couple of layers of cement over it. He would be trapped for eternity. I hoped.

On the way back from Tybee I had called Rennie to meet Connie, Mole, and me with the necessary equip-ment and supplies. We'd brought Mole back with us for his own protection and to help us ride herd on Reedrek for the drive back to Savannah.

We weren't worried about Sharona since she'd been fine when we left her, and Mole had been careful not to show any affection toward her in front of the other vampires. As far as they knew, she was just a by-stander with bad taste and not the love of Mole's evi-

dently long life. So we didn't have to worry about
Diana taking her hostage to try and get to Mole.

Rennie was a little bit freaked out by Reedrek's
snarling and fang-baring, but he got over it. For years
I'd managed not to involve Rennie in vampire business. But in recent months, I'd had to call on him
more and more, and he'd responded like a real
trouper. I was just sorry I had to bother him, what
with him being sickly and all. He never complained,
but he was clearly in pain from his ulcers again.

So we put Reedrek to bed. No muss, no fuss. Well,
okay, there was quite a bit of fuss from the old bloodsucker himself, who cursed and struggled the whole
way. With Connie and me controlling him, and with
Rennie to wield the blowtorch—which came in really
handy for forcing Reedrek into the box—the old bastard didn't have a chance.

As Connie, Mole, and I were walking Rennie back
to his truck I told them my idea for exploiting
Reedrek's in with the Council. "So, Rennie, do you
think you could engineer a way for us to get a tele-
phone to Grandpa?"

"I'll think on it, Jack. It might be as simple as
drilling a hole into his box and running a fiber-optic
cable in there. I'll talk to some telecom people and see
what I can come up with."

"Thanks, man. Take it easy with those ulcers,
huh?"

Rennie tried to smile, and went back to his truck.

Once we were in William's vault and out of
Reedrek's considerable earshot and mind-reading
powers, I could finally let my guard down and think.

I wanted to ask Mole some questions like we'd intended to do in the first place. We couldn't get into all the issues in the car because Reedrek could overhear us. Now we could finally put our heads together.

Deylaud had given Mole a change of clothes from his own closet. The shape-shifting canine's human form was not as tall or muscular as me, but Mole still had to roll up the khakis and the sleeves of the pullover.

When Mole had had a chance to wash up and change, I gave him a glass of blood spiked with some of William's best brandy and got drinks for Connie and me as well. I urged him to get comfortable on the chaise and put his feet up. He swirled the drink in the snifter and sighed with contentment before taking a sip.

Diana would assume Mole would not go back to the bar they had attacked him in, which meant it was perfectly safe for him to do just that. I wouldn't have been surprised, however, if the quartet who had escaped from underneath the table earlier found a new and less terrifying watering hole. I wasn't too worried about them talking. By the look of them, anyone they might tell about being menaced by vampires would certainly chalk the adventure up to demon rum, not actual demons.

When Mole seemed cozy enough, I sat beside Connie on the couch. "What a night, huh?"

Mole rubbed his chest where he had been semi-staked with the pool cue. "They thought I had blown up the boat. They had no way of knowing that I'd lost my body to Eleanor, and naturally they wouldn't believe me when I tried to tell them. Thanks to you both for coming to my rescue. One more moment and Sharona would be sweeping what was left of me up off the floor of the billiards room."

"Connie deserves your thanks more than I do. She did the heavy lifting," I said.

Mole held up his glass. "To the Slayer," he said. "Congratulations on dispatching one of the most evil vampires that ever stalked the earth. You were magnificent, my dear."

I raised my glass as well. "Hear, hear. I'm really glad you're on our side."

"Thanks," Connie said.

"What you did was an extremely big deal," I said. "William tried twice to kill Ulrich and failed both times. You did it easily."

"Remarkable," Mole added.

Connie said, "I can't believe it was only a short time ago that I didn't even know vampires, shape shifters, and faeries existed. Who knew there were creatures just beyond my understanding, and they are living all around me. And now I *am* a creature I don't understand."

"I think you understand plenty. In fact, you're amazing," I said. "And not because you've got superpowers, but because you've got the mental toughness to deal with them. I have to ask—what did it feel like? Killing him, I mean."

Connie shook her head and smiled. "It was an unbelievable rush. I can't really describe it."

"You avenged a lot of good people who were slain

by him. That is indeed something to be proud of," Mole said.

"If I hadn't let Reedrek get the drop on me, you might have been able to kill Diana, too," I said. I'd always prided myself on my fighting ability. It was a weird feeling, getting out shined by a girl. I had been William's right-hand man for so long that when he died I figured I'd take over as the baddest bad-vampire killer on earth. I guess I'd just have to get used to the idea of being someone else's understudy again.

"What do you think Diana's going to do now that she's on her own? Do you think she'll go back to Europe?"

"Definitely not," Mole said, shaking his head vehemently. "You don't want to go before the Council having failed to complete a promised task."

"So what do you think she'll do?" I asked.

"My guess is that she'll come up with a new plan. Her other option is to go into hiding, and I think she's much too ambitious for that. She'll only go before the Council when she has something else to offer them. And, of course, she'll blame the latest failures on Ulrich since he's no longer around to defend himself. That's my prediction."

"What can she do on her own, without help?" Connie asked.

"Yeah," I put in. "On this side of the pond there's nobody for her to recruit. We're the good guys over here. Even if she makes her own vampire, a fledgling is too hard to control. Look what happened to Eleanor. William thought he could keep her on the straight and narrow, and she went completely off the rails at the first sign of trouble."

"Don't underestimate Diana," Mole warned. "She can cause plenty of mischief without help. She's a very powerful vampire in her own right. My only advice is to stay alert."

I sighed. My life had been on code red alert for months now. "We still need to discuss what happened to Olivia's coven."

"Such a tragedy," Mole fretted. "When she and her remaining family are settled into a new home, I must talk to her and find out who among them lived and who died. I worked with several of her vampires, and I'm highly distressed about the attack."

"What else could Eleanor have told the Council when she tapped into your memories—besides ratting out Olivia's cover?" I asked.

Mole thought for a minute. "Nothing comes to mind. I hadn't been spying for Olivia that long, and for my own protection, I didn't ask her for any of the coven's information. The less I knew the safer I was."

"So you weren't spying for any other vampires?" Connie asked.

"Oh, no. Olivia's group are the only nonevil blood drinkers in Europe that I'm aware of. There's nothing else of a damaging nature that Eleanor could have told the Council that might have come from me."

"That's a relief, at least," I said. "Do you have any special knowledge about the Slayer?"

"What kind of knowledge?" Mole asked.

I filled him in on Connie's and my trip to the underworld and what I'd seen and heard. Connie still couldn't remember a thing from her time there.

"Oh, my," Mole said. "I had no idea you'd had such a difficult time of it. So you haven't had much guidance in the way of the Slayer, then?"

"No. Do you know very much about the Slayer that we don't?" Connie asked. "Uh, I mean about me, that is. I'd be grateful for anything you could tell me."

"I know enough to be able to confirm that Reedrek was telling the truth about how the Slayer—that is you, uh, Connie—could be killed," he said delicately. As if it pained him to put a sore subject into words, he drew a finger across his throat.

"I get it," Connie said. "Do you know anything else about slayer lore and prophecy?"

"I've had very few opportunities to sneak looks at the archives of the Council. For decades I attempted to view the writings on a catch-as-catch-can basis. I was eventually caught and punished, so I stopped making a habit out of it. What I did see was so piece-meal that I'm afraid I couldn't make much sense of it. I'm really sorry I can't help you. I promise that if I re-member anything that might be of use I'll tell you im-mediately."

"Thanks," Connie said.

"May I have another drink, please? You're ever so kind." I mixed Mole another blood and brandy and handed it to him. "You know, Connie, your story is fascinating. Jack, have you ever been able to figure out what propelled Connie from the underworld and back here to earth?"

"Never have," I said.

"From what you told me, if I had to guess I'd say the force of your own will accomplished that, Jack. At the risk of appearing romantic I might even say it was the force of your love." The wizened little vampire smiled so warmly he looked almost human for a second or two.

So my feelings for Connie were that transparent. I looked at her, but she couldn't meet my eyes. Would Seth have risked his life and soul to save her like I had? I guess that was an unfair question. Still, I couldn't help but think it. It didn't matter, though. Connie had made her choice, and it wasn't me.

"Maybe I screwed up by going to get you back," I muttered to Connie. "If I'd only left you there to be slayerized the way you were supposed to be, maybe things would have been different somehow."

"Don't second-guess yourself," Connie said, shaking her head. "It's over and done."

"Quite right," Mole chimed in, and took a long drink of his cocktail.

I sighed. Had my actions doomed William to everlasting death? How would things have played out if I had not been so headstrong? That thought was just too painful, so I banished it from my mind. I knew it would haunt my nightmares though, probably for the rest of my undead life.

There was no telling who else's fate I'd changed without even knowing it by my bullheadedness. I just hoped I hadn't gotten the ball rolling in the wrong direction in ways I couldn't fathom yet.

Mole was getting a little tipsy. He'd had a tough day, what with being roughed up by Reedrek and Ulrich, and I could tell he was exhausted. Judging by the angle of his shiny little head, he was probably in greater danger of nodding off from fatigue than of passing out from alcohol. I suggested he hit the hay, and he let me help him into the spare coffin.

Connie was putting the glasses in the sink when I closed the lid on Mole. "I should go," she said.

"Are you sure you don't want to stay here tonight? Diana's going to be extra pissed because you killed her man today. It wouldn't be too hard for her to figure out where you live."

"Maybe I should, since it's so late," she said. "I'll have to call Seth and tell him."

"Tell Seth?"

"He's staying at my place now."

"Oh," I said numbly. "Sure."

"Tomorrow morning he can pick me up and take me to get my car at Werm's club. Where do you want me to sleep?"

I stifled the urge to say, *With me.* Instead I said, "The guest room is on the third floor. Second door on the left."

"Okay," she said. "See you . . ."

"Tomorrow night," I said. "I'm thinking of having a meeting with the people on our side. Eleanor's house—geez, I'm going to have to stop calling it that—anyway, it's finished now. We can meet there. We need to discuss the idea that Werm came up with, and we can get everybody up to speed about what happened tonight. Be there at sundown, and bring Seth."

"All right," she said. "See you then." She turned to go but looked back at me.

"What?" I asked.

She took my chin in her hand and inspected the wounds in my jaw and brow, running her fingers over the small dents Seth had put in my flesh. They were already almost healed. "You'll be okay," she said.

I listened to her footsteps as she climbed the steps and closed the door to the vault behind her. I went to William's desk and sat down in his chair. *No, I won't be okay. I'll never be okay again.*

Nineteen

So much had happened in the last couple of days. I realized I needed to set up a conference call to fill in Iban and Tobey, and I would have to do so before I turned in, while everything was fresh in my mind. They were relieved to hear that Connie had come back to her senses and that the double-dead threat was gone. When we first learned Connie was the Slayer, I had reason to worry that even the good vampires would try to kill her before she had a chance to kill us. That danger was over. I could tell that Iban and Tobey were sincere when they said they wished Connie well.

I told them what happened with Mole and the others aboard William's boats, and I described how Connie had killed Ulrich.

"She killed him with one blow?" Iban asked. "That must have been impressive."

"You got that right," I said.

"Ulrich was legendary," Tobey exclaimed. "He was said to be immensely powerful."

"That's right," Iban agreed. "He struck fear into the hearts of even the most ancient vampires. I wonder how the Council will react when they find out he's dead."

I shared with them Mole's speculations on that score. They urged me to proceed with caution and assume that Diana was capable of anything.

"She hasn't survived to be hundreds of years old—especially as a female—without being extremely clever," Iban pointed out.

"Yeah," Tobey said. "She's bound to have some tricks up her sleeve. You and your people have to be hyper-vigilant. There's no telling what she might be planning."

"I hear you," I said. "I'm not satisfied to sit back and wait, though. I want you guys to have a powwow with your people. Try to generate some ideas as to what the old lords might be planning next based on what they've done in the past. We need to start being proactive."

They said they would do what I asked. Then I remembered my conversation with Connie on the way out to Tybee. "Have either of you guys heard anything from Travis? Now that Connie's back in her right mind, she has a lot of questions for him."

"I can understand that," Iban said. "But I haven't seen or heard from him since the last night we were all in Savannah."

"Me neither," Tobey said. "And we've been asking around. We're kind of curious about the situation with Connie's mother, too. We'll let you know immediately if we hear something."

"Thanks," I said. Now I needed to broach the really tough subject—the one I'd saved for last. "There's one more thing. We need to talk about how to get more help here."

"I don't know, Jack," Iban said. "As you know, my entire clan was wiped out by the plague. Since I've joined Tobey's people, we lost another vampire when Damien murdered Freddie Blackstone so he could masquerade as him."

"I knew there would be problems sending any of your people out here," I said. "I'm talking about making more vampires. Very carefully, of course."

There were a few moments of silence on the other end of the line before Iban said, "That's against everything we stand for, Jack. You know that."

"Yes, I do. But desperate times call for desperate measures." I told them Werm's idea about recruiting people with useful skills and no family.

"I think it's wrong," Iban said flatly. "I'd rather come out and help you myself."

"You're welcome to do so, but with all due respect, you're not enough. We need to build a team that can be ready for anything at any time."

"Jack, no," Iban insisted.

"Listen!" I exploded. "I know your people are spooked. But this is going to be the hot spot when the Council strikes again."

"We may have more people, but you have the Slayer at your side," Tobey pointed out hotly. "We're not immune to trouble out here ourselves. An entire colony was wiped out."

"Look, the bottom line is this," I said. "I'd love to

have your blessing to do whatever I need to do in order to fight off the old lords. But I don't *need* your blessing. This is fair warning."

"We've been allied with William since he came to the New World," Tobey said gravely. "Don't throw all that away, Jack."

"Are you threatening to cut ties with me if I go forward with what I must?" I could barely get the words out.

Iban sighed. "Let us all take a step back here. I, for one, trust Jack not to do something we will all regret. Jack, whatever you decide, just go slowly and be careful. Do you agree, Tobias?"

"Yes," Tobey finally said. "Be careful, Jack." I almost relaxed, but I sensed he wasn't finished. "I'm sure I don't have to remind you what happened when William went against his own policy and made Eleanor."

"No," I said. "You don't. If it wasn't for her, William might be here right now. I'm not likely to forget."

"I'm glad," Tobey said. "Good night, Jack."

"Good-bye, my friend," Iban said.

"Yeah. Bye," I said.

I finally made it to my coffin, but as exhausted as I was, I couldn't get to sleep. The events of the evening—getting the shit kicked out of me by Seth, witnessing Connie kill Ulrich, having a long-distance fight with Tobey and Iban—kept going through my head over and over.

Being the guy in charge wasn't easy. I regretted all the times I'd given William a hard time for his decisions. He was barely gone and I already had more understanding of him and what he must have gone through than I'd had in the entirety of my existence while he was alive.

I may have slept for a couple of hours, but I finally gave up on getting a full day's rest by eight or nine in the morning. I crawled out of my coffin, showered, and found Connie drinking coffee in the kitchen, evidently waiting for Seth to pick her up. Even though it was daytime, Deylaud and Reyha had for some reason chosen to be in human form. Deylaud sat at the table with Connie, politely answering questions about his background.

Reyha, predictably, was more standoffish, leaning against the wall in the farthest corner and twisting her long pale hair nervously. I couldn't help but feel sorry for her and her brother. In a few short weeks they'd lost William, Melaphia, and Renee. They were creatures of habit, and their world had been turned completely upside down. I was the only constant they had left, and I'd invited the woman who killed William into their home.

It would take time for them to accept Connie. When I entered the room Reyha didn't approach me as she usually did. I'd locked her out of the vault the night before in my attempt to get some rest.

"Good morning, everybody," I said, trying to sound as natural as possible for the twins' sakes. I got some fresh blood from the refrigerator and poured it in a glass.

"Deylaud's been telling me some interesting stories," Connie said.

I turned my attention to her for the first time and noticed that she had one of her shirtsleeves rolled up and a bandage on her arm. "What happened there?" I asked.

Reyha gave a little cry and bolted from the room. Connie sat calmly, saying nothing. Deylaud was the one who spoke. "Reyha bit Connie," he said. He couldn't have any more shame in his voice if he had taken a bite out of her himself.

Anger flared inside me, and I started around the table after Reyha, but Connie caught my arm. "Let it be," Connie said. "She feels bad enough already."

"I can't let her get away with this," I said.

Poor Deylaud lay his head down on the table and sobbed. "Please don't hurt her," he said. "I couldn't bear it."

Connie stood up and handed me back the glass I'd slammed onto the table. "Calm down and finish your drink."

I downed the rest of the blood in the glass, then reached for Connie's arm. I slid the bandage away from the bite and inspected the wound.

"Wow," Connie said. "It's almost healed."

I'd seen Reyha's handiwork when she really meant business. This wound was barely a scratch in comparison, but it was probably no thanks to Reyha herself. "You must really be coming into some heavy-duty *dhampir* powers. You're healing fast."

Deylaud had perked up again, sensing that the danger to his littermate was over. "*Dhampirs* are supposed to have many of the powers of the blood drinker since they're half-vampire," he said.

I'd forgotten what a fount of information Deylaud could be. "How did you know that?" I asked.

He shrugged. "I read some of Melaphia's texts on the matter, but she took them with her when she left. That's about all I know."

Connie asked him a few questions and they compared notes, figuratively speaking. Deylaud didn't know much more than she did except for the healing thing. When Connie asked him to let her know if he remembered anything else, he gave her a quizzical look. I explained to her that he had perfect recall, and he never forgot a thing. His brain was a treasure trove of information—some useless, some vital.

"If he says that's all he knows, that's pretty much the end of it," I said. "I'm glad the bite's almost healed, but I still have to talk to Reyha."

"Let me do it, Jack. Please?" Deylaud begged. "I know I can make her see the error of her ways."

Connie tossed the bandage into the trash and rolled her sleeve back down. "No harm, no foul," she said. "I have a feeling that was just something she had to get out of her system. Let Deylaud talk to her. Give her the rest of the day to think about what she did. Then we'll have a heart-to-heart."

I sighed. "All right. Deylaud, just make sure she understands that her new job is to protect Connie, not be a danger to her."

"I'll make sure," Deylaud said, and excused himself. "We have to change. We've been in human form too long in the daylight. After she bit Connie, I forced

Reyha to change into human form so that we could reason things out. She was mortified by what she'd done. But I'll talk to her again before the transformation."

"Changing twice in so short a time must be pretty stressful for them," Connie said.

"Yeah, it's a brutal process."

"Speaking of stress, shouldn't you be asleep right now? Yesterday was a pretty rough one for you."

"I couldn't sleep. It was no use. I just had to get up." I started when she touched my chin again. I was going to have to tell her to stop touching me. Maybe I'd get around to that one day.

"You hardly healed at all last night. Is that because you didn't sleep?"

"Yeah. We need sleep to heal."

Suddenly there was a crash at the front door. I could smell gasoline. I ran toward the foyer, but had to stop in my tracks. Light was streaming from the panes around the door, because the drapes were pulled back in the daytime.

I staggered back into the kitchen, helpless as Connie ran out the door past me. The twins, in canine form, flew down the stairs and outside after her. When I heard human screams and the snarling of the dogs I nearly lost it. I stuck my head into the foyer to try and see what was happening on the lawn. I came away with a stabbing pain in my eyes for my trouble.

"Connie!" I yelled at the open door, but the only thing I heard was more shrieking and growling. Thank the gods the human voice wasn't Connie's. But neither was the snapping and snarling all the twins either. Who was out there and what the hell was happening?

I tried again to look out the open door, but burned my face and eyes even worse. I ran blindly to the sink to splash water on my face, trying to think what to do. I heard Mole come up the stairs from the vault. He'd evidently had a hard time sleeping as well. He froze when he got to the kitchen doorway.

"What's happened?"

"I think it was a Molotov cocktail by the smell of it. Since it's daylight, Diana must have hired some thug to firebomb us. She couldn't do it herself."

"Is the house on fire?"

"I don't think so. The smoky smell is getting weaker."

When the screams and snarls started again, Mole clasped his hands to his chest. "What's happening now?"

"By the sound of it, I'd say somebody's getting their ass chewed off."

"Is Connie out there?"

"Yeah, and if she doesn't come through that door pretty soon and tell me what's happening I'm going to lose my mind."

I grabbed the end of the linen tablecloth and pulled. A cup and saucer flew across the room along with the salt and pepper shakers. I soaked the cloth in the sink and was wrapping it around me when Seth burst in carrying Reyha. Deylaud followed literally on Seth's heels and Connie was right behind them.

"Give me that wet cloth," Seth said as he laid Reyha on the table. I could see now that she was badly burned along her right flank. I quickly spread the cold cloth over the burn. She yelped but quieted quickly, settling into a rapid pant, her eyes wild. Deylaud circled the table, whining.

"She saved the house, and us," Connie said.

"What happened?" I asked.

"I saw it all," Seth said. "I parked and got out of the truck just in time to see a guy throw a bottle of gasoline with a rag wick against the front of the house. Reyha ran right through the fire and her coat caught, but she didn't even slow down."

Connie took up the story. "Deylaud and Reyha raced past me and jumped on the guy. They were chewing him up pretty good by the time I got there. I ripped down the curtains and beat out the fire."

Seth continued, "I joined Reyha and Deylaud to finish off that guy."

"Did you change?" I asked, dumbstruck. "It's daylight out there. Did anybody see you?"

"I didn't have to change," Seth said with a murderous look. "It was over in seconds. Nobody saw. There wasn't even any traffic. But there *is* a body under that tarp by your back door. It's in several pieces. You're going to need a Hefty bag."

"I'll take care of it," Mole said, retreating toward the vault.

"Good," I said, pointing to the pantry where the garbage bags were. "Put the bag outside the door to the vault that leads to the tunnels. When you get finished, get back in the coffin. You're going to need your rest. I'll take care of the body from there." Mole hurried to do as I'd told him.

"Who the hell was that?" Seth asked.

"That was Mole," Connie said. "Long story." She went to Reyha's side and stroked her head. The injured sighthound licked her hand.

I bent down so Reyha could see me. "Thank you, girl. You're going to be all right." I mentally thanked the gods I hadn't punished her.

Reyha's gentle eyes fixed on mine for a moment before rolling upward.

Seth felt for a pulse in Reyha's neck. "She's in shock," he said. "We're losing her!"

Twenty

"Get that cold, wet cloth off her," Connie said. "She needs to be warm."

Seth carried Reyha to the den and laid her on the floor. The front door was closed, so I was able to follow them by dodging the sunlight coming from the windows. Connie and Seth wrapped a couple of throw blankets around Reyha and we all gathered around her.

"Do they heal as fast as other shape shifters?" Seth asked.

"Yeah. Especially when they stay in animal form. Just like wereanimals," I said.

"Good. Then she'll survive the burns if she survives the shock," Seth said.

Deylaud hovered over his sister and began to howl. I gathered him into my arms to comfort him.

"What do we do?" Connie asked.

"Look, I know a vet that can be trusted. He's a werewolf himself. I'm going to take her there." Seth picked up Reyha, and Connie and I helped wrap the blankets tightly around her. "Can you come with me?" Seth asked Connie.

"Yeah. Jack should go back to, uh, bed anyway."

"Call us on your cell when you know something," I called after them. I made a mental note to get a replacement cell phone since mine was still at the bottom of the river.

I held fast to Deylaud when he tried to follow them and walked him back into the kitchen. He whined and fretted while I stroked his head.

I was never sure how much Deylaud understood when he was in dog form, or even if he remembered once he changed back into a human being. I needed to talk to Deylaud the young man right now, but I didn't know what it would cost him to shape shift yet again. "Deylaud, look at me," I said, gently cradling his narrow head my hands. "I need to talk to you. Do you understand? I need you to be human now. Can you do that without hurting yourself?"

By way of an answer, Deylaud's slender body convulsed and the shape-shifting process began. I always had a hard time watching the change. It was brutal, painful. I don't know how they did it twice a day. I know the twins—and Seth, too, for that matter—considered their dual nature a blessing. I'm afraid I would consider it more of a curse than being a vampire.

When he was transformed, Deylaud opened a cabinet for some clothing, but started talking immediately. "Is she going to be all right, Jack?" he asked as he pulled on his pants and a sweatshirt. "Please tell me she's going to live. I don't know what I would do without her."

"Seth's going to make sure she gets the help she needs," I said as soothingly as I could. "I'm sure she's going to be fine."

"What can I do?" he asked, still frantic, putting on his socks and shoes. "I should have gone with them."

"I need you here," I said. "I'm going to have to go back to the coffin, but I want you to wake me the minute you hear anything about Reyha, understand?"

"Yes, Jack," he said.

"I need you to stay in human form in case one of the neighbors called the police. If anyone—the police or someone else—comes to the door asking about what happened here, tell them there was a prowler, but you ran him off."

"What if they ask me for a description?"

"Tell them you didn't get a good look at him. Act really calm and say everything's under control. Explain that you work for Mr. Thorne and that he's in Europe."

Deylaud nodded. "I get all that, but what if the evil ones send someone else? What will I do?"

"Get on the phone to Tarney down at the docks. Tell him to send one of William's men over there to act as a security guard. But I doubt Diana will send anyone else. They won't expect me to stay here."

"What? What do you mean?" Deylaud looked alarmed. "You're not leaving, are you?"

"No. She won't be expecting me to stay here, so that means I can. I'll use reverse psychology on her."

Deylaud wasn't relieved for long. Soon he began to sob. "My sister may not live."

I'd never seen a creature more heartbroken. "I'm so sorry, Deylaud. I wish I could protect you, but I have my hands full trying to keep a step ahead of the old lords. And that means I'll be depending on you to take care of Reyha when she gets back. Maybe you should hire some security guards to help you and Reyha feel safe."

Deylaud bristled. "Do you not think we can take care of ourselves and the mansion? We foiled this attempt on our lives and William's property. When Reyha gets well, we'll . . ."

"Shhh. It's all right," I said soothingly and patted his shoulder. "Of course you can take care of things. I don't know what I was thinking." Deylaud and Reyha's sole purpose in life was to guard me and the property, and they did their job well. I should have realized that suggesting they needed any help with their sworn sacred duty would go against Deylaud's grain.

"I'm also counting on you to handle all William's business matters, including the maintenance of all properties and assets," I added quickly. "You know what to do. If you need business help, you can hire someone."

Deylaud had served as William's clerk since the days when books were kept in, well, real books. When the computer age came along, Deylaud adapted to technology as quickly and easily as he adapted to everything else. He knew as well as William had himself what it took to run William's many business interests. In addition, he had all the legal authority he needed. He also had a talent for forging his former master's signature.

Deylaud nodded and wiped his eyes with the back of his hand. "You can count on me, Jack. I'll handle everything. We just make sure that Reyha's okay first."

"I give you my word," I said, and squeezed his hand. "I'll make sure that Reyha has everything she needs to recover. I'm sure she'll probably be fine by the time she gets back here."

Deylaud took a deep breath. "After all the danger that you and William have found yourselves in, not to mention Melaphia and Renee, I never believed that Sister and I would be in danger, too."

"I'm so sorry, Deylaud," I repeated. I was sorry I'd let these trusting, loyal creatures down. And I was sick to death of being sorry. I was beginning to feel like turning a whole army of vampires, and damn anyone who tried to stop me. Enough was enough.

Deylaud sat up straight and tall, but his eyes were still full of misery. "You should go back to sleep, Jack. You need your strength. I'll tell you when I hear from Seth and Connie about Sister."

As I headed back downstairs, Deylaud called to me, "Jack, are we ever going to be a family again?"

"Yes," I said. "Absolutely." I hoped he couldn't sense the bravado I heard in my own voice.

Downstairs I climbed back into my coffin, still rattled by everything that had happened but too exhausted to do anything but fall into a deathlike sleep. *Finally.* I was only vaguely aware of Deylaud opening the lid to my box some time later to tell me that Reyha was back home and getting better.

I woke at precisely sundown. Connie was waiting for me in the vault. "Reyha's going to be fine," she said. "Come upstairs and see."

Reyha, still in dog form, was resting comfortably on Melaphia's bed, covered with a down comforter pulled up to her slender neck. I stroked her, murmured soothing words of thanks to her, and kissed her head. "You rest now," I said, and left a much-relieved Deylaud watching over her.

"Oh, man, what a load off my mind," I said.

"Mine too," Connie said quietly.

"Are you all right?" I asked her.

"Yeah. Just tired."

"You didn't get much sleep last night."

"I'll be fine. I wanted to stay with her until you woke up."

"Thanks for helping Reyha. I know Deylaud is grateful. I am, too."

Connie smiled and nodded, but didn't say any more. She might be fine, but she was definitely subdued. I wondered what she and Seth had talked about during their trip to the vet and back. I couldn't worry about that now, though. I had plans to make.

"I think it's time for that team meeting I told you about."

I called Rennie and told him to get the irregulars together and meet us at Eleanor's house. Then I called Werm and told him to be there, too. I instructed both of them to go through the tunnels so as not to draw any attention to themselves.

"I forgot to tell Seth to come," Connie said after I got off the phone with Werm.

"Go ahead and call him."

She did, and I pretended to be interested in whatever it was Mole was telling me while Connie talked to Seth. She hung up and said, "He'll be there."

I had to get rid of this burr under my saddle where Seth was concerned. What they talked about was none of my business. They were together now. Connie and I were business partners of sorts. Nothing more.

"Let's go then," I said, and we set off.

We were the first to arrive at what was to have been Eleanor's house. William had recently ordered the place built, after Reedrek had torched her first brothel. With all hell breaking loose, the house had remained vacant. I hadn't had a chance to think about what to do with it now that Eleanor wouldn't be coming back.

The bottom floor had a large parlor on one side and a spacious reception area on the other, complete with a circular desk. Upstairs were eight bedrooms and another big common area. There were kitchens on both floors and a generous laundry/utility room on the ground floor in the back of the building. The whole setup was like that of a small, exclusive hotel. The most important feature to those of the pointy-toothed persuasion was the light-tight basement with steel-reinforced doors and its own secure entrance to the tunnels.

"I can practically see the wheels turning in your brain. What are you thinking?" Connie asked as we looked around the main floor.

"I was thinking that all we need to do is furnish this place and it would be a dandy facility for a big group of blood drinkers."

"Indeed," Mole observed. "This would make lovely accommodations. Depending on the appointments, it could be quite posh."

Werm came through the door. "How're things at the mansion?" he asked.

"Fine now," I assured him.

"I'm glad to hear it." Werm glanced around and whistled. "Wow. This is a nice place. Mind if I explore?"

"Help yourself."

"I shall join you," Mole said.

Werm shyly squeezed Connie's arm on his way past her to the stairs. "It's good to have you back."

"Thanks. It's good to be back."

Seth was the next to arrive. As soon as he came through the door, he stationed himself between me and Connie. "How's Reyha?" he asked.

"A lot better. She's going to be fine, thanks to you," I said.

Seth shrugged. "You look like hell," he said.

"Again, thanks to you." I fingered the wound on my chin. It was nearly healed, but he kicked my ass and I guess he had to rub in that fact. Especially in front of Connie. I wanted to point out that I let him beat me because I knew I had wronged him, but of course I couldn't say that. Instead I tried to lighten up the tension convention I seemed to be chairman of. "I hope you're up to date on your vaccinations," I said.

"I'll be fine if you have rabies. I don't know if they make inoculations for evil dead. It's not catching, is it?" Seth said.

"Boys," Connie said, looking away.

"I was talking about *my* health," I said, ignoring her. "I'm living proof that your bite's worse than your bark—or howl or whatever. I probably have a whole bloodstream's worth of dog germs right now."

"Hope you don't get an infection," Seth said with a snarl. "Oh, I forgot. You're already dead."

The door opened and the boys from the garage filed in. "Oh, good," Connie said. "Everybody's here."

After folks had a few minutes to look around, I asked everybody to go into the parlor. Some of the guys sat on the floor or the hearth and some leaned against the wall. Connie perched on the reception desk while Seth leaned on it as close to her as he could get. He was so determined to mark her as his territory I half-expected him to hoist one leg and pee on her at any minute.

I started by introducing Mole to the ones who didn't know him and explaining his background. The others couldn't help but stare. I thought since they'd gotten to know Werm they might well figure they'd seen it all where funny-looking vampires were concerned. But Mole raised the bar on the vampiric creepiness factor, and that was no small feat. I went on to catch everybody up on the events of the last few days—most of the events, that is.

The irregulars expressed alarm at the firebombing, relief that the real Connie was back, and awe to hear that she had killed Eleanor and Ulrich.

"You should have seen her bitch-slap him before she stabbed him," I recounted. "Actually, it was more of a pimp slap. It was inspiring, I'm telling you."

There were whoops of approval all around. Seth looked at Connie. "You didn't tell me about that. Way to go, honey," he said.

"What do you think this Diana is going to do now?" Jerry asked. "I know it was scary and all, but hiring somebody to throw a Molotov cocktail at William's house seems like a lame kind of a move for a self-respecting vampire."

"Yeah," Rufus agreed. "Seems someone like her would be able to think of something more—I don't know—impressive."

"She was so pissed that the Slayer killed her man, it was the only thing she could think of on short notice," I said. "That's my theory anyway. I'm not looking forward to the day she gets her act together."

"Do you have any idea what the Council's next move is?" Rennie asked.

"No, but that's what I called y'all here to talk about. I figure all of us have a stake in the future of this city and the well-being of the citizenry. I know I've called on all of you at one time or another to help out with fending off the bad vampires. Y'all have really stepped up to the plate, and I thank you. But with William gone and with the Slayer in Savannah, we're going to be the target of who knows what in the future. I mean, look at the earthquake, for example. The old lords tried to harness the forces of nature, of the elements themselves, to raise hell and they very nearly succeeded."

I looked from face to face. They were duly concerned, but there was not a coward among them. I was proud to be their friend. "I'd like us to continue working as a team, but our numbers are thin. I think we need to consider adding some new recruits."

"What exactly are you talking about?" Seth said, his yellow-green eyes narrowing.

"I'm talking about making new vampires. Very carefully, of course."

"That's a damn fool idea," Seth said. "William wouldn't have approved of that and you know it."

I had to catch my teeth between my fangs to keep from telling him off. "Things change," I said. "We need help, and the western clans can't spare any. Werm thinks we can recruit every vampire-to-be discreetly and selectively from some of the young people he knows. We'll look for people who have skills we can use, people who don't have any family."

"I don't know, Jack," Otis said. "Won't a bunch of fledgling vampires running around Savannah be hard to keep tabs on?"

"It's true we have to be very careful. This is going to be a slow process," I said. "We're not going to go off making vamps half-cocked. And of course we would never turn anyone against their will."

"This is against everything William stood for," Seth said, his muscular arms crossed in front of his massive chest.

I looked at the ceiling and tried to keep my temper under control. "William's not here," I said deliberately. "I have to defend this city—hell, this *continent*—the best way I know how. I'm in charge now, but if any of you have better ideas, I'd be happy to hear them."

Seth ran a hand through his hair and looked at the others. Nobody said anything. Connie let herself down from her perch on the desk and walked to the bay windows at the far side of the room. It struck me that she was reacting to my reminder that William was dead. Her guilt and sorrow were palpable. Seth had respected and looked up to William almost as a father figure, just as I had done. He had always been in awe of what William had been able to accomplish for good, how he'd overcome his nature as a demon.

"You may be large and in charge," he said at last, "but if you go through with this scheme, you're half the man William was."

I glared at him. I wondered how much of his anger was about making more vampires and how much of it really was about me having sex with Connie. The others were looking back and forth between Seth and me like they were expecting a fight to the death to break out any second. That wasn't going to happen if I could help it. "You're entitled to your opinion."

"I'm not going to participate in this unholy fiasco,"

he said. He stalked toward the front door and put his hand out for the knob before he realized that Connie wasn't following. She remained standing with her back to him, her spine ramrod straight. He hesitated for a moment before leaving and slamming the door behind him.

Twenty-one

When he was gone I looked around at my remaining friends. Not only did the situation put Connie in an awkward position, it was also potential trouble for Jerry. As Seth's second-in-command, his loyalty to Seth in the pack's business was a given. But when it came to outside matters he was a free agent. I was particularly touched that he didn't make a move to follow Seth.

"The last thing I want to do is to twist anybody's arm," I said. "If any of you have a problem with this idea, you're free to go without involvement and with no hard feelings. I promise you that."

There was only a moment's silence before Huey piped up. "I'm with you, Jack. I'm not sure what you're talking about exactly, but whatever it is—count me in."

Out of the mouths of zombies. Huey's affirmation broke the tension, and there were chuckles all around except, I noted, from Rennie. Even Connie laughed. She turned around and rejoined the group, sitting on the floor right in front of me. Nobody else left. They waited to hear more about my plan. I relaxed, grateful that I had so many true friends. So many more than I felt I deserved.

"Thanks, guys," I said. "I'm going to turn the floor over to Werm. He's been planning how we should go about this and he's going to tell you what he thinks we should do."

Werm stepped forward and rubbed his hands together. "Jack covered most of it. We're looking for skills, talent, and people who are misfits with no family."

"However will you find such people?" Mole asked guilelessly.

Rufus laughed but Otis elbowed him in the ribs. "He's not kidding, is he?" Rufus muttered.

"I think what Rufus means is that Werm's nightclub, the Portal, attracts . . . unusual people."

"Enough to have plenty of candidates to choose from, I expect," Jerry said. "But here's what I don't understand. How are you going to approach them? You can't rightly go up to any old nerd with a dog collar around his neck and say, Hey, man, you look like solid vampire material. Want to sign up? No offense, Werm."

"None taken," Werm said cheerily. "Here's the thing. As the bartender, I get to know people. I know who's dissatisfied with their human lives, who's yearning for more out of their existence—a purpose, a mission."

"Gee, Werm, now you're making me wish *I* was a vampire," Otis said, and the irregulars laughed. All of them except for Rennie. Maybe he was in pain again. Or maybe he just didn't want to get involved. If so, I didn't blame him one bit.

"It sounds like you've got candidates in mind already," Connie observed.

"As a matter of fact, I do." Werm grinned. "And I also have an idea of how to conduct the competition."

"Competition?" I asked, not liking the sound of that word in this context. "You didn't say anything about a competition the other night."

"My idea has kind of . . . evolved," Werm explained.

"Please tell me you're not planning to make a circus out of this."

"No, not at all. But I am thinking it would make a great reality show."

I waited for Werm to give some kind of sign that he was kidding. He didn't. "What," I asked, "are you talking about?"

"I propose we hold a kind of a contest where three or four people have to prove who'd be the best vampire."

"Oh, *hell* no," I said. I was tempted to go over and box Werm's ears. "That's the stupidest damn fool idea I've ever heard. For starters, people aren't supposed to know vampires even exist, remember? What are we going to say to the losers? Thanks, but no thanks? Enjoy your lovely parting gifts and have a nice life?"

"Of course not," Werm said. "You just use your glamour on the ones we don't choose and wipe out their memory of the contest."

"I can see it now," Connie said, making a sweeping gesture with her hand. "*American Vampire!*"

"You're not helping," I accused her.

"Hey, can I be a judge?" Jerry wanted to know.

"Me too!" Otis chimed in.

"Yes!" Werm said.

"No!" I thundered.

"I have no idea what you're all on about," Mole said.

"It's so crazy it just might work," Huey, of all people, said.

"Time out, dammit!" I said. "We're not putting on an *American Vampire* pageant!" I pictured nerds on parade, complete with banners and tiaras.

"Why not?" Werm insisted. "Seriously, Jack, think about it. We can get them to demonstrate their skills or abilities that might help the team. Then we could quiz them about their family situation. And finally we could test them to see how hungry they are."

"Hungry for blood?" Jerry asked, clearly irked, which he had some nerve being since he was a werewolf.

"No," Werm said. "I mean hungry as in how much they *want* the life."

"You mean the *death*," I corrected. There was a world of difference in how Werm and I were thinking about this. I had chosen to be a blood drinker, yes, but I didn't know what I was getting into. If I had known, I would have rather died on that battlefield. There were times throughout my existence when my hindsight wavered on this point, but losing Connie in the last couple of days had finally decided the matter for me. Not that my newfound certainty did me a damned bit of good at this late date.

Werm, on the other hand, had desperately wanted to become a blood drinker, although he didn't know what he was letting himself in for either. Over and over I tried to tell him that he didn't want to be a creature of the night like me. But he just couldn't hear me. He was convinced that being a vampire meant never being pushed around again. But he discovered after it was too late that being a vampire just meant that the dudes kicking you around had longer and sharper teeth.

I think Werm had second-guessed himself plenty on whether he had made the right choice. Right now he seemed pretty chipper about it. I hope he didn't have cause to change his mind.

Werm sighed. "Yes, I mean we have to make sure they want death."

"That's heavy," Huey said solemnly, as if he wasn't as dead as a doornail himself.

"Another big thing they'd have to understand," I said, "is that the process of being made into a vampire isn't particularly pleasant. And there's a significant chance that the person might not make it. Remember what happened with Shari."

"Of course," Werm agreed. "We have to make that crystal clear. Speaking of Shari, and at the risk of sounding sexist, we can't turn any women. The odds are stacked too strongly against their survival."

I sighed. "What do you all think?"

Rennie finally spoke up. "I'm for it," he said. To

my surprise, the irregulars to a man nodded their agreement.

"Connie?" I asked.

She surprised me by saying, "Go for it."

"Mole? You have a lot of experience, and you know a lot about vampire lore. What do you think?"

Mole cleared his throat. "I would trust few vampires with such a grave undertaking, if you'll pardon the pun," he said. "But I think that you and Werm are most capable of successfully turning a small number of good candidates and guiding them in a righteous direction."

"Thanks," I said. "I can't believe I'm saying this, but okay. Let's do it."

"Great!" Werm said, beaming so broadly his fangs glowed white. "You won't regret it, Jack. Are you ready for my next idea?"

"I don't know, am I?"

Werm ignored my sarcasm. "Just look around you at this place. Wouldn't this make a great team headquarters? It's got everything we need."

"Yeah," I admitted. "It really does."

"It's like a clubhouse," Jerry declared.

"Yeah, no girls allowed," Otis said with a wink toward Connie.

"Hey," she warned. "None of that sexist crap. Besides, I have a feeling I'm going to wind up the den mother around here."

"Not to mention weapons instructor," Werm enthused. "We've got plenty of room for martial arts training—"

"As if," I said. I'd been trying to talk Werm into some kind of fighting lessons for months.

"I promise I'll do it this time, Jack," he vowed.

"What are we going to call this place?" Connie asked.

"Ideas, people!" Werm clapped his hands.

"Dorm of the Damned?" Rennie suggested.

"Hell Hotel?" Jerry said.

"We're not looking for bad horror movie titles," I said.

"How about the Nest?" Huey put in.

"Why 'the Nest,' Hugh-man?" I asked. Huey might be a few brain cells short of a full load, but his ideas always had a kind of tortured logic.

"Baby vampires are called fledglings, like little birds, am I right?" asked Huey, the avian expert. "And birds live in nests."

"Huh, not bad," I admitted.

"Hey, I like it!" Werm said.

"Me too, actually," Connie added.

"It seems appropriate," Mole said.

"And downright homey," said Otis.

"All right," I said. "The Nest it is. Werm, how soon do you think you could come up with some candidates for this vampire contest?" I could barely believe what I'd just said.

"No more than a week or so," he said. "We can hold it onstage at the club. I can charge a cover!"

"Hey, wait a minute!" I said. "I've put glamour on a whole room full of people before, but what if somebody sneaks out and spreads the word?"

"You don't get it, Jack," Werm said. "The regular

customers will think it's a *pretend* vampire contest. It is a goth club, after all. They'll think it's just entertainment. They'll never realize it's dead serious."

This was just getting farther and farther out. I could tell the whole idea really appealed to Werm's theatricality. I had to wonder again if the boy was straight. "You'd better be damned sure that the contestants know it's real," I warned.

"Oh, don't worry. I'm going to take care of everything," Werm said with confidence.

"That's what I'm afraid of," I muttered.

It was decided that Mole would move into the Nest immediately. He and Werm volunteered to pick out the furnishings and coffins and handle the decorating. If Werm's taste in decorating the Portal was anything to go by, the place would wind up looking like the brothel it had been meant to be in the first place.

Connie excused herself to go back to her apartment. She had a lot of work to do to smoothe down Seth's ruffled fur, or werewolf hackles, or whatever. I chose not to think about it anymore for one night. Either Seth would come around or he wouldn't. He had Connie, so as far as I was concerned, he had a lot of nerve to complain about anything.

Werm went off to check on the bar and help Mole gather his meager belongings from his rented place on Tybee. The fair Sharona would just have to be content with a longer-distance relationship with her leathery beau.

When the irregulars and I got back to the garage, I went to the kitchen to make a fresh pot of coffee.

Rennie joined me while the other guys started up a card game.

"Uh, Jack, can I ask you something?"

"Sure, man. What's up?"

"I know vampires are really strong and all," he began hesitantly. "Let's say something is wrong with somebody. Maybe he's got a bum leg or he's deaf or has webbed toes or whatever."

"Yeah?" Remembering his earlier mood, something told me this wasn't just a philosophical question, and I wondered where it was coming from.

"Well, if that person got turned into a vampire, would he be well again?"

"Hmm. I've never known any vampires with any physical problems like that. Except for maybe body odor." I chuckled. Rennie didn't crack so much as a grin, so I continued. "I guess it would depend on what was wrong with him. I mean, if he's missing an arm I don't know if he could grow it back or not."

"What if he was just sick?" Rennie asked.

"In that case, I'd say he'd get well. That is, he'd be as well as you could be for a dead guy."

"What if he had cancer?"

Startled, I looked hard at Rennie. His eyes were as rheumy and unreadable as ever behind his thick glasses, but I'd known him long enough to know that he was very, very serious.

"Rennie," I began carefully. "You don't have ulcers, do you?"

He shook his head. "No."

"How sick are you?"

"I've got pancreatic cancer."

The news struck me like a body blow. I hung onto the sink to steady myself. As shaken as I was, I couldn't even imagine what it had been like for Rennie, living with this news. "How long have you known, Ren?"

"A couple of weeks now. I started the chemo a few days ago."

Rennie didn't have a wife or kids. In fact, he didn't have any family at all that I knew of. I'd often wondered what he did with his time in the daylight hours. I hated to think of him hooked up to tubes, being pumped full of poison. I was struck again by how fragile and fleeting human lives are. Pancreatic cancer was the worst kind you could possibly have, the hardest to survive. I'd lost hundreds of human friends over the decades, including a lot of close ones. I'd cried buckets of tears over their loss, but I couldn't bear the thought of losing Rennie.

"Oh, man. I'm really sorry. Is there anything I can do?"

"Yeah," Rennie said. "You can make me a vampire."

Twenty-two

I was nearly too stunned to speak. "Are you sure? Rennie, this is a big step."

"And dying isn't? Yeah, I'm pretty sure."

If anybody besides the twins, Mel, and Renee knew the drill where being a vampire was concerned, it was Rennie. I wasn't going to insult him by pointing out what it would be like to survive on blood, to never be able to go out in the sun. Hell, for all I knew he didn't go out in sunlight anyway. He was at the garage from sunset to sunup. He had to sleep sometime.

Yes, Rennie had seen the life close up. He knew about all the trouble we'd been having lately with the bad vamps, the double-deads, vampire plagues, and all the other threats we still faced. He understood about William's death and how a vampire's second death is final. He knew he'd be giving up his soul. And he still wanted to play. How could I deny him?

I nodded my head slowly. "All right," I said.

Rennie smiled. "I knew I could count on you, Jack."

"Give me a few days to build up my strength and rest. I think that would give you a better chance of survival." I squeezed his shoulder. "Don't worry about a thing. I'll fix you right up, man."

Rennie smiled and thanked me again, and we both went to join the card game. We sat down at the table as Huey was dealing a new hand. An argument between Rufus and Otis was in full swing.

"Get out," Rufus said.

"I'm telling the truth," insisted Otis. "I saw it once. It's an island right between Tybee and Wassaw that only faeries can get to. Nobody else can even see it."

"So what happens when boats come along? Do they run into this invisible island? Next thing you're going to tell me is that it's part of the Bermuda Triangle."

"It's a magic island," Otis said. "Boats don't bump into it."

"You're so full of shit," Rufus said, scooping up his cards.

"Otis, what are you talking about?" I asked, my interest piqued.

"I was just telling the boys about this island I saw once, years ago."

"How many years ago?"

"This was back when I came here the first time, right after the English colonized Georgia."

"That's a fer piece back all right," Huey said.

"Did I understand you to say that only faeries can see it?"

"Yeah, that's right. Until you get there, that is. Once somebody's actually *on* it, well, then they can see it. But only faeries can find it."

"Did the faeries ever live there?" Jerry asked.

"For a while. Just until they could get on a ship going back to the Old Country. See, when the English started colonizing North America, the rumor got out among the faerie community that it was a happening place. They must have thought the streets were paved with gold or something, because a dozen or so decided to stow away on a ship and come over here to start their own colony. Little did they know that not only were the streets *not* paved with gold, but there weren't even any *streets*."

"Faeries sound pretty gullible," Rennie observed, sorting through his cards. He adjusted his glasses to make sure we couldn't see his hand in the reflection. Rennie was clever that way. The more I thought about it, the better a vampire I figured he'd make.

Otis gave him a sour look. "The other thing the faeries didn't know was that the Native Americans had their own fey folk, called Yundi Tsundi."

"So?" Rufus said.

"The Cherokees thought the Yundi Tsundi were as cute as pie and got along with them fine. But the Indian faeries turned downright nasty when they saw another race of little people trying to move in on their territory. No amount of peacemaking and gifts offered on the part of the Irish Sidhe did any good. The Yundi Tsundi came after them with spears, clubs, you name it.

"The legend goes that the Sidhe had to combine all

the magic they could muster and conjure themselves an island where they could escape the Yundi Tsundi until they could figure out how to get home. They put a spell on the place so that their enemies couldn't find them, and when a suitable sailing ship headed back to Ireland they literally jumped on it. I came over a few years after that when the frontier was pushed back west of Macon. When the normal-sized Cherokee left, the Yundi Tsundi went with them."

"But you got sent over here to spy on the vampires, right?" Rennie said.

"Not at first. Initially I was just a scout, a kind of advance man in case the Sidhe ever wanted to try colonization again. Nobody wanted to repeat that first mistake. I was supposed to report back to the Sidhe nobility about the other kinds of little people here and whether they were friendly. Even though it was safe by the time I got here, the Irish fey never did immigrate in big numbers. Faeries are big on storytelling, and in our oral tradition the ferocity of the Yundi Tsundi got passed down over the generations until most of the fey were too shit-scared to come here."

"You must be really brave," Huey said, putting a chunk of his day's tips in the pot. "I raise."

Rufus snorted.

Ignoring Rufus, Otis said, "Thanks, Huey. I guess I had the wanderlust in those days."

"So how did you get started spying on the blood drinkers?" Jerry asked.

"It wasn't until much later—when the fey started seeing signs of the apocalypse—that they sent for me to return to the Old Country. That's when they gave me the assignment to watch the undead," Otis answered.

"Do you ever get homesick for Ireland?" Jerry wanted to know.

"Not really. I had some . . . misunderstandings over there, so I was glad to be able to come here."

"So when was the last time you saw this island?" I asked, throwing two quarters into the kitty.

"Oh, man, it was many human lifetimes ago, before I was called back to the Old Country. I went out there to see if anyone got left behind. One of the fey folk had gone missing and never made it to the ship." Otis laid his hand on the table. "I'm out."

"Did you find them?" Jerry asked.

"Nope. Not a sign of 'em, or of anybody else either."

I scratched my chin. "I call," I said, and put my three queens on the table.

"It's yours," Rufus grumbled, throwing down two jacks.

"Lost again," Huey said, sounding as surprised as ever, although he never won.

"What are you thinking, Jack?" Rennie asked, gathering up the cards for another round.

"Just that if somebody ever needed a place to hide, an invisible island would be pretty sweet."

Otis shrugged. "I'm not sure I could even find it again, to tell you the truth."

I've always been convinced that whenever anybody said *to tell you the truth* they are very likely to be lying. I gathered my winnings as Otis eyed the coins over his new hand of cards. Something told me that if any of us ever needed to disappear for a while, Otis might be persuaded to miraculously remember how to get to that island. The only question was, Would he be more motivated by a carrot or a stick? That is to say, a really, really sharp stick.

When I got back to the house, I entered as usual by the side door and was greeted by an eerie silence and a rock-solid knowledge that something was bad wrong.

The kitchen was deserted, so I walked through to the foyer. The door to the formal parlor was closed, so I continued on to William's den at the end of the hallway. What I saw made my heart jump into my throat. I froze. It couldn't be.

It was William.

"Cheers," he said, turning fully toward me and raising his glass in my direction. "If it isn't the estimable Jack McShane."

Will Cuyler, son of William Cuyler Thorne, leaned against the wet bar swirling a highball glass full of blood. He stared at the twins, who were huddled together on the sofa in petrified silence. The last time I'd seen him his hair had been dyed red, almost orange. Now he'd let it go natural, a tawny blond. Damn, but it made him look like William.

It took me a few seconds to get over the shock and compose myself. "What are you doing here?" He'd been painfully thin and drawn when I first met him. He looked like one of those heroin addicts you see in the movies. Now he had filled out some and the dark circles under his eyes were gone. All that made him look even more like his father.

"Is that any way to greet William's son and heir?"

When he'd been here before, Will had treated me like a hired hand. I wasn't about to let him get by with that. "I've been more of a son to William than you ever were," I said.

"Through no fault of my own, mate. I didn't even know my natural father was undead until a few months ago. Speaking of dear old Dad, where is he?"

Reyha yelped and ran from the room. Deylaud said, "Excuse me, please," and trotted after her. I heard them run up the stairs to the bedrooms. I felt like joining them. I couldn't believe Will didn't know his father was dead. And I was going to have to tell him.

"What's with them, then?" Will asked. "I could barely get the mutts to speak to me."

"Don't call them that," I said. "Maybe they're upset because the last time you were here your mother and Hugo broke Reyha's legs and nearly beat her to death."

Will drained his glass without looking at me. "That was Hugo's doing and he's in hell, thanks to my father. I was nearly dead myself with the vampire plague at the time, remember? Besides, I'm a Jedi now, haven't you heard? I've turned away from the dark side."

I remember what Olivia had said: Will was one of us now, no longer the vicious killer of humans that he'd been for hundreds of years. I didn't buy it—maybe because I'd seen him rip out a defenseless human's throat. "I'd sooner believe a leopard could change its spots."

"What a surprise. You've never been my biggest fan."

"That's right. Especially since you helped kidnap Renee."

Will slammed his empty glass onto the bar. "Again, not my idea, mate. You are a hardheaded sod then, aren't you?"

"Maybe it wasn't your idea," I said, ignoring his jibe. "But you charmed her into going along with you and Diana and Hugo."

"What can I say? She loves me. And don't forget my role in helping my father rescue her."

I heard a snarl beginning in my own throat. Will had somehow bewitched Renee, and she was usually the one who did the bewitching. I hated to admit it, but he was right. She loved him.

"So tell me, where is the little angel? I can't wait to see her."

"You're lucky they're not here. Melaphia would kill you with her bare hands if she were."

"Sounds like I have a bit of fence mending to do," Will remarked with a shrug.

"I'll ask you again. What are you doing here?"

"The last time I saw him my father invited me to come. I want to get to know him."

"Why didn't you come with him when he first invited you?"

"I decided to do some traveling. I haven't spoken to any other vampires since I left Olivia's coven." He glanced out the window for a moment with a puzzled look on his face as if he were distracted by some sight or sound in the backyard, then shrugged. From where I stood, I couldn't see anything. "I want to help my father with his work—you know, join up with the Force and all that rot."

My mouth had gone dry. I hated Will, but I hated even more being the one to tell him his father was dead. How did I even begin to do that?

"Not that catching up with you isn't always fun, but I really want to talk to my father. Where is he?"

"I have bad news," I finally said.

"Eh?" He blinked his cat-green eyes—so much like William's—a couple of times.

"William is dead."

Will just stared at me for a few awful seconds. He cocked his head to one side as if his hearing had failed him. "What do you mean? He can't be dead."

"He was killed not long ago."

"No." Will's body went rigid and he fisted his hands at his sides. "You're lying."

"You have no idea how much I wish I were."

"I don't understand." Will shook his head and took a step toward the center of the room and then back again. "How could this happen?"

Now this was the tricky part. No way did I want Will to find out that Connie had killed his father. "Shortly after he came back from Europe, he was . . . staked."

Will stood still, his eyes round with shock. He'd gone even whiter than his normal pallor, making his cross-shaped scar, the top of which was just visible at his open shirt collar, stand out in vivid relief. Will's bravado was gone in an instant. His chest heaved a couple of times and he stammered, "But—but I'd only just found him after hundreds of years. I wanted to learn from him. This can't be happening." He threw his head back and bellowed, *"No!"*

The sound vibrated with unhuman agony and loss. I heard the dogs start to whine upstairs and wanted to cover my own ears. "I—I'm sorry," I stammered.

"Who? Who killed him?"

"I don't know," I lied.

There was a loud crash as the bay windows exploded inward. I thought for a second that Will's scream had caused the glass to shatter, but then I saw what—*who*—had entered the room like a wrecking ball.

It was Diana.

Twenty-three

Diana sailed into the room like a Valkyrie on the warpath and landed a few feet from me. "He lies! He knows full well who murdered your father!"

"Mother!"

With Diana's entrance, Will's world was doubly rocked. If he was telling the truth about not having spoken to any vampires since he left London he couldn't know his mother was still undead. The last he knew, she was buried under tons of rock in a cave-in underneath the city.

"You don't know what you're talking about," I said. "You weren't there."

I knew I had to take advantage of Will's disorientation before what was going on really sank in, and I had to silence Diana if I could. I grabbed a floor lamp, the closest thing at hand, and swung it at her. It caught her in the midsection and she crashed against the wall behind the sofa. Then I leaped on her as she was sliding down the wall and pinned her shoulders against the oak paneling. My fangs were an inch from her throat when Will grabbed me by one arm and pulled me off his mother.

"If you know she wasn't there, you must know who *was* there," he roared.

I wrenched my arm out of his grasp and punched him hard on the chin with a left. He flew backward and hit the wet bar but was on his feet again at once. I wrapped my hand around Diana's throat, but not before she shouted, "He saw who killed William. It was his lover, the vampire Slayer!"

I tried to crush her throat, but she kicked out and connected with my knee hard enough to force me to release her. "Don't listen to her," I yelled. "She only wants to control you again."

"Vampire Slayer?" Will hissed. "Who is this vampire Slayer?"

I tried to grab a fistful of Diana's hair but she darted away and landed beside her son in a move so fast I could barely see it. "It's the policewoman Connie Jones. The one he saved from you. I wish you had killed her that night you killed the filmmaker. If you had, your father would still be undead."

I got to my feet. "It's not as if you didn't try your damnedest to kill William yourself, you whore," I said.

"So you don't deny it?" Will said to me, his eyes wide and bloodshot with rage. "Your lover is the Slayer who killed my father."

"While *he* stood by and did nothing," Diana charged. "And now you'll never be able to spend the time with your father that you could have."

"That's a lie," I said. "I did everything I could to

save him. And as for you not getting to know your father better, Will—it was Diana who kept you from each other for hundreds of years while she whored around with any vampire she thought could help her with her ambitions."

Will glowered at both of us. I hoped I was getting through to him. I couldn't get a clear strike at Diana now that she stood an arm's length away from Will. If I attacked her and he decided to come to her rescue, they would double-team me. "I tried to stop what happened that night," I insisted. "The Slayer had just been activated, and William had been injured in the earthquake. The Slayer was wild, inhuman, uncontrollable. She's matured now, and she's sorry for what she's done. She's sworn to help us."

"Help you?" Diana mocked. "She helps you fight and kill your own kind!" Sensing an advantage, she turned to her son. "Come with me, my love. Join me in working for the old lords. Help me gain favor with the Council. Glory is ours for the taking."

"What the hell are you on about?" Will looked annoyed and bewildered.

"She's a politician now," I charged. "She wants a seat on the vampire Council, and she's been bribing every vampire she meets to join her, promising she'll let them ride on her coattails—even me."

"Don't believe him, my son," she simpered. "Who will you trust? Your own dear mother or the man who helped kill your father?"

"You *bitch*! I'll kill you for that!" I launched myself at Diana, but Will dove forward, blocking me. I wound up on my back on the carpet, and Will landed hard on the floor not far from me. I reached up and grabbed a fistful of Diana's clothing and pulled her down on top of me like a lover. I seized her neck, brought her throat to my mouth, and bit down fiercely.

She howled like an injured animal, and Will scrambled to his feet. He hesitated a moment. If he pulled his mother away from me and her carotid artery stayed in my fangs, she might not recover. But if he couldn't get some kind of clear shot at me, I could kill his mother within seconds.

He wedged his hand between his mother's neck and mine and squeezed my throat so hard a human would have died of a crushed larynx. I only bit down harder and deeper. Will panicked, grabbed his mother's shoulders, and pulled. A chunk of flesh remained in my fangs.

Diana's hands flew to her throat to try and stanch the massive bleeding. Her mouth worked but she couldn't speak. The sight of his mother's injury seemed to drive Will around the bend. He looked at me with rage. "You helped murder my father and now you've tried to kill my mother. I'll destroy you for this, McShane."

Effortlessly, he picked up Diana and carried her out of the house through the window she'd just obliterated. After a few seconds Deylaud appeared, sobbing.

"I guess you heard," I said, staring at the demolished den.

"Yes," he said, trembling. "That was Diana—one of the ones who beat my sister—and her son, Will."

"That's right. I did my best to kill her, but she escaped."

"Thank you, Jack. I know you tried." He stood up straight, visibly trying to pull himself together. "I'll put this room to rights."

"That would be great," I said.

While I wondered what my next move should be, I began righting the furniture that got upended in the struggle. Will would take Diana somewhere and patch her up, and the both of them would come for me. Then they would go find Connie. And Connie wouldn't leave the city. What the hell was I going to do now? Even if I told her she was pregnant, which I couldn't, she still might not agree to find a safer place than Savannah.

"Jack?" Deylaud said with a tremor in his voice.

"Yeah, buddy?"

"I've got to tell you something."

"What's that?"

"Sister and I have . . . made a decision."

I looked at him, sensing something bad coming down the pike. "Tell me."

"Our mystic bond to protect William was broken the night he died," Deylaud began. Unable to meet my eyes, he bent to pick up a shard of glass.

Suddenly more weary than I could ever remember, I sat on the ottoman near William's easy chair. I couldn't bear to sit in his place. "Go on," I choked out, already knowing what my old friend would say. He and Reyha had been given to William by one of the former pharaohs of Egypt—who had just happened to be a vampire. The littermates were to guard William's daytime resting place for as long as he remained undead, which they did for hundreds of years. Now their duty was over.

Deylaud's voice broke. "Sister nearly died the other night. And now this—this invasion by someone who nearly killed her once before."

"I know," I said. "It's all right, Deylaud. Say what you have to say."

"We have to leave now. We're in so much danger, and it's so sad here without William, Melaphia, and Renee. But we love you so much."

I looked up to see a trembling Reyha standing in the entrance to the den. I gestured for her to come to me, and she did. She knelt next to the ottoman and threw her skinny arms around me. Deylaud joined her and snuggled up to my other side just like he would have if he'd been in four-footed form.

"It's okay, you guys. You have my blessing to leave. I want you to be safe and happy just like Melaphia and Renee. And for the record I love you, too."

I stroked their silky hair and listened to them sob, all the while assessing what my so-called life had become. If my situation wasn't so pitiful and sad I might have to laugh.

You know you've reached a new low in life when even your dogs desert you.

Twenty-four

I gave the twins each a kiss and sent them to bed with a promise that we'd talk about the details of their departure in the next couple of days. Deylaud would hire and train a team of managers for William's business interests and properties so I wouldn't have to take time out from my busy schedule of trying to remain in one piece.

As soon as the twins left, I picked up the phone. I couldn't wait until morning to warn Connie, but I also couldn't talk to her directly. She'd just killed William and Ulrich—two of the most powerful vampires on the planet. She wouldn't be alarmed that Will and his mother were after her, but she should be. The pair of them were much more dangerous than Ulrich had been alone. Ulrich relied on raw brutality. Diana and Will would use treachery.

I called Seth's cell phone. "Yeah," he said.

"Shut up and listen good," I began. "Tell Connie this is a wrong number. Then meet me in the tunnels under her apartment in ten." I hung up and went downstairs to the vault's entrance to the tunnels. It was almost daylight, and I didn't want to get stuck topside.

Seth was there waiting. He didn't ask me what I was playing at or give me a hard time. He knew it was important or I wouldn't have called him at dark-thirty and demand to see him without Connie. In turn, I didn't beat around the bush.

"Will's back," I began. "I had to tell him William was dead. I was making up a lie about how it happened when Diana busted in and told him Connie murdered William. I managed to put a pretty bad bite on Diana, but the two of them got away. When they left they were yammering about revenge. As soon as Diana recovers they'll be coming after Connie tag-team style."

"Shit," Seth muttered. "What do you think we should do? I know she won't leave Savannah. She thinks she's ten feet tall and vampire-proof."

"Yeah, I know. I've got a plan, but I need your help."

"Let's hear it."

Even with everything that had happened, I finally got a decent day's sleep, knowing that Seth and I had hashed out a plan that should keep Connie completely safe—at least until I could figure out how to get rid of Diana and Will. I got up at the crack of dusk and hurried to meet Otis at the marina closest to the island he called Tara.

At first I wondered why the faeries named the island after Scarlett O'Hara's house, but Otis pointed out that Tara was the name for the most magical place in Ireland. That made more sense.

As I drove, I mentally rehearsed the plan that Seth and I had agreed on right before dawn. He was to make an excuse to Connie and go directly to gather up all the provisions he and she would need to be marooned on an island for a few weeks. I had to use every ounce of strength I had not to obsess over the idea of Seth and Connie cooped up on a faerie island for weeks on end with nothing to do but . . . I wouldn't let my mind go there or I'd lose it. I forced myself to stick to reviewing what I had to accomplish.

Otis had agreed to rent a powerboat, guide Seth to the island, and help him set up camp and unload the supplies. As soon as Otis was back at the garage, I had called Connie and told her that I'd gotten a tip on Diana's whereabouts. I explained that it was on an island only Otis knew how to get to and told her to be prepared to go with me to check it out as soon as the sun went down. Of course I knew full well that she wouldn't wait for me but would go to Otis immediately, which was exactly what happened.

As I'd coached him, Otis put up enough resistance to keep Connie from smelling a rat and then caved in and agreed to take her. To make sure she didn't pull a fast one, I'd told him in no uncertain terms to insist she leave her cell phone with him. He had to convince her that the faeries who owned the island disapproved of cell phones so she would have to leave hers behind.

He would let her out on the island close to where he had dropped off Seth, and as soon as she was out of earshot of the motorboat, he would come back to the mainland, stranding her there with the werewolf.

I was now on my way to pick up Otis at the marina where he turned in the rented boat and to make sure the plan had gone off—please, gods—without a hitch.

The lanky redneck faerie was waiting for me in front of the boat rental office when I pulled up in the 'Vette. He opened the door and got in on the passenger side. "Well?" I asked.

"Everything happened just like you planned," he said. "Peanuts?" He offered me some from a foil bag. I flashed my fangs. "Oh, yeah. Sorry."

"Did you see them meet up?"

"Yeah. I saw Connie and Seth talking on the beach right before I revved the motor. They'll be fine."

"And you've got her cell phone?"

"Yep." Otis handed it to me and I pocketed it.

I sighed. "All right then. Don't get those peanut hulls in my upholstery."

"Okay."

I peeled out of the parking lot and headed back toward Savannah, giving myself a moment to enjoy the relief of knowing that Connie and my baby were safe, at least for a while. She would discover any day now that she was pregnant. Best-case scenario would be that Seth could talk her into staying on the island for the sake of what he thought was *his* baby until it was born. As a lawman, he was more than capable of delivering an infant. I knew for a fact he had been called on to do it a couple of times before in the course of his job.

Pangs of jealousy and loss gnawed at my gut as I

thought about what I'd given up. Connie would be angry at first, but Seth would calm her down. He was probably having mind-blowing makeup sex with her right now after confessing his part in the scheme to get her to the island. I got an awful vision of my girlfriend gloriously naked on the beach, her black hair spread out on the sand, her new lover moving eagerly between her thighs.

If Otis hadn't been in the car with me I would have been tempted to drive into a tree. Instead I whipped out my cell phone and dialed Olivia. "How are you?" I asked.

"Better than when we last spoke," she said.

"You've found a safe place?"

"Yes, thank goodness. I went to Ireland in advance of the others and found a perfect place for us. The others are going to join me as soon as they've packed our archives and our few belongings that survived both fires."

"Wow, you move fast," I said. "Tell me about your new home."

"It's not far from where Melaphia and Renee are living," she said. "I hope to visit them soon. Discreetly, of course. We're going to be leasing a farmhouse with a large cellar. It's on a hill so there's good visibility all around for security."

"It sounds great," I said. "I'm glad you're going to be close to my girls. You can all keep an eye on one another."

"By all means. Listen, Jack, can I call you back in a bit? I'm having a meeting with some of the fey elders here. I set it up as a courtesy to them. I don't think they'll have any objection to us moving into their territory, but it can't hurt to do some little public relations, yeah? I'm literally standing in the foyer of their headquarters waiting to be called in as we speak."

The unpleasant news I needed to tell her about Will could wait. "Sure," I said. "One more thing real quick and I'll let you go." Without mentioning Will I told her about the scheme I'd just pulled on Connie.

"Oh, my. You *are* a brave man. I don't know if I'd want to piss off the Slayer to that degree."

"I'll take my chances. When you meet with the faeries, would you ask them what they know about the island? I'm kind of curious about it." Beside me, Otis started choking on a peanut.

"Are you all right, Jack?"

"Yeah. That's not me." I slapped Otis on the back and he gagged.

"It sounds as if you're strangling someone."

"I'll explain when you call back. Just ask the Sidhe about the island in general and see if anyone remembers anything about it."

"Will do. They just announced me so I've got to go. I'll call you back directly. Cheers."

"Bye, babe. Good luck."

Otis coughed violently. "Why do you want her to talk to the Sidhe about the island?"

"Like I said, just curious is all."

Otis stuffed the rest of the nuts in his pocket and stared out the passenger-side window into the darkness.

"Is there something you're not telling me?"

Otis sighed. "Uh, well, way back in the day when

they sent me to see if anybody was hiding out on this island . . ."

"Go on," I urged. I was starting to get a bad feeling.

"When I reported back to the nobility that I didn't find anybody, there was this one guy who didn't believe me."

"Is that the misunderstanding you mentioned before?"

"Um, yeah."

I waited for him to continue, beginning to think that I was going to have to stop by the side of the road and beat the story out of him. "Out with it," I demanded. "What are you tiptoeing around telling me? What was it about this guy?"

"The thing is, there was this gold involved."

"Involved in *what*?"

"In the disappearance."

"The disappearance of *who*?" I stomped on the brakes in the middle of the deserted road and stared at Otis.

"The princess," he said haltingly.

"I swear to the gods if you don't tell me exactly what you're talking about in complete sentences in a minute or less I'm going to reach down your throat, tear your tonsils out, and feed them to the fish. Go."

Otis's eyes got as round as saucers as he took a deep breath and started talking. "The princess was the faerie I mentioned—the one who went missing. Her folks, the king and queen, refused to give their permission for her to go to the New World, but she ran off anyway and stowed away on the boat with the others. I think she was in love with one of the guys. Anyway, being a princess, she wasn't about to rough it with everybody else so she took a bag of gold with her.

"When she turned up missing they sent me to look for her like I said. By that time it was a hundred years later, so the trail was pretty cold, and—"

"Whoa! Back up," I said, starting the car up again. "That doesn't make a dab of sense. Why did they wait a hundred years to send you to look for her?"

"I don't remember."

"What the hell? Faeries are supposed to remember everything!" This was just lame. William used to tell me that the fey were powerful, talented, clever creatures. Otis must have gotten left under the Blarney Stone when the brains were given out.

Otis hung his head. "I guess I'm not a very good faerie."

Just my luck that the only faerie in my orbit had to be one with deep-seated competency issues. Not only that, but this whole situation was just unbelievable. A faerie princess and a pot of gold? How cliché was that?

"Look, I'm sorry. Go on with the story."

Otis sighed. "I remember it was about this time of year—Saint Patrick's Day . . ."

I gritted my fangs and suppressed the urge to slap him upside the head. "Get on with it."

"So I went to the island, searched for the princess, and didn't find a trace of her. But when I was called back to the Old Country to give my report, this one guy in the royal family accused me of doing away with the princess in order to steal the gold."

"That's crazy. A hundred years had passed. If the princess was still alive, surely she would have come back on her own, gold or no gold."

"You'd think so."

"Okay, so what's the upshot of all this? Why don't you want Olivia to ask about the island?"

"I just don't want to open old wounds. I get along pretty good with the people I report to. I try to keep my head down and maintain a low profile when it comes to the higher-ups. And you can't get any higher up than the king and queen. I think they believe me, but this prince who accused me of offing her was one of her cousins. It was him she was running away from according to the gossip."

"Why was she running from him?"

"They'd been betrothed since they were infants. She was going to be the queen someday and he would have been her consort. When she disappeared, his path to power went up in smoke, and he never got over it."

We were coming into the outskirts of Savannah and it occurred to me that despite how long Otis had been hanging out at the garage I didn't have any idea where he lived. For all I knew he lived under a toadstool or something. "Where do you want me to drop you off?" He gave me an address on one of the nicer squares.

I took a few minutes to let everything Otis told me sink in. By that time, we were at the address he'd given me. The place wasn't a mansion like William's, but it was a nice town house in a historic building. A man with a clipboard under one arm was training the beam of a flashlight along an ornate wrought-iron handrail at the door. The sign on a van parked at the curb read ACME WELDING.

"This is a good-looking place," I remarked as Otis opened the car door. "Bet it costs a pretty penny."

Otis laughed nervously. "Oh. Yeah. I'll see you later, Jack. Thanks for the ride." He walked quickly past the man inspecting the railing to the entrance.

I began to pull away, but something stopped me. I paused to listen as the man spoke to Otis. "Oh, hello there, Mr. Fey. I just came out to personally inspect the work our man did for you this morning. Would you like to take a look? I think he did a very good job."

"Uh, it's fine. Just fine," Otis said. "I really have to go now."

"Sure. If you'd just sign the work order right here where it says 'owner approval,' I'll be on my way."

I was out of the Corvette and at Otis's side by the time he'd finished signing his name. I nodded to the welding man as he turned to go and grabbed Otis's elbow. "I need to talk to you, Mr. Fey."

Otis looked a little pale, even for a faerie. He shimmered a little like he was in danger of losing his glamour, but he toughened up and held on.

"The faeries must have you on quite an expense account, huh?" I asked him.

"Uh-huh." He nodded.

"Otis, do you know what happens to someone who lies to a master vampire?"

He shook his head gravely. I was totally bluffing. Oh, there'd be hell to pay if another vampire lied to me but as far as I knew that threat didn't extend to other types of creatures. But Otis had always had a healthy fear of me, and he always fell for my bluffs when we played cards, so sure enough I could tell that he believed me right now.

"What they give me wouldn't keep a bird alive," he said.

"And you didn't save a lot of money from your show business days as a glam rocker in the seventies, did you?"

"Nope." He shook his head.

"You stole that gold, didn't you, Otis?"

"I didn't steal it! I found it!"

I clapped my hand over his mouth as a couple out walking crossed the street in front of us. "I'm a vampire, dammit, I can hear a fish fart at a hundred yards. Keep your voice down." I removed my hand and the couple kept going.

"I didn't do anything wrong, Jack," Otis whispered.

"You could have taken the gold back when you were called back to the Old Country."

"I needed that gold, and I knew they wouldn't miss it. They've got tons of the stuff. Plus, I figured if I got in trouble for failing to bring the princess back with me, I'd need it to run as far and as fast as I could."

"But surely you didn't know that that one guy would accuse you of harming the princess at the time you found the gold."

"Listen, Jack, when the faeries send you to find

something—especially if it's a member of the royal family—and you come back empty-handed, well, let's just say they can punish you in ways you don't want to think about. I had to come back here and stay for my own protection. I barely got away in one piece, and I had to have something to live on."

I looked at him hard and he didn't look away. "But you're telling the truth about not finding the girl, right?"

"On my honor as a faerie."

"And that is just so very valuable. Geez."

My cell phone rang. It was Olivia. I didn't even have time to say hello before she said, "Jack, go and get Connie off Tara now!"

"What? Why?" I asked, immediately alarmed at the panicked tone of her voice.

"Because that island is about to disappear for one hundred years!"

Twenty-five

"What the hell are you talking about?" I demanded even as I grabbed Otis by the shirt collar and propelled him back toward the car.

"The island is cursed. It could disappear at any moment."

"What do you mean 'disappear'?"

"What—" Otis began.

"Get in the car, Otis!" We got back in the Corvette and I headed it back in the direction we'd come from. I plugged my cell phone into the gizmo attached to the cigarette lighter so the sound would come through the speakers and Otis could hear what Olivia had to say.

"Otis was right when he said only faeries could see the island. But what he didn't tell you is that the island is only reachable, even by faeries, once every hundred years."

"I didn't know! I swear!" insisted Otis.

I steered the Stingray with one hand and reached

out to throttle him with the other but then figured it wouldn't do any good. "Were they sure?"

"There's no doubt."

"How much time do I have to get them back?"

"I'm not sure. All I know is that the only time you can access the island when the hundred years is up is a week or so before and after Saint Patrick's Day."

I let loose with a string of expletives. I was worried about Connie being trapped on the island with Seth for a few weeks and now Olivia was telling me it could be a century! "My God. It may already be too late."

I turned a corner so fast the car went up on two wheels. Otis covered his eyes and screamed like a girl. "Shut up!" I yelled. "Not you, Olivia. What am I going to do if I can't get them back? They'll get old and die there."

"Not necessarily," Olivia said.

"What do you mean? If a hundred years goes by—"

"Jack, did you ever see *Brigadoon*?"

"Maybe it's me, but is this the right time to discuss the musical theater?"

"Humor me. The story was about a small town in Scotland that appeared every hundred years. Only for that hundred years, the people who lived there only aged a day."

"Are you saying that somebody made a movie about this island?" I asked, totally confused.

"Yes, but they changed the name and the setting. Tara—that is to say the real island in question—is legendary."

I gave Otis a murderous look. He shrugged apologetically and said, "I've been over here so long I haven't exactly kept up with the Irish legends."

"So you're saying that even if I have to wait a hundred years to get her back, she'll still look exactly like she does now."

"And she'll think it's . . . tomorrow," Olivia said.

"What if I can't get to her? Did you explain the situation to the faeries?"

"Yeah, but they said there's nothing they can do to intervene."

"What about those two gods you sent for? Do you think they might still be here in Savannah?"

"I heard they returned to Europe. They wouldn't be able to help you anyway. They're pagan, but they're not part of the Sidhe, so they couldn't remove the curse."

"Why was the island cursed in the first place?"

"The faeries I talked to weren't privy to that but it may have something to do with a missing princess."

I pulled back my lips and showed Otis my fangs and he covered his face again.

"But listen," Olivia said. "I did ask them to speak to their higher-ups about the situation. They said they'd take it all the way to the monarchy if they had to, as a special favor to me."

"I'm glad you're hitting it off with them," I said glumly.

"Me too. It bodes well for the future. Speaking of that, I've got to get back to the meeting. I still have a lot on my agenda to go over with them."

"Wait. I've got some bad news for you, too," I said.

"Oh, my goodness. What is it?"

"Will showed up here last night. He had no idea William is dead. He didn't take it well."

"Oh no! The poor thing!"

"Poor thing my ass. Now he wants to kill me. His mother showed up and convinced him that I helped Connie murder William. I think she got a whiff of Will's scent somewhere and tracked him to me. She'd probably been watching the house anyway, waiting for a chance to get the drop on me."

"That's dreadful! What happened?"

"I nearly tore out Diana's throat, but when Will took her away she was still alive. I expect he let her feed on him. She's probably almost gotten her strength back by now."

"What are you going to do?"

"I don't know."

Olivia groaned. "I had such high hopes for Will. I was sure he was one of us now. The shock of losing his father must've been too much for him."

"Yeah. Whatever. You'd better get back to your meeting."

"I'm so very sorry about all this, Jack. What a rotten series of events."

"You can say that again." We said our good-byes and I flipped the phone closed.

I snarled at Otis and it scared him so badly that his glamour completely disappeared. There he sat in his true faerie form, three feet tall and in that shimmering blue getup. His skin had an unnatural glow and his hair glittered like it was shot through with stars.

"I'm really, really sorry, Jack," he said.

"Get a grip on yourself, you shiny little bastard. We've got to go get the Slayer back."

We searched until it was almost sunup without finding any sign of the island. I made Otis promise to keep looking through the daylight hours and made sure he had plenty of cash on him for gasoline.

He apologized so many times I finally told him to shut up. Since it was closer than William's mansion I went back to my old place next to Bonaventure Cemetery to spend the day. After a quick call to make sure the twins were all right, I laid on the couch.

In my mind I replayed all the trouble I'd caused everyone I loved—Connie, Seth, the twins, Melaphia, Renee, William. Of all the mistakes I'd made in the last few months, this latest just took the cake. I'd trusted an incompetent faerie with the lives of the woman I loved, my child, and my best friend—and now they all might be lost to me. The only positive was that inside of the next hundred years I was pretty sure that I'd be no more than a pile of dust. With my luck one of the bigger, badder vampires would have put the bite on me, and I would finally stop being a danger to those around me.

I must have dozed off, because at some point I heard a faraway tinkling sound and wondered why somebody didn't make it stop. After a few moments I woke up enough to realize it was my cell phone. I fished it out of my pocket and saw that it wasn't ringing. Connie's phone, in my other pocket, was the one that was making that racket. My phone didn't play "Another One Bites the Dust."

By the time I'd figured that out, the ring tone had stopped. I flipped it open and pressed the button for the voice mailbox. Diana's recorded voice startled me completely awake. "We have McShane surrounded. If you want to see him again, come to his warehouse home at sundown."

Surrounded? What the hell was happening? I could tell it was still daylight outside. Where were Diana and Will? If they were checking my usual haunts they would have seen my car parked outside and figured they had me trapped. Or if I'd been particularly careless in my distraction over Connie they might have followed me. Either way they would have had to find shelter from the sun shortly after they found me; I'd barely made it inside with my own hide intact. Which meant that they'd called Connie from somewhere close by after having glamourized someone at the cop shop to get her number. I had to get out of here as soon as the sun went down, and I had to be smart about it.

I called the garage, hoping Rennie had already opened up shop. He answered on the fifth ring. "Midnight Mechanics," he announced.

"Rennie, listen close. I need you to drive the wrecker to my place at the storage warehouse. Bring the boys and tell them to arm themselves."

"With what?" Rennie asked, alarmed.

"Pointy sticks. Y'all are going vampire hunting."

"Say what?"

"Diana and Will have got me pinned down in here, but they don't know that I know they're out there. What I need for y'all to do is create a diversion, but be ready if they come at you. They're dangerous, so be careful, but there are more of y'all than there is of them so watch one another's backs. I'm going to be ready to fly out of here and then I'm going to try my damnedest to kill both of them."

"I got it, Jack."

"Thanks, buddy. I owe you one."

"Yeah, you do. But you know what I want."

"Consider it done, man."

"See you in ten minutes."

I went to the door and listened, but I couldn't hear anything unusual. Why hadn't I installed some kind of peepholes out of the same material William had installed in his boats? At least I had a second way out installed in the back, but I still felt like a sitting duck. There wasn't much I could do but sit tight and wait for the sun to go down and the boys to show up.

I dialed Werm's cell phone. It rang for a long time before he answered. "Yeah?" he said, clearing his throat.

"It's Jack. Look, I'm in some trouble and I wanted you to know what's going on."

"What's happening?"

"Well, Diana and Will have me trapped in the mini warehouse."

"Will's back? Holy crap!"

"Yeah. I had to tell him Connie killed his father and he's pissed. I've called Rennie and the guys to come over here with some stakes and give me a hand. They ought to make it here by sunset," I said, glancing over at the wall clock. "If they do I'll be fine."

"Look, I'll head over as soon as it's dark."

"No! I don't want you anywhere near this place. I—I just wanted you to know what was happening. You know?" I actually just wanted to hear his voice but that sounded kind of gay.

"I don't know what to say, Jack. I feel so helpless."

"It's going to be okay. But while I've got you on the line I just wanted to say I'm sorry for not doing more to protect you."

"What do you mean?"

"I feel like I should have done more to scare you away when you first asked me to turn you. If I had roughed you up a little maybe you would have given up and Reedrek never would have gotten ahold of you."

"You're apologizing for not beating me up?"

"Yeah. Or biting you just enough to bring you to your senses."

"Jack. You couldn't have discouraged me if you'd tried. Besides, I was only kidding that last day we were demon hunting. I *like* being a vampire. If I had it to do over again, I would have made the same decision. In fact, I would have come to you even earlier."

"You would have? Really? Why?" I couldn't imagine what the little guy was thinking.

"Because I want to be just like you."

"Huh?"

"You're the bravest dude I've ever met. You try to protect everybody, no matter who they are—from Eleanor's prostitutes to the average Joe on the street who's been body swapped or menaced by double-dead demons."

"Did I tell you I just ruined Connie's life by trusting her fate to an inept faerie?"

"Huh?"

"Never mind."

"Like I was saying, you take the weight of the world on your shoulders no matter what kind of danger it might put you in, and you never give up, especially when someone you love is in trouble. That's why you're my hero. If I'd had a real brother I'd want him to be just like you."

Now it was me who didn't know what to say. So I just said, "Thanks. Uh, the sun's almost down, so I've got to be ready."

"Give 'em hell, Jack," Werm said.

"I will, buddy. Count on it." I hung up feeling lucky for the first time in days.

A loud crash and shout startled me into high alert. I unlocked the double-bolted door and opened it a fraction of an inch, earning me a searing pain right between the eyes. I slammed the door shut again, but not before I'd gotten a glimpse of what had caused the ruckus.

I realized too late I should have warned the guard at the front gate to expect company. When he was challenged, Rennie had evidently decided to save time and ram the wrecker through the ten-foot chain-link fence at a speed high enough to turn it into what looked like a huge wad of tinfoil. The next sound I heard was booted feet—lots of them.

"Let's go, boys," I heard Rennie say.

I opened the door again, more carefully. The irregulars, armed with broken-off broom handles and jagged shards of lumber, had formed a gauntlet on either side of the doorway, ready to stab any vampire who dared get between me and the wrecker.

As I waited for the sun to disappear completely, I thought how lucky I was to have such brave friends.

Then came the explosion.

Twenty-six

I came awake with a knifing pain in my neck and a constricting weight on my chest. It felt a lot like the night I died. "William," I muttered. "Are you there? Where are we, William?"

A feline growl reached my ear from somewhere close by. Very close. My eyes flew open to see Diana sneering at me from mere inches away. Her fangs were dripping my blood.

How long had she been feeding on me?

I tried to raise my head but I didn't have the strength. My arms and legs felt like they were tied down, and I knew that trying to get to my feet would have been useless. I'd lost so much blood I could barely see.

Someone kicked me hard in the ribs. "It looks as if your lady friend doesn't give a toss about you," Will said.

"You're probably right about that," I groaned. She had chosen a werewolf over me, after all. Even after unbelievably awesome sex. Maybe it hadn't been as good for her as it was for me.

"Where is she?" Diana hissed.

"Even if I knew where she is, why would I tell you? I'm half-dead anyway. Just finish me off and be done with it."

"Why did you call out for my father?" Will asked.

I blinked, barely able to see him. "I thought I felt him close by."

"Fool," Diana said. "He's dead and gone, but it's not too late for you. If you tell us where the Slayer is, we'll set you free."

"Then I really would be a fool. Besides, as I said I don't know where she is."

"Liar!" Diana bit me hard in the throat and I yelled in pain.

As she sucked my blood, I knew that soon I wouldn't be able to speak. Then I remembered the explosion. "Tell me before you drain me—did my friends live through the bomb blast or whatever it was?"

Will stood over me while his mother fed. Sounding bored, he said, "I suppose so. They were setting up such a fuss they'd have to be alive, now wouldn't they? Dead men don't scream like that. Although one of them looked to be all crispy around the edges. Too well done for me, I'm afraid. I like my meat rare."

Why oh why had I called the irregulars? I should have known a handful of humans were no match for Diana and Will. I was just convinced that if the boys could help me get out of my house without being am-bushed I could save all of us. Instead they were injured, one of them possibly burned to death. It was just like I'd been thinking earlier. I was a curse to everybody I cared about.

"This is no fun," Will complained. "You're not even putting up a fight. Why don't you do something interesting, like beg for your life?"

"No."

"Right. Finish him off, Mum. I'm bored."

Diana bit down harder, but this time I didn't even wince. I was glad. I'd had a good long run, but it was time for me to go before I got anybody else hurt.

If Olivia couldn't figure out a way to get Connie and Seth back, then at least they'd be safe for a hundred years. Maybe by that time the vampire wars would be over, and humankind would be entirely safe from the likes of us. Or the whole planet would be overrun with blood drinkers, and everyone would be doomed due to the loss of the prophesied vampire Slayer and her services. When I thought about it that way, I realized I had potentially screwed up the lives of everybody in the whole cotton-picking world—not just those of my loved ones, especially my child. Damn, I wonder what I could have accomplished if I'd been a *bad* vampire.

Will sighed. "Any last words, McShane?"

"Yeah," I whispered with the last of my strength. "I knew William was wrong about you."

"What the hell is that supposed to mean?" Will demanded.

"He said you had the potential to be one of us."

He blinked a couple of times and his face broke out into a snarl. "Like I'd want to." He kicked me in the side again, but at the moment his foot connected with my ribs, I heard a whirring noise and all of a sudden a shiny spiky thing became stuck in his neck just to the right of his cross-shaped scar.

In the instant I recognized the ankh symbol on Werm's throwing star, a bigger fork-shaped object came sailing end-over-end in my direction and struck Diana in the head with such force her whole body flew from on top of me, breaking her grip on my neck.

Will was prying the metal star out of his neck while he went to his mother's side. With what felt like the last of my strength, I moved my head to see that the two shorter tongs of Werm's sai had gone clean through Diana's eyeballs and the long one was buried deep in her forehead. Instead of pulling it out she screamed and waved her hands.

Werm materialized at my side. "Move, Jack!"

"I can't."

Werm lifted me and put me over his shoulder in a fireman's carry. Since I outweighed him by a hundred pounds, he wouldn't have been able to do that as a mortal. He might not be the strongest vampire I'd ever come across, but he managed to lift me and run just the same.

As we were making tracks I got an upside-down view of Diana and Will. He glared at us but didn't give chase. Instead he tended to his mother. Each time he touched the sai to try and remove it, she screamed louder. It wouldn't do any lasting damage, but it was still a pretty grisly injury.

"How did you find me?" I asked.

"I got out to the warehouse as soon after sundown as I could. The place was a madhouse, covered with police and fire units. I saw Will and Diana carry you off. All the humans were running every which way and nobody tried to stop them. I turned invisible and followed. I stayed upwind of them, but I don't think they would have smelled me anyway over the odor of the accelerant they used for that bomb."

"What happened to the guys?"

"The paramedics were working on them. I was concentrating on where Diana and Will were taking you, so I can't say for sure."

I peered into the darkness but couldn't tell if Will was coming for us or not. "Can you run very far carrying me? I'm awful heavy."

Werm picked up speed to prove that he could. "You're not heavy. You're my brother."

I must've passed out again, because when I woke up, I was in yet another strange place. "Where am I?"

"You're in the hospital blood bank," Werm said.

I was lying on a cot with an IV in my arm. "What's this?"

"Since you'd passed out, it was the quickest way to get blood back into you. You've already had eight pints. You'll be fine in a few minutes."

"Since when did you get to be a phlebotomist?"

"I have lots of skills."

"I'm beginning to appreciate that more and more."

Werm grinned. "Thanks. Since it's the middle of the night, nobody's here in this part of the hospital. It was easy to sneak you in."

The hospital. "Oh, hey, this would be the place they brought the guys, right?"

"Yeah. I've been waiting for you to wake up so we could check on them. See how you feel when you sit up." He helped me to an upright position.

"I feel fine," I lied.

"You don't look so fine. Let's see if we can clean up that wound. You look like you've been attacked by a rabid wolverine."

"You don't look so good yourself. My blood is all over both of us."

"I'll see if I can find us some scrubs to change into while you bandage that wound."

I washed away the blood and taped a wad of gauze across the gash in my neck with the adhesive tape that lay on the counter. Werm was back in seconds with surgical scrubs. We shucked our clothes and put them on. His pants were too long and mine were too short, but he rolled his up and we set out.

After inquiring at a couple of nurses' stations about anyone injured in an explosion, we were directed to the intensive care unit. The elevator of the ICU floor opened out into the waiting room where Jerry, Rufus, Otis, and Huey sat around looking dazed and drinking coffee out of Styrofoam cups.

The only one missing was Rennie.

"How's Rennie?" I asked immediately. Though all of them were bandaged and scorched-looking to some degree, they clearly were going to be okay. It was my partner's absence that struck fear in my gut.

Jerry inclined his chin toward the ICU entrance, a pair of double doors covered with all kinds of signs whose messages all boiled down to the same thing: *keep out.*

"He's bad, Jack," Rufus said. "Third-degree burns. And his immune system isn't up to snuff because of the chemo he's been taking."

"Rennie has cancer?" Werm asked, shocked.

I nodded. "How long have you guys known?"

Otis shrugged. "A couple of weeks. He didn't want to tell you, what with William's death and everything else you've had on your mind."

I groaned. "I'm so sorry I got y'all into this."

"We couldn't turn our backs on you, Jack," Jerry said. "Not after everything you've done for us."

"Yeah. What are friends for?" Huey said.

"Are you guys okay?" Werm asked.

"Yeah, we'll be fine," Rufus said. "You know we're . . ." He looked around to make sure no humans had entered the waiting room. "Special," he finished.

"Yeah. Special," Huey said, wiping hot chocolate off his upper lip with his sleeve.

I was especially glad to see that Huey hadn't gotten anything blown off in the explosion. The others could heal extra fast—maybe even regenerate limbs for all I knew—but Huey the pet zombie would have just limped along with his missing pieces, well, missing. Depending on what was blasted away, it could have been downright off-putting for the customers at the garage.

"I've got to see Rennie," I said.

"They'll only let two people in at a time and then only every half hour for ten minutes," Jerry complained. "But you and Werm could probably sneak in with those getups."

"Yeah," I said. "Come on, Werm."

We pushed our way through the double doors and nearly ran into a nurse carrying a bag of IV fluid. "Who are you?" she demanded, her eyes narrowing.

I looked into her eyes and did my glamour thing. "We belong here. We're here to help," I said.

She nodded and continued on her way. Nobody else from the nurse's station in the center of the ICU cubicles even looked at us. Rennie was in the second room we came to.

He was unconscious, deathly pale, and hooked up to too many tubes to count. I took a deep breath. "He's dying. I can smell it," I said.

"What are we going to do?"

"We're going to turn him. It's what he wanted. That's what he said when he told me about the cancer."

"We can't turn him here."

"I know. We've got to move him."

"Where to?"

"I've got an idea, but we have to act fast. He doesn't have much time left."

"Are you sure this is going to work?" Werm asked, peering out the tiny window of the morgue into the corridor. He was watching for anyone who might come along and catch a vampire draining a defenseless man's blood.

"It's got to. I imagine that the pathologists around here mostly work nine to five so we should be okay.

I'm going to drain Rennie's blood right here. Then I'm going to let him feed on me. Then he'll pass out, and we should have just enough time to get him back to one of the coffins at William's before daylight and before he starts . . . screaming."

Werm turned around to face me and Rennie. "Is there anything I can do?"

I'd already started sucking Rennie's blood, so I disengaged from his throat to say, "Just make sure nobody comes through that—"

The door hit Werm in the back so hard he flew a couple of feet into the morgue, bounced off a stainless steel table, and landed in a heap on the tile floor.

". . . door," I finished.

A tall slender woman with honey-colored hair and blue eyes halted right inside the door and blinked at me, her lips parted in shock as she tightly clutched a clipboard loaded with medical forms. She wore a small name tag that read DR. SANDRA BARTON, PATHOLOGIST.

I glanced down at myself and Rennie. His blood stained the front of my scrub top and his hospital gown, and my chin was sticky with it. Werm cringed and crawled under the autopsy table.

"Uh, this isn't what it looks like," I said hastily.

After a moment's hesitation, she said in a sultry voice, "Oh? What is it, then?"

"I, um, that is—" I came around the gurney Rennie lay on and looked deeply into her eyes. "There's nothing wrong here," I said soothingly. "Everything's fine. We're just here to help."

"Oh, yeah? Because it looks to me like you're trying to drain that guy's blood and turn him into a vampire like you. I don't necessarily call that helping."

I stared at her in shock. For the first time my glamour hadn't worked. She grabbed a sharp pencil from under the clipboard's fastener and held it in her fist pointy-side out.

"Tell me I'm wrong," she challenged.

"Uh, not exactly."

"Jack!" Werm shouted from under the table. "Are you crazy?"

Intrigued, I ignored him. "You're not supposed to believe in vampires."

"I believe my own eyes."

"Nobody else does. Most people would be able to think of a normal explanation for this in no time flat."

"I'm not most people."

Now this was downright extraordinary. Not only was she absolutely sure of herself and her own sense of reality, but she showed no fear whatsoever. Not even an inkling. Her flinty gaze never wavered as she stared at me.

"Jack! What are you doing?" Werm cried.

I looked back and forth between Werm and the doctor. I had exactly no time to weigh my options, not that I had any good ones, so I went with my gut. "Listen, lady, er, doc—it's like this. That's my best friend over there on that gurney. He was injured in a bomb blast earlier tonight trying to save what passes for my sorry life. I only have a couple of minutes to start the process. I know it's what he would want. In fact, he's got pancreatic cancer and he told me so awhile back. I was going to turn him anyway, but I have to do it now or he's not going to make it.

"Now, you can try to stab me with that pencil, but you can't stake me and my little friend under the table there both at the same time. Whichever one you go for last will put the bite on you. I promise if you let me work on my buddy over there, we'll be out of your way in fifteen minutes and you can forget you ever saw us. Do we have a deal?"

The lady doctor shifted her weight on her feet, still holding the pencil in an offensive position. She drew her plump bottom lip between her even white teeth and thought for a couple of the longest moments in my existence. Then she thrust out her chin and lowered the pencil.

Finally, she said, "We have a deal. But only if I can watch."